All Worlds Unseen:
Book One

Aurora

N.W. Twyford

For Jenny and Carrie,
My favourite things.

Chapter 1
Red Cards and Blue Wolves

Wolves make the best imaginary friends.

They're loyal, fierce, and just a bit scary. They're fast and strong, have long teeth and sharp claws. They can tear you to shreds. You don't mess with a wolf.

Aurora's was massive and blue, and, like all good imaginary friends, only she could see it.

It had always been like this. Her first words were "blue doggie," and as soon as she could hold a crayon, she worked her way through scores of blue ones drawing it. She never realised it wasn't meant to exist; it was always nearby, but it only turned up when no one else was there.

When she was three, she disappeared for an entire afternoon as her parents watched football. It was only when the doorbell rang that they realised she had been gone. Upon asking where she had been, the happy toddler offered her favourite phrase: blue doggie.

When she turned five, her parents grew concerned. She was too old to have an imaginary friend; it wasn't normal. This prompted the first of an ever-increasing series of visits to doctors, child psychiatrists, and even opticians, but the results were always the same: "Mr and Mrs Card, there's nothing wrong with your daughter. She's very smart, she's very imaginative; she just claims to see a blue wolf from time to time. She'll grow out of it. Not every child is into football."

This was unacceptable, they said. *Everyone* should be into football.

Around her seventh birthday, it dawned on Aurora that perhaps having an imaginary friend was an inconvenience. She had grown tired of the constant questions, worried looks and the complaints from her parents that she wasn't growing up. Frustrated by their failure to understand, she decided it would be best if she stopped mentioning the wolf. It seemed to work; her relieved parents never brought up the subject again and the questions stopped.

But pretending she couldn't see the wolf wasn't as easy as she thought it would be. Being the only one who ever saw it and never being able to talk about it gradually made her blue wolf feel less real, and she found herself beginning to ignore her lifelong friend. The unfortunate consequence was that, over time, the visits from the wolf reduced, making it even harder to believe in.

By the time she was twelve, the blue wolf had become something strange, infrequently glimpsed out of the corner of her eye, but far as her parents were concerned, everything was as it was meant to be and life could go on as normal.

For the Card family, normal meant an obsessive amount of football. Aurora didn't mind it, but even she had her limits. Watching it at home, in the pub, going to premiership matches, and – worst of all – watching her brothers play in the local team was deathly boring, especially when this meant they had time for little else, and actively discouraged anything that wasn't football.

This was a problem, as Aurora's passion was for stories. Yes, she liked hanging out with her friends like any normal twelve year old.

She liked sport and going out. She watched a lot of movies. But more than anything else, she loved reading books. They were her escape into another world, and one that only she could control. Her parents might hold sway over what was on the TV, but were powerless to stop her reading. They could never understand where this passion came from, and they didn't particularly care.

Perhaps it was *because* of the wolf that she had such an active imagination. She was always on the lookout for extraordinary and unusual things, seeking them out, hunting for an alternative to the relentlessly dull existence her family lived. That the visits from the wolf diminished only made her read more, to compensate for the absence it left in her life. Her imagination was strong, and often she would find herself drawn into the stories she read; wandering the ocean floor, escaping from forbidden castles, roaming underground labyrinths and exploring all manner of alien worlds.

And so it was that she found herself standing in the pouring rain on the sidelines of a football pitch on a cold October evening, and not minding one bit. She was immersed in an adventure story; a thrilling escapade in the jungle, and she swung on a vine across a raging river, with natives hot on her heels as she neared a ruined temple. The sun beat down, the winds whipped at her face as she swung.

It was all she needed. She was content.

And none of this meant a thing, she realised, in the very instant that the football nearly broke her nose.

Its impact knocked her off her feet, yet she was too stunned to feel its sting. She flopped to the ground like a dead fish, her auburn hair flailing and her hazel eyes blank.

As Aurora remembered who she was, the world realigned itself, blurring and shifting piece by piece from an otherworldly sunset to a grey autumn evening.

Looking up from the puddle she lay in, she saw her brothers, Eric and Ryan, howling with laughter as if this was the funniest thing they had ever seen. Eric was responsible for sending the ball in her direction, but it wasn't skill that had made the ball hit her, only luck.

The ground of the football pitch was slushy and freezing cold, made only worse by rain that refused to let up, and Aurora got to her feet as quickly as she could, relieved the downpour would hide the tears that rushed to her eyes. Wiping the mud from her swollen cheek proved little help; her hand was as dirty as her face. *Never mind*, she told herself. *Adventurers didn't mind a bit of mud.*

It's war paint, she thought, trying to work her way back into the jungle. *I'm wearing war paint; I never left the jungle. The worst tropical storm in history has just hit, and the natives are closing in. They know I stole their jade idol, and are about to sacrifice me to their heathen god, unless I can perform the most daredevil…*

It was no use. It was too cold and her knees ached. Her fingers were numb, so she buried them deep in the armpits of her large coat. The real world was here to stay and she had better get used to it, no matter how miserable it made her.

Speaking of the real world, a six-foot reminder of it was headed her way in the shape of a man everyone, including his children, called 'Red.'

Roger Card, professional referee, part time coach and full on football obsessive, was renowned for his lack of humour.

"What was that?" he barked, oblivious to any pain his daughter might be in.

"Apparently the boys think I'm better as a target than a linesman," she deadpanned, dusting herself off with a forced air of casualness. The rain meant this was more like spreading cold, muddy paste.

"Don't blame them," he scolded. "You weren't paying attention."

"I'm bored!" she moaned. "It's freezing and I'm soaked. I've got homework to do. Why can't I just go?"

"Because this team needs a linesman," Red told her, "and none of the others we've had have been any good. So you're it." Aurora knew exactly what this meant; Red had been so unbearable that anyone else who had tried it out, child or adult, had quit before long. Being part of the family, Aurora didn't have that luxury.

"I'm really the best you could find?" she asked, trying to get a rise from her father.

"Just keep your head in the game," he snapped, having none of it. He took the ball and marched off. "The sooner you grow up and stop daydreaming, the better."

"I'll stop pretending when you do."

"What's that supposed to mean?"

"Eric and Ryan: they're rubbish. Hitting me was the first shot they made tonight."

Either Red chose not to hear, or the comment was lost on him. Aurora sighed. Talking to her dad was like talking to a wall: a wall that turned everything into a conversation about football.

The game resumed.

Before long, Aurora's mind began to drift. It was too cold to return to her fantasy world, but the game was too boring to watch. Despite Red's best efforts to install the principle of teamwork, the players embraced an 'every man for himself' policy, which meant trying to score as soon as possession was achieved.

The result was not pretty: a mass of talentless, sweaty teenagers huddled round the ball, aggressively hacking away at one another while Red bellowed ignored instructions. The only break from this monotony was the occasional stray kick that sent the ball off, redeploying the mob of players further up or down the pitch in the exact same formation.

Aurora longed for distraction; she longed for summer, when it was dry and light and (without Red knowing) she could discreetly read while the team punted the ball around with all the skill of a three-legged cow. Reading was her favourite thing, and being forced to endure the game with nothing else to do seemed like a torture her father had concocted specifically for her.

Her vision drifted to the edge of the pitch where woods bordered the school field and dense gorse prevented entry to the trees beyond. The more she stared, the deeper the woods became and the more was revealed to her.

In a gap in the gorse was something that should not have been there. Apparently oblivious to the wet, rain dripping from its nose and ears, was her blue wolf. It was sat utterly still and watched her patiently, more like a stone statue than a living being. Under the rain, its fur was almost grey blue, yet it remained dignified and poised. Not even its tail moved as it watched her.

Aurora wondered why she kept seeing this one peculiar thing, and why it seemed so real. Usually she would ignore it, as she had taught herself to do, but boredom and the frustration she felt at her father made her want to rebel. Besides, she felt fond of the wolf, her constant companion and first friend: so what if it wasn't really there? In the only movement Aurora noticed, the wolf tipped its massive head in a kind of nod, directing her attention towards the pitch. She followed its gaze and –

Just managed to catch the football in her hands. She held it in front of her for a moment, trembling under the force of the shot but amazed at what she had done, her palms stinging from the contact.

Eric kicked at the ground with frustration, angry at failing to catch his sister out once again. His foot struck an especially soft patch and was enveloped, causing him to trip as he tried to pull it out. Despite his best efforts to regain his balance, he quickly found himself face down in the mud. Karma. Aurora smiled and Ryan must have agreed with her on some level, snorting at his brother's misfortune.

The wolf had gone, but Aurora dwelled on how it had warned her. As much as the idea appealed, the logic her parents had drummed into her since birth prevailed. She must have heard Eric kick the ball, sensed it flying towards her, or caught it in the corner of her eye, she concluded.

Aurora looked over at Red who gave her what at first she took to be a nod of approval. She felt proud until she realised what the nod *really* meant. The previous shot hadn't been a fluke; Eric had hit her deliberately, and had nearly done so again. Red's thuggish star player had proved her wrong, and they both knew it.

Rather than let this get her down, Aurora took the opportunity to channel all her frustrations, kicking the ball to centre field with precision. It arced through the air towards Ryan, who, still laughing, was caught unprepared when it struck him on the head.

His moment of triumph spoiled, Red rubbed his temples in despair, then looked over at Aurora. She gave him such a look of defiance that he realised for the briefest and most fleeting of moments that he didn't know his daughter at all, and maybe, just maybe, that was his loss.

Chapter 2

A Mystery Worth Investigating

Everyone knows the greatest place in the whole world is Your Bed, and leaning against a wall of pillows, with a book resting on her lap, Aurora was in no position to argue.

Her room was her sanctuary, and her bed was its heart. This was the place she had read countless tales of faraway lands and alternate worlds, or occasionally explored them in her dreams. It was here she realised the first day of the school holidays had arrived, or had woken up far too early on Christmas morning when she was little.

Her family were usually noisy, but tonight proved to be worse than normal. It was parents' evening and Aurora assumed that right then her parents were either sitting numbly through praise of their daughter's progress, or tuning out concerns about Eric's (lack of) academic ability and Ryan's toilet dunking of Year 7 boys, (many of whom Aurora knew and felt she had to apologise to).

Unfortunately for Aurora, both parents presented a tracksuit wearing front that declared 'football first, everything else later.' This meant that despite trying hard and being one of the smarter pupils in her class, Aurora knew a bit of acknowledgement from her parents would be too much to ask for.

Worse, her parents' absence left Eric and Ryan free to do as they pleased, and this meant computer games and pounding music. The bass vibrations would make anyone leaning against the wall find themselves lying slumped before they realised it. This was nothing new to Aurora, and an occasional wiggle to readjust herself every few minutes was easy enough, if only slightly annoying. Headphones tuned out most of the noise.

Aurora's shelves were stacked beyond capacity with books: anything to take her mind away. Her parents didn't approve and rarely bought them for her, but they couldn't stop her spending her pocket money on battered paperbacks from second hand bookshops, or borrowing extensively from the library. Stories of far off planets; adventures set in our world, but twisted slightly; or lands that couldn't or shouldn't exist, it didn't matter; she soaked it all up.

The walls of her room displayed the imagination of which her parents so despaired. Cuttings of fantasy worlds taken from magazines competed for space next to film posters, photos of unusual locations from geographical magazines and images from the Hubble telescope. Every picture was somewhere to escape to and never return.

Cunningly concealed on their reverse were football pictures and league tables, ready to be flipped over at a moment's notice should she hear her parents approach. Part of her welcomed the charade; she was a prisoner, and the pictures obscured the maps that would one day lead her to freedom.

Tonight Aurora tried something different: Raymond Chandler. It was a library recommendation, and the master of detective fiction was making a mixed impression, although not through any fault of his. Aurora struggled to understand many of the words, which were unfamiliar, associated with trends popular decades ago, and this frustrated her more than she would admit. As a result, she hadn't made much sense out of the last sixty pages.

It didn't matter. Her determination bordered on stubbornness. She hadn't given up on a book yet and wasn't intending to start now. Regardless of whether she understood what was going on, she *loved* the world Chandler's hero Marlowe lived in. Plus technically, although it was fiction, it wasn't fantasy, so her parents couldn't complain.

As she read, she allowed her imagination to take over like it had on the football pitch. Her room became a private eye's office; Venetian blinds broke the light from outside into strips across her wall. Her brothers' relentless music became a train passing. Everything was, of course, in black and white. Sultry jazz played in a bar downstairs. Maybe she'd investigate a murder there later, uncovering a conspiracy so deep that the corruption's roots spread from the streets and led back all the way to the mayor's office. She concluded she had moxie, whatever that was, and that while private investigators were always poor and frequently beaten up, they said whatever they liked.

Aurora concluded she would make a good P.I. She was however at a fundamental disadvantage; ignoring the fact she was a twelve-year-old girl from Watford, the main problem that stood in her way was that, traditionally, P.I.'s had *clients*. She did not; no one had asked her to find anything out. Well, that wouldn't stop her, she decided.

She would do the mandatory research that most cases involved, and something would present itself to her.

Depressingly, this research took the form of a family history project she was required to do for school. The project wasn't very interesting, Aurora noted with disdain, as she traced the roots of her family tree as far back as she could.

Aurora would have loved to be part of a large family, with a history that could be traced back ten generations. To know what she could have been like if she was born a hundred years ago; to see the sort of people she came from. Sadly it was not to be.

The Cards were a boring family. Her grandfather worked as a mixer in a paint factory in Bracknell, and retired with her grandmother in Marlow, before dying peacefully ten years ago. Rumours were that due to his experiences in the factory, he hated colour, and subsequently everything in the house in Marlow were muted shades of brown and beige. Aurora always wanted to point out that when you mix all shades of paint together, you get brown, and maybe that was why everything in the house was brown, but the remark would have fallen on deaf ears. They visited her grandmother infrequently, and she was a pleasant, but mostly sleepy, old lady.

So Aurora decided to research her mother's family instead. She had asked her mum if they could look through the family pictures and files together, but her mum had claimed she was too busy to help; Aurora could do it herself. At least, that's what Aurora chose to take from her mum's brisk "I'm busy love, do whatever."

Aurora's mother, Joan, was tight lipped about most things – generally speaking her sentences did not run longer than five words – but when it came to family, she was practically mute. Aurora had tried to ask her about them a couple of times in the past, but had been met with a series of brief non-committal answers. Clearly Joan's family were not football fans. Aurora assumed her mum's parents were dead. There were certainly never any phone calls, Christmas cards or birthday presents to contradict this theory.

Delving through old photos of her mum looking as sullen then as she did now (albeit sporting some truly appalling fashion choices) and worse, some of Red with what could only be described as a ginger afro, she finally hit pay dirt.

It was an adoption certificate. Apparently a man named Jim Hayhoe had adopted Joan at a young age. Aurora realised she'd never heard of him before, scouring her memory for any reference to a 'Grandpa Jim,' or similar. She didn't even know her mum had been adopted. Hayhoe was an odd name, and she wondered what he had been like. She looked through the rest of the files, hoping to find something of use; a picture, maybe some newspaper cuttings, anything that could shed light on this mysterious figure, but there was nothing. It was as if this man had been erased from history altogether.

Aurora carefully combed the contents of the box again, and found a letter at the top of the pile. It was dated only last month, from a place called St Elmo's Nursing Home. She had heard of St. Elmo's before; Eric had nearly been forced to volunteer for work experience there earlier in the year, but at the last minute had managed to work in the school canteen instead. The near limitless supply of chips at his disposal had made the escape all the more worthwhile, he had bragged, but she suspected it had played a large part in developing the acne that made his face resemble an out of focus photograph of itself.

This idea of a mysterious Grandfather ignited something in Aurora's already fertile imagination, and a myriad of ideas ricocheted round her mind. Her first instinct was to picture a kindly old man like Father Christmas, but she quickly moved on from this idea. She already had one dull grandparent; she had no desire for a second one. The much more appealing reason her parents wouldn't talk about him was if he was dangerous.

Maybe this Jim Hayhoe was a spy with secrets that could never come to light. Or a criminal mastermind, and St Elmo's was secretly a secure facility.

Maybe he had stolen jewellery from the Royal Family.

Perhaps he had killed a man.

Whoever he was, she felt pity for him. As far as she knew, her mother never went to see him, and neither did the rest of the family. She wondered what could have happened for their relationship to be so strained.

In her heart, Aurora realised another truth. Although he wasn't a blood relation, maybe he was like her, in which case she wouldn't feel so different from the rest of her family.

She headed back upstairs towards the room her brothers shared. The door was open, and she could hear them talking.

Entering Eric and Ryan's room was not something Aurora did lightly. It was a world that smelled of boys; old takeaways and sweat; sneaky cigarettes poorly masked by the liberal spraying of cheap deodorant. The music that blasted out made it hard to think. Once inside, she was no longer in neutral space. This was their domain, subject to their rules. There would be no Marlowe-style interrogation from her here; she would have to use her brains.

Eric and Ryan were not twins, although they might as well have been given everything they had in common. Neither one looked as if they had completed evolution, and they were both thuggish and dull eyed.

Eric was the eldest, having recently turned sixteen, his face a mess of red and white spots. Mostly red, as he constantly picked them. He could be mean, but mostly he was disinterested in everything he laid eyes on, including his twelve year old sister.

Ryan was fifteen and although fair skinned in comparison to his brother, his voice was breaking. His monotone observations became more entertaining as his voice flailed wildly in pitch. Unfortunately this had not given him the hint to shut up.

At times Aurora wondered how these two could possibly be related to her, and what it said about her that they were.

Sprawled in front of the TV, video game controllers in hand, they were in the midst of a zombie cull, the sound of shotguns mingling with their music. Aurora stood patiently.

"What do you want?" asked Eric without looking at her, slouched in an inflatable chair.

"Did you know we had a Granddad?"

"Paint maker," Eric replied. "Dead."

"Another Granddad. Mum's dad."

"So?" grunted Ryan, perched on the bed. He hammered the controls and his character pitched a grenade into the zombie horde. Rotten limbs pelted the screen.

"Well, I didn't know we *had* a granddad."

"Where do you think Mum came from, stupid?" Ryan snorted,

"Cloning?" His voice broke, adding an extra syllable to the word.

"Did you know he lives at St Elmo's?" she asked Eric.

"Bothered," Eric mumbled, scratching at a particularly juicy spot on his chin. Fit to burst at any moment, the spot gave his dull chin a small yet sinister point that would not survive the night.

"Is it too much to ask to get an answer out of you?" Aurora asked, careful of her tone. If she showed stress, it would only encourage them further. If she did nothing, however, they would continue to ignore her.

Eric belched. Ryan grunted in approval. Aurora rolled her eyes.

"Cook us something and we'll tell you what we know," Ryan said, reaching into a mini fridge for a coke.

"Mum left you microwave pizzas," Aurora replied. "They're not rocket science."

"Yeah, well, it's your job. Woman. Get you ready for domesticated life. If anyone'll have ya."

A wave of anger washed over Aurora. She didn't like being teased.

"New plan." Before the boys could react, she snatched the remaining coke from the mini fridge. Gripping the can tight, she shook it violently for several seconds. The brothers watched with interest, their game momentarily forgotten as the zombies shuffled ever closer, ready to eat their (tiny) brains. Stretching her arm out, she held the can above the console.

"What are you doing?" asked Eric, a hint of panic entering his voice. Under the red of his spots, he had gone rather white.

"I'm only little," Aurora said, putting on a dainty voice. "My arm's already tired. I may drop this well shaken, *slippery* can at any moment."

"Rory, whatever you're doing…"

"I don't think your X-Box would like getting covered in coke, do you?"

"What do you want, Rory?"

"Make it all sticky…"

"Rory!"

"Mum's dad," she ordered, pleased she was getting somewhere. "Jim Hayhoe. Talk."

"I don't know *anything*!" Ryan said. Once again, his voice broke comically, giving the 'any' in anything a generous extra two syllables.

"Eric?"

"All I know is that mum doesn't talk to him," Eric said, ignoring his brother's look of confusion. "Red doesn't like him much either."

21

"Why haven't we ever seen him?"

"He never sends us anything for Christmas, who cares?"

Ryan nodded in agreement. This logic worked for them. Aurora felt a bit guilty for having observed the same thing moments ago.

"Don't you think that's a bit weird?" Aurora asked, abandoning her threat and setting down the can. Both boys gave a sigh of relief and shrugged, quickly ignoring her again. The zombie cull resumed, but Eric did take the can and quickly set it away from his sister, giving her a wary eye as he did so.

A door slammed downstairs: their parents were home. Ryan hastily ejected the zombie game, replacing it with the latest FIFA title while Eric turned the music down and sprayed a generous helping of deodorant. Too much deodorant was better than even the slightest trace of cigarette smoke. Aurora couldn't mock them for this; in moments she would be flipping all her posters over. Her cell would be back to normal.

"You can ask them yourself now," Eric said.

So that was exactly what Aurora did. She may not have had a client, but she had a mystery to look into, and for an aspiring investigator, you couldn't ask for more than that.

Chapter 3
Interrogation

"Who's Jim Hayhoe?" Aurora asked her parents as casually as she could.

In her defence, she hadn't intended on ambushing them. She had started off by asking them how parent's evening had gone, but only received a nonchalant "fine, love," from her mum, which extended into a slightly exasperated, "you did great, Rory," under duress.

That was slightly better: Aurora hadn't worked that hard for "fine, love," even if her mother's enthusiasm had most likely been dampened by one son's intellectual deficiency and the other's tendency to treat twelve-year-old boys as toilet brushes.

Joan only called Aurora 'Rory' when she was feeling affectionate (rarely) or fed up (likely). This was the latter. Aurora wondered why she and her mother had so little in common. Most of the time she felt her mum saw her less like a daughter and more like a visiting exchange student, or maybe an odd pet.

The mood changed when she asked about her grandfather. Her parents shared an oddly harmonised groan, as if the thought of Joan's father brought about the exact same frustration.

Now Aurora really was hooked. A hidden relative was interesting, one who her parents didn't care for, much, much better.

"So when were you planning on telling me I had a granddad?" she asked indignantly.

"I don't see him much," Joan said.

Aurora raised her eyebrows, trying to will her to go on. "And? Can I meet him?"

"Why?" Red sniffed. "He doesn't send you anything at Christmas."

"What is this family's obsession with Christmas presents?"

"He's a bloody pain," Red said knowingly.

Aurora shot her father a look she hoped read 'Keep going like this and I won't visit you when you end up there,' then she realised: *I'm standing up for a man I've never even met.*

"He's not very well," her mum offered. In her way, she was trying to diffuse the tension. Aurora's inquisitive nature didn't mix well with Red's bluntness, and her mum couldn't be bothered with any more conflict after an evening of teachers discreetly trying to tell her they had a strong dislike of her eldest two children.

"I'd like to see him anyway," Aurora announced. She knew her mum held the power here and she concentrated her efforts on her. "Please," she begged. "Even if it's for ten, no, five minutes."

Joan looked uncertain.

"It's for *school*," Aurora added, hoping this particular straw might break the camel's back.

"When?" her mum sighed.

"Tomorrow?" Aurora's voice was so high by this point it was practically a squeak.

"Fine," her mum relented. "I've got forms to fill in there anyway."

Wow, Aurora thought, *an eight-word sentence.* For her mum that was practically a record. Things were getting interesting already.

Chapter 4

The Road to St Elmo's

The next day at school dragged like Christmas Eve. Aurora was so excited that every lesson seemed to take hours to pass. Her friends asked her why she was in such a weird mood, but she refused to tell them. She loved having a secret, and saying it aloud would spoil it somehow.

So she was going to see her grandfather. So what. People did that every day.

How often do they meet him for the first time, though? Aurora asked herself, knowing the answer was only once.

Finally, three thirty came and she went to wait with her brothers outside the school gates.

"You're weird," Ryan told his sister.

"Why?" she asked, "'Cos I wanna meet my granddad? I think you're weird for *not* wanting to meet him."

"Whatever," Ryan grunted, unable to articulate a better response. He hacked up a globule of phlegm and tried to spit it as far as he could. He seemed dismayed when it limply dangled from his lips like a large white tadpole before landing on his shoe. "Aw," he moaned.

Eric snorted at his brother but shared his indifference, rolling himself a poorly made cigarette with all the skill of a man wearing boxing gloves.

Aurora ignored them. Until recently the three siblings had been allowed to walk home unaccompanied. It took just under an hour on a good day. However, Eric and Ryan had recently thought it a good idea to take out a few windows with a football on route. They knew that because they had used a football Red wouldn't really mind, but unfortunately for them, their mum was slightly more long sighted and agreed with the school that a lift home would prevent any future incidents. How Aurora fitted into this escaped her, and she missed walking home with her friends.

While she continued to imagine what sort of a man her potential adventuring-mass-murderer-jewel-thief-slash-spy-criminal-

mastermind grandfather was, her brothers wrestled and jabbed one another with a playfulness that poorly concealed their malicious nature.

Aurora let them continue, staring down the road and devoting all her power into trying to will her mum's car to appear. No sign. The street was empty. The Card siblings were the last to leave, the deserted school at their backs like an abandoned street in a Wild West movie. All it was missing was the tumbleweeds.

Aurora watched it sullenly. Schools without children were strange things, like empty swimming pools with their undisturbed water.

Something strange drew her out of her thoughts. Passing between the old science block and the humanities building moved a shape she recognised but never expected to see.

The massive blue wolf stopped its prowling and sat, watching her. Aurora turned to her brothers, wondering if they could see it too, but they were still engaged in a squabble of ever-increasing severity:

pinching was involved now. They were alone, together. Sitting perfectly still, the wolf's eyes locked onto her.

A shiver ran through Aurora. She felt small, unworthy of its attention, yet she stared back. There was something about this creature that, at her core, felt so familiar. It felt so right. If she didn't know better, she would say what she was experiencing was trust, but without any rhyme or reason.

It was like remembering a flavour long forgotten and unable to be articulated. She was close to recognising it. She could almost –

Her eye contact with the Wolf was suddenly broken as Eric and Ryan fell into her, still fighting. She fell to her knees and picked herself up again, immediately searching for the animal. It was nowhere to be seen, which didn't surprise her. It couldn't be real, and she couldn't tell a soul. She would literally be crying wolf.

Still wrestling, Aurora's brothers sloshed through a dirty puddle, sending a line of filthy brown water up Aurora's leg and onto her skirt.

Right, she thought, that tears it.

*

Two minutes later, Joan Card arrived in her people carrier. Over the years Joan and Red had always owned cars with lots of storage space. Red's sole demand in a vehicle was that "it had to hold enough kit for a football team."

Aurora stood between Eric and Ryan, who were both on their knees in some discomfort. One of their ears was tightly gripped in each of her hands, twisted to keep them on the ground.

The boys silently piled into the back of the car as Aurora released them.

"Everything alright?" her mum asked.

"Fine," Aurora beamed, climbing into the front seat. Eric and Ryan simply grunted, unprepared to admit that their twelve-year-old sister had put them in their place.

Aurora could tell, despite how annoyed her mum was at having to visit her father, that this was one of the few moments where they felt connected. If she didn't know better, she would say her mum seemed proud of her.

*

"Why didn't you tell me about him?" Aurora asked, breaking the uneasy silence that dominated the drive. Even Eric and Ryan were silent.

"Who?" her mum replied, feigning ignorance.

"Our granddad. *Your* dad."

"He's not your real granddad," her mum corrected her.

Aurora chose to ignore the comment. "Is he mean?"

"Not really, no."

"Then what?"

"He's not the easiest person to know," her mum said, apparently forgetting she was talking to her daughter. "I didn't see much of him growing up. He was away a lot of the time."

"Doing what?"

"You don't give in, do you?" Joan said, and Aurora couldn't tell if she was impressed or annoyed with her tenacity. Maybe a little of both.

The car left the main road and snuck through a series of winding streets. They turned a corner and went up a hill, towards a large old house, half obscured by trees.

"This is it," her mum said, switching off the engine and unbuckling her seatbelt. Turning to Eric and Ryan she added, "Stay in the car." Fortunately for her, they were engrossed in their portable consoles, and grunted without looking up. At least they weren't fighting.

"Stay with your brothers," she told Aurora, who had just undone her seatbelt as well.

"What?" Aurora asked with disbelief, "I thought I was going to meet him!"

"I've changed my mind," her mum said, "Sorry."

"You're joking."

"No," her mother replied. "Maybe one day, but not today. We've got a lot to do and don't have the time. I'm only going to be there for a minute."

"Why can't I see him?" Aurora asked, stricken.

"Because I said. Don't push it, young lady."

Joan got out the car. Aurora watched her mother enter the house, and could feel the frustration mounting in her chest. She'd spent the whole day looking forward to this, and now it had been taken away from her at the last minute. She tried to tell herself it did not matter; it was just some old man she'd never met. Who cares? But the truth was it mattered an awful lot to her. The frustration became a lump in her throat, and Aurora did what always came naturally when she felt upset: she disobeyed.

She opened the car door.

"Uh-oh," came Eric's voice from the back seat, "Going to see the old man?"

"Hope you like dribble, Rory," Ryan cooed, joining in, "You gonna chew his meals for him?"

Eric hit Ryan on the arm, silencing him. His tone became grave as he leant towards his little sister. "Rory, you've never been to a place like this before. I nearly did my work experience here. From what I've heard, everyone there is crazy. Michael Robinson's gran lives here, and he says it's like a haunted house. People shout at nothing all the time, like they're seeing ghosts. It stinks, and it's really, *really*, creepy."

He sat back, forcing the look of concern to stay on his face. Aurora could tell he was trying his hardest not to look proud of himself, and it was mostly successful.

She swallowed hard, trying not to picture the place. If she thought about it too much she would lose her nerve; it was the drawback of having such a powerful imagination. If she were to go, it would have to be now. Finally, as if stepping out of a plane, she went for it.

"What's the worst that could happen?" she shrugged, jumping out of the car.

Her brothers watched her for a moment with a mild look of disbelief, and then, as if endowed with a goldfish's memory, resumed their games.

"I give her five minutes," Eric muttered.

Aurora approached the home. She only allowed herself to look back at the car once, knowing full well that the grief Eric and Ryan would give her if she turned back would be unbearable. Passing through the cluster of trees, the building was revealed to her.

St Elmo's nursing home was a large Victorian manor that had been hastily converted into a retirement home. Mainly red and black in colour, Eric might have been right, she thought; it did resemble a haunted house more than a care home. It had a range of tall chimneys that gave the impression of a castle's spires.

A breeze picked up for the first time that day and pulled a thin shower of leaves from their branches, and Aurora walked through a cascade of red, yellow and brown, before passing through the main doors of the home, expecting to be stopped at any time. However, she was small and fast enough to remain hidden from the staff and moved through the home undetected.

The inside of St. Elmo's was a mix of patterned ancient red carpets, whitewashed walls and elaborate old lights that desperately needed replacing. As she walked past what she took to be a communal room, some of the residents watched her with mute curiosity from their armchairs. She shuddered as she heard a moan from down the hall break the silence.

31

They're just people, Aurora thought, trying to convince herself.

Her mother emerged from a room down the corridor, and Aurora ducked round a corner to avoid being seen. Her mum was most likely leaving her grandfather's room, she concluded, feeling a pang of satisfaction that her detective skills were paying off.

She watched Joan approach the main desk and start talking to a handsome doctor. Aurora rolled her eyes; her mum's attempts at flirting were as painful as they were unsuccessful. Still, in this case it would work to her advantage.

As quickly and as quietly as she could, she snuck past her mum and the doctor, moving down the corridor and entering her grandfather's room unseen.

Her heart leapt when she saw his name on the door: *J. Hayhoe*.

There it was, in black and white.

He's real, she thought, *and I'm really going to meet him.*

Chapter 5

The Man Himself

To Aurora's disappointment, the room appeared to be empty.

Aside from the predictable contents of a bed, some chairs and a wardrobe, it held little more than a bookcase with a few tattered paperbacks, various ornaments on shelves and some photos on the walls. Old people junk. It was a lifetime's collection of items, destined to become the stuff of charity shops and car boot sales that would lie unsought and unclaimed. The thought saddened her.

She wondered what to do next; she had to learn *something* or the whole journey would be a waste. Looking around, she tried to get a better sense of who this man was and what his life had been like. As she looked, something bothered her; an old fashioned radio sat on one of the shelves, emitting a constant but irregular low buzzing that immediately gave her a headache.

A slow realisation crept up on her as she scoured his shelves, and she wondered how she had missed it. It wasn't a lifetime's collection of junk, it was a lifetime's collection of *stories*.

Scraping a thick layer of dust from a musty old bottle sitting between the radio and a pocket telescope, she was amazed to find the coiled body of a cobra preserved in wine, watching her with jewelled dead eyes, its open mouth betraying a chipped fang. She stepped back, expecting the cobra to jump to life upon being disturbed. Of course it did not. It was dead and had been for years.

Carefully lifting an old globe off a shelf next to an unusually shaped twelve-stringed instrument, she was surprised to see many countries were in the wrong places, or missing altogether. There were several dotted outlines all over the globe, marking places that did not exist, the largest of which filled a large portion of the Atlantic Ocean.

Replacing the globe, she moved on to the photos on the wall, and saw pictures of a handsome man in his forties, presumably her grandfather, taken from all over the world: up a mountain; in the Arctic; on safari and on a camel in the Sahara.

Finally, she inspected the contents of his bookcase, something she always did whenever she entered a house. It was her best way of seeing what someone was like. She was used to disappointment; her parents' bookcase contained nothing but footballers' autobiographies, but she kept an open mind.

On the shelves was a collection of dusty and battered paperbacks. She did a double take as she realised the author of every book was the same: Jim Hayhoe.

Aurora's jaw dropped. She was stunned. A writer in the family! She could hardly believe it.

She stepped back to admire the wall, trying to take it all in within a glance. It was strange to see the contents of a man's life summarised by a few pictures and ornaments, and Aurora hoped that when she reached this age (however old that was) she would have a collection to rival it. It was apparent that regardless of wherever he was now, Jim Hayhoe had led a very eventful life. She couldn't wait to meet him.

Without looking, she sat down in the chair behind her. A noise from beneath her made her jump to her feet with alarm.

An old man was slumped in the armchair. She had not noticed him when she entered; he had been sleeping and practically blended into the furniture. He moaned.

"I'm sorry," she blurted out, hugely embarrassed, her heart pounding, "I didn't see you!"

The old man seemed not to notice her, but groaned in discomfort. He stared off at nothing.

Was this him? Jim Hayhoe himself? Aurora had no reason to believe otherwise, but hoped she was mistaken. The old man was pale and sickly, clearly in distress. What must have once been a strong frame was now bowed and hunched. It was a shame to see anyone looking like this, but the contrast from the man in the pictures to this was particularly disheartening.

"Granddad?" she asked, gingerly. He did not reply. "Are you Jim Hayhoe?"

A moan. She took this as confirmation.

"I'm... I'm your granddaughter."

His eyes lifted for a second, met hers, then glazed over.

This was useless. Aurora felt despair tug at her.

"I'm Aurora," she tried. Last attempt.

"...Awe-rah..." he whispered, a ghost of a smile attempting to light his face. He blinked a few times, then grimaced, as if fighting off the pain he was in.

He forced his gaze to meet hers, and Aurora felt herself tremble under his glare. Somehow the strength of will in those old eyes was something to be reckoned with.

"You *are* Jim Hayhoe," she said with confidence.

Trembling, his hand reached out and settled on her arm. She gave it a reassuring squeeze.

"I didn't know you were a writer," she said. It was as good a place to start as any.

He nodded, then whispered, "… All true…"

"What are? The stories?"

He raised his eyebrows in a knowing manner and gave a sickly laugh that ended as a frail cough.

"Come off it," she scoffed; quite pleased he had a sense of humour despite everything.

"See for… yourself…"

"Really?"

His hand left her arm and nudged her towards the bookshelf. She allowed herself a proper look. All but a few of the books had the name Jock Danger in the title.

She read aloud: "Jock Danger and the Nightmare Locomotive. Jock Danger and the Curse of the Nazi Tomb. Jock Danger and the Phantom Oilrig? Granddad, what are these?"

A cough was his reply, and at his urging Aurora took three slim paperbacks off the shelf and tucked them into her coat pockets. It was a big coat, shapeless and worn at her parents' insistence. For once it had come in handy; no one would spot the books in there.

"How many did you write?"

He shrugged, and then clutched his forehead. Aurora felt for him and wished there was something she could do.

Aurora looked around the room helplessly and again became aware of the low buzzing emitting from the radio on the shelf.

"Is it this?" she asked, pointing at the radio. "Is this bothering you?" She reached up and grabbed it from the shelf.

Despite appearing half a century old, a small red light blinked infrequently on the machine. Stranger still, it didn't seem to be plugged in, so how could it have a flashing light? It seemed too old to be battery operated.

She felt around and found the off switch. The red light died out and with the buzz of the radio gone, a real silence settled.

"Better?"

The old man's eyes seemed to sharpen, as if coming out of a trance. His eyes began to flicker round the room, and it seemed to Aurora like he was seeing it for the first time.

Aurora would remember thinking what followed was like a tightly wound spring uncoiling.

Her grandfather lurched to his feet and stumbled forwards, gasping. To her surprise he was much taller than she thought he was, well over six feet. She was worried he was having some sort of attack, a stroke maybe, but it wasn't that at all.

"What the devil's going on?" he yelled, suddenly articulate, spinning round to take everything in.

How could this be the same person? A moment ago he could barely sit up; now his energy seemed limitless.

"Granddad?" she asked, tentatively.

"Oh god, they did it!" he said with horror, apparently to himself. "They actually did it. I can't believe they would stoop so low, those sick —"

"Granddad!" Aurora interrupted. He was frightening her.

"Oh!" he started. It seemed to stop him, and he paused momentarily, before the urgency returned and his eyes widened once more.

"It's not safe here," he said, grabbing her by the shoulders, "You have to run. They got me, who knows where they'll stop! It may be too late already!"

Before he could say anything more, several orderlies and a doctor burst into the room. The doctor was the same handsome one her mother had been talking to. He looked especially concerned.

"Your plan's foiled," the old man snapped at the doctor. "You knew you couldn't hold me here forever."

"Oh good lord," the doctor sighed. "Not again. Restrain him."

The orderlies did as instructed, and within moments they had her grandfather under their control despite his best attempts to the contrary. The doctor ushered Aurora out of the room; the last thing she saw was an orderly prepping a syringe while the others held the old man down.

"You can't keep me here!" he shouted, "I'll get out! And when I do, I'll expose the lot of you for what you've done!"

The doctor closed the door softly behind them, muting her grandfather's cries.

"What are you doing?" she demanded.

"He gets agitated," he explained, "and when he does he's at risk of hurting himself. What happened?"

"I don't know," Aurora said. "We were talking, and he suddenly came to life. He said someone had got him."

"Paranoid delusions," he confirmed with a voice like silk. "It's very sad, but quite common given his condition. I'm sorry you had to see that. It must have been rather distressing for you."

"It was fine," Aurora lied, not wanting to be patronised. "I wanted to meet him."

"You must be Aurora," the doctor said. "I'm Dr Goode. Jack."

He smiled, revealing a row of perfect teeth. "I imagine your mum will be looking for you. She said you were waiting in the car."

"My brothers were in there," she explained, "and I wanted to meet him. What's wrong with that?"

"Brothers," he nodded, "I can relate. Bane of my life."

Aurora smiled, but something made her uneasy. For reasons she could not express, there was something about Dr Goode that made her suspicious. Not only was he was incredibly well spoken, but he was *too* well dressed. His haircut was immaculate, there wasn't a wrinkle in his clothes, and his shoes were new and well-polished.

In short, he was too good to be true.

"Anyway, I'd like to say it can't cause much harm," Dr Goode continued, "but you saw how he reacted. Another time, maybe. For now I think it's best we find your mum."

"There you are!" barked Joan moments later, storming down the corridor like a hurricane in a tracksuit. "You were meant to stay in the car."

"I wanted to meet him," Aurora explained. She'd said that three times in the last three minutes. Why did people struggle to understand? Was she saying it wrong?

"Maybe some other time," her mum suggested, echoing Dr Goode, "We're very busy at the moment. Football season," she added as an explanation, glancing at the doctor.

"Every season is football season!" Aurora moaned.

"We're off," her mum told her, leading Aurora out by the wrist and giving the doctor an embarrassed look.

Aurora wrestled her hand free.

"I left my phone in his room," she lied.

"Is that okay?" her mum asked Dr Goode.

"As long as you keep it quick," he said kindly.

"Thirty seconds," her mother warned Aurora.

She ran back into her grandfather's room. The old man was subdued and back in his chair, and it was as if their meeting had never happened.

Aurora didn't know why she had gone back in. The old man was a little scary, if she was being honest, and there didn't seem to be

40

much she could say to him. Maybe it was pity. Maybe it was curiosity. Either way, she wanted to say something to him.

"I'm sorry I got you in trouble."

No answer. She had not expected one, but it was still disappointing. She went to leave.

"Awe-rah…"

She stopped, returning to his side. "Granddad?"

He leant forwards, the strain on his face apparent. Clutching her wrist, his knuckles whitened.

"Don't… trust him," he warned, "Everyone's in danger... Read. Learn… I'll be here…"

And with that, he seemed to pass out.

A chill ran through Aurora, and she left the room in a hurry.

In her haste, she failed to notice the red light on the radio was blinking once more.

Chapter 6

The Adventures of Jock Danger

Eric and Ryan tried in vain to tease Aurora on the journey home, but their jibes were not solely malicious. There was a twinge of curiosity in their voices, and she could tell they were wondering what had happened in the home. She ignored them, and when it became apparent she wasn't going to tell them anything they soon lost interest.

Her hands stayed under her coat, clutching the three paperbacks her grandfather had given her. For her mum to learn she had them would most likely have been a disaster.

The boys tore up to their rooms when they entered the house. Aurora removed her coat, hung it by the front door and started upstairs too. Something thudded beneath her: one of the paperbacks had got caught in her pocket and fell to the floor.

"What's that?" her mum asked, only half paying attention.

"School stuff," Aurora lied, scooping the book off the floor before her mum could look closer. "Extra reading." It wasn't a bad lie and her mum seemed to buy it; Aurora often brought back more novels than any sensible person could carry.

"I'll be in my room!" she yelled as she ran up the stairs. "Homework."

Closing the door behind her, Aurora clutched the books to her chest. Her heart was pounding.

Why does it feel like I'm doing something wrong? She didn't know. It wasn't because she was defying her parents; she did that on a daily basis, although not to this extent. Maybe it was Dr Goode. He was a doctor, after all. They were about as grown up as it got, and he had warned her not to encourage her grandfather.

Whatever it was, she quite liked the feeling. Her grandfather was alone, and she was all he had, even if he didn't know it.

She spread the three thin, battered paperbacks out on her bed. They shared the same style; the bold font, faded colours and dramatic cover that screamed classic adventure story. All three showed a chiselled hero locked in action against nefarious villains, or escaping from treacherous landscapes. She read each back cover, deciding which one to tackle first.

Jock Danger and the Forgotten Forest told the tale of (unsurprisingly) a forest deep in the Congo which, it was rumoured, held a great treasure from another world, but was haunted by a terrible monster that could disguise itself as the very trees of the forest, and only Jock Danger was man enough to go in.

Sounds okay, Aurora thought. She'd heard of better.

Jock Danger and the Phantom Oilrig (which Aurora had noticed in her grandfather's room) made mention of, yes, a ghostly drilling platform, which appeared in the North Sea at night. It spelled certain doom for those who saw it, and only Jock Danger was man enough to go in.

Really, Granddad? You'll have to do better than that.

In *Jock Danger Must Die!* a vicious warlord dispatches a group of assassins to finish off the adventurer once and for all. Hidden on his remote island, the warlord holds a terrible power, and poses a threat to the whole world. Should he survive the assassins, only Jock Danger was man enough to go in.

I'm starting to detect a formula here, Aurora noted, suddenly feeling reluctant. The books felt terribly unoriginal. Still, it wouldn't hurt to give one a try, would it?

And with that, she opened the battered copy of *Jock Danger Must Die!* and began to read.

```
As the small jet plummeted from the sky, hurtling
towards the mountainside and bursting into flames
engine by engine, the pilot, Jock Danger, while
wrestling with a dwarf cage fighting champion,
finally realised he had bitten off more than he
could chew.
"Unhand me, Danger!" the dwarf yelled desperately
in his thick Austrian accent. He had stopped
biting Jock's ankle when he saw the mountainside
gradually growing larger through the cockpit
windows. "If you don't, we'll both surely die!"
"Not a chance, Hans," Jock grimaced. "You're my
only link to the Nameless City, and I'm not
letting you go until you tell me what I want to
hear!"
```

44

"I can't!" Hans screamed. "They'll kill me!"

The dwarf twisted and turned, trying to break Jock's grip. Jock knew the technique, he had been unfortunate enough to tackle a cage fighter in Mexico four years earlier, while trying to break a smuggling ring that dealt in rare cacti, and although this fighter was much smaller than his last opponent, the principle remained the same. He countered Hans' move and slammed the little man into the control panel. He heard a crack, and did not know if it was the dials on the console or one of the dwarf's teeth.

"Don't make this harder than it needs to be, old son," Jock yelled over the roar of the engines. "Give me a name!"

"It's them!" Hans sobbed, realising his attempts to fight him off were futile.

"Who?"

"You *know* who!"

"Say it!"

"It was the Neh —" the word caught in his throat, and the assassin struggled to breathe. He clutched at his collar, choking, eyes wide, and Jock knew exactly what this meant.

Before he could take action, the dwarf was dead.

Knowing there was nothing he could do, Jock grabbed the only remaining parachute and leapt from the burning aircraft as flames engulfed the last engine. The chute opened, yanking the straps

45

hard against his shoulder, knocking the air from his chest and sharply slowing his descent as the plane exploded against the mountainside.

Things were not going well. He would land shortly, and wherever it was, it would be in the middle of nowhere. It was freezing out, he could feel the cold getting to him already, and night was coming. He had a lighter, his hat and a watch: more than enough to survive.

But that was not what chilled him to the bone. What did that was knowing who killed Hans.

Only one group had the power to do that. Only one group could kill a man halfway around the world for even mentioning their name.

The Ne'er DuWells.

And with that, Aurora was hooked.

Jock Danger, the tough-as-nails explorer whose wit was matched only by his right hook had her captivated. She spent the next hour and a half reading through the (admittedly thin) book; following Jock scour the earth in search of mystical relics, staying one step ahead of criminals, dangerous women, mercenaries and thieves alike.

And to top it all off, as exciting as the character of Jock was, there were two references in particular that kept her wanting more. The mysterious cabal known as the Ne'er DuWells were as fascinating as they were evil. They were everywhere, they were all powerful, and they were utterly anonymous, yet everything seemed to lead back to them, one way or another. For a hero like Jock to dread taking them on only made them seem even more terrifying.

The other reference was even more cryptic, if that was possible. Whatever the Nameless City was, the champion explorer regarded it as the ultimate goal. This was a man who had climbed every mountain, plundered every tomb and rescued artefacts beyond comprehension, and still this one prize eluded him.

Aurora put the book down and immediately set to choosing the next one, when a shrill voice from downstairs called "Dinner!" cutting her escapism short.

Chapter 7
Pitching Danger

The Card's dinner table was unique in that it consisted of two sofas angled towards a huge TV which dominated the living room. The actual table was buried under a heap of assorted football-related paraphernalia; kit bags, plastic cones, filthy socks and match programmes, and Aurora unsuccessfully tried to remember a time when it hadn't been.

The Cards were, as usual, gathered round the TV to watch football. It was as close to a family event as they got.

The temptation to scoff down her food and rush back upstairs was almost overwhelming, but Aurora didn't want her parents to grow suspicious. Putting the brakes on like this was torture, like being forced to very slowly unwrap the world's greatest birthday present.

Halfway through eating, the temptation became too much for Aurora, and she decided to share. It was a long shot, but rather than take issue with them, maybe her family would find the books interesting. She would regret *not* mentioning it. What was the worst that could happen?

"I read one of Granddad's books," she announced to her family, who sat slack-jawed in front of the TV.

"You took one of his books?" her mum asked, eyes not leaving the screen.

"He told me to."

"What book?"

"One he wrote. Have you read any of them?"

"No. I don't know," she said, distracted. Then Joan processed what her daughter had said and tore her eyes from the screen: "He wrote a book?"

"He wrote a lot of books," Aurora told her. "I want to see him again. When can we go?"

Maybe it was a pause as the captain lined up a free kick on the TV, maybe it was the unexpected question, but either way, her family all turned from the screen to look at her. Even Red.

She had their attention. She could not believe it.

"See... Granddad?" Ryan asked.

"Yeah, I want to talk to him," she continued, quite amazed everyone was paying attention to her. *Let's see where I can go with this*, she thought. "He's got these villains, called the Ne'er DuWells -"

"Sound like City fans," her father interrupted, turning back to the game. The others, except for Joan, followed suit. Aurora's heart dropped.

"Well, they kind of are," she continued, trying to keep her mum engaged, "They're looking for this Nameless City..."

"They will be if they stay two-nil down," Eric said, trying to adopt the same tone of nonchalance as his dad. Aurora frowned, confused until she realised he was referring to the football team.

"Did you like him then?" Joan asked, actually curious.

"Yeah, he was nice."

"Pretty boring nowadays though," Joan said. "He just sits in that chair."

Aurora nearly contradicted her mother until it struck her: Joan didn't know about the outburst with the radio. That must mean that Dr Goode hadn't told her. Why would he do that? Was he trying to stop Aurora getting into trouble, or was there more to it?

It was then that the captain took the free kick. The ball shot across the heads of the players and was deflected off the striker's waiting foot with surgical precision into the back of the net. The whole family, including Joan, was swept up in the excitement, cheering noisily and captivated once more.

Aurora was disappointed but what did she expect? The important thing was she had tried, and Aurora would not make the same mistake again.

In that moment she made a decision about what to do next that would change her life forever.

Her appetite lost, she climbed the stairs and returned to the fantasy world of Jock Danger. If she had waited a moment longer she would've seen her mother glance around, briefly wondering where she had gone before returning to the match.

Chapter 8

Upon Further Investigation…

Aurora dedicated the first Saturday of the Half Term holidays to learning all she could about Jim Hayhoe, Jock Danger, and the mysteries of the Nameless City and the Ne'er DuWells.

To her, there was only one place this investigation could be carried out: the library.

Her love of books meant she was on first name terms with the staff, who had recommended dozens of stories to her over the years, and were only too eager to help her research the mysterious old man.

A search through the library's catalogue yielded no results. Widening the search, there were no results for Jim Hayhoe or Jock Danger on the internet. He was more than forgotten; he seemed to have never existed; any trace of him or his stories scrubbed from the history books.

"But he's written loads of them!" Aurora told the librarians. "How can they simply not be there?"

"It happens sometimes," said Barbara, one of the librarians. She was Aurora's favourite; interesting and funny, and (compared to the others) young. She seemed to make working in a library cool. "Given your granddad's age, they would have been released pre-internet, and sometimes things like these aren't recorded properly. Not everything is remembered as a classic, especially if they don't sell well." Aurora thought she wanted to add 'or aren't very good,' but hadn't, afraid of hurting her feelings.

51

She had had the foresight to bring the three paperbacks with her, and she scoured them for information, looking at the publisher, the ISBN number, where they were printed, the lot.

Nothing.

One search result – many pages in and far later than any reasonable person would think to search for – linked the name Jim Hayhoe to a publishers called Salmon & Son Books. Aurora had already searched for Salmon & Son; their name and logo of a fish leaping into the air were on all three novels, but the link was broken, the page gone.

Salmon & Son, needless to say, never seemed to have existed either.

Growing frustrated by her lack of success, Aurora tried changing her approach.

Despite a plethora of mythical cities in popular culture, searching for the Nameless City was fruitless. However, searching for the Ne'er DuWells under various different spellings turned out some interesting results.

Or lack of results, to be more accurate. She found lots of entries such as "Ne'er DuWell conspiracy," but upon selecting the links, found that the websites crashed or had been removed altogether. Only a few conspiracy theorist sites made any reference to them, and they were almost entirely useless. Several times she found quotes like "This had all the fingerprints of a Ne'er DuWell affair," and she realised that their name was thrown around almost like an urban myth. Likewise, when she tried searching for images, she only found patches of graffiti bearing their name.

Wholly unsatisfied with her search, she thanked Barbara and the rest of the staff for their assistance and left.

*

Aurora's evening was dedicated to reading the remaining two Jock Danger novels, and she set to this as soon as she got in.

Jock Danger and the Forgotten Forest was an entertaining enough read, but it did not shed any new light on the Ne'er DuWells or the Nameless City.

Like *Jock Danger Must Die!* it was a mix of classic heroics and rip-roaring yarns with a twist of humour. The narrator clearly found the adventures fun but somehow preposterous. A distinctly British tone was present throughout the book, and Aurora found herself cringing at the constant use of phrases such as "Crikey!" or "Gosh!"

It was not hard to see that the resemblance her grandfather bore to Jock Danger was clearly intentional. She thought about the wilful glare in his eye, the way he dressed; that dated suit with khakis. It did however remain quite obvious that Jock was deliberately too good to be true. The adventurer was tough, brave and witty. Her grandfather might have been the same as a younger man, but those days were clearly behind him. Now he was trapped in a nursing home, alone.

If anyone was meant to read his books, Aurora was.

As late afternoon turned to evening, she finished *The Forgotten Forest*. The adventure concluded with the sentiment that nature should not be trifled with, as the thieves who followed Jock into the woods met a grisly demise, the adventurer himself barely escaping with his life.

The tribe who lived on the edge of the forest made Jock an honorary member of the clan, and gratefully awarded him a twelve stringed musical instrument that Aurora recognised from her grandfather's room.

She knew she should stop there; it was late and she should sleep, but there was a feeling that persisted, and she grabbed the last book, *Jock Danger and the Phantom Oilrig*, migrating under the covers to read by torchlight.

It was there she found what she was looking for.

Chapter 9

High Stakes Games

"Well chaps," Jock Danger announced, a stack of poker chips and a terrible hand of cards in front of him, aiming a pair of pistols at some of the world's most dangerous individuals, "We're in a bit of a sticky spot, aren't we?"

He was terrible at bluffing, and hoped no one could gather from the bead of sweat that was subtly working its way towards his brow that both guns were empty.

The room contained a single round table with a light hanging directly above it, casting stark shadows onto six people with weapons raised at one another. The poker game had been an unusually tense one and tempers had been pushed to the brink until finally the standoff had occurred.

It was an interesting gathering. Around the table was Jock; his friend and sometimes sidekick Julio Knives; a huge man in his sixties with a braided beard; an aristocratic young man with a murderous disposition and immaculate suit; and an infamous crime lord. Standing behind the crime lord was her bodyguard, silent and menacing.

"Whose bet is it?" Jock asked innocently.

"I bet last," Julio smirked, keeping his guns trained on the crime lord's bodyguard and the aristocrat. "It's the shaman's turn."

"It's not me," the large man corrected him, "My bet's what got you all fired up in the first place."

The 'shaman' was the huge man in his sixties, who bore more of a resemblance to a Viking warrior than a magic man. Of all the figures gathered round the table, he was the only one who did not have a weapon drawn on any of the others. A wolfish smile was plastered onto his face, and he watched the players with eager eyes.

He also had the single largest knife Jock had ever seen carefully placed next to his diminishing collection of poker chips. Jock had seen a lot of knives in his time, and was tempted to reclassify this one as a sword.

"Well, what do you expect, Ragnar?" Jock scoffed, "When your bet was to reveal the name of the Nameless City?"

"My hand is just that good," Ragnar grinned.

"Or you're bluffing," the aristocrat suggested, speaking up. Of slim build, the young man had a three-inch, vertical scar on his right cheek, blue grey eyes and a cruel mouth. Although his words were directed at Ragnar, his eyes were fixed on Jock with murderous intent. "Avalites are not renowned for their poker faces."

Without moving his eyes from those gathered around him, Ragnar grabbed the huge knife from the table and stabbed it down with considerable force. The blade had, quite remarkably, pierced the heart of the Ace of Spades, which lay upturned on the table.

"Word of advice, son," Jock told the aristocrat. "If that's how you treat your clients, you might want to rethink your approach to hospitality."

"How *dare* you talk to me like that!" the young man spat, removing the safety from his gold handled pistol. The light gleamed from the gun and his ornate cufflinks, and Jock could make out a crest with the initials N.D.W written in gold letters. "I should kill you now."

"And why should you do that?" Jock asked.

"You know why. You murdered my father!"

"Prove it," Jock shrugged. "I never did anything of the sort. Maybe he just had enough of you and your whole rotten family."

The young man's temper was ready to boil over and everyone knew it. Fortunately, help came from an unexpected quarter.

"Let's get on with it," purred the crime lord, who was as beautiful as she was dangerous. She held a tiny but ornate revolver, and waved it like a cigarette holder as she spoke. "I don't care if you all kill one another, but not on my time. I've got a prize to win."

"Works for me," Julio put in. "It's getting a little close in here."

"Fine," agreed the aristocrat, finally. He impatiently pushed his small mountain of chips into the centre of the table. "All in."

Everyone placed their bets, and more than chips were on offer. The crime lord slid forward a curiously shaped bottle of wine with a dead cobra coiled inside, the contents held in place by a wax seal. The aristocrat put in the keys to his car, an Aston Martin.

They revealed their cards. Jock's hand was the worst, which was why he had brought Julio with him. His friend was an excellent player, and laid a full house that outmatched both his hand and the crime lord's.

The aristocrat sneered as he revealed his hand. Straight flush: he had Julio beat.

Jock groaned internally. If the aristocrat learned the name, all would be lost. They all held their breath as Ragnar turned his cards over.

"Royal flush," he beamed. He hadn't needed to bluff after all.

Moments later the crime lord had departed with her bodyguard in tow. The young aristocrat was ready to leave too, but had something to say.

"Well played, sir," he growled, swallowing down his anger and nodding at Ragnar. "It appears I was… wrong."

"It comes with age," Ragnar said stoically, although it was obvious he got some pleasure from antagonising the young man. "I would never risk the City's name for something as trivial as a card game."

"As you say. I look forward to dealing with you again in the future."

"Tell *her* I said nice try," Jock advised the young man, who shot him a murderous look as he left.

Once the aristocrat was gone Jock returned his attention to Ragnar. "You can't trust him, old wolf," he told the shaman, "Any of them."

"Thank you for your concern, Mr Danger," Ragnar said, greedily scooping up his winnings with massive hands, "but we've been through this. I know your feelings towards them and would not trust them with the City's name for all the treasures of All Worlds Unseen. But I'll keep the company I choose. Here, for your troubles."

He handed Jock the bottle of snake wine, which the adventurer took gratefully, admiring the contents.

"Now," Ragnar said, getting to business, "Have you ever been out to the North Sea?"

Chapter 10

All Worlds Unseen

And so Ragnar, Chief of the Avalites, (whatever they were) sent Jock Danger on a mission to find the Phantom Oilrig, which plagued sailors on the North Sea. But that was not what captivated Aurora.

"*A crest with the initials N.D.W. written in gold letters.*" She read the quote again, and then the whole passage for good measure. There could be no doubt; the young man who so clearly despised Jock Danger was a Ne'er DuWell. He *had* to be. What did this mean? Were the Ne'er DuWells an organisation like she first suspected, or – from what Jock said – were they a family?

Who was this "*she*" that Jock mentioned to him at the end? What made her special?

Aurora's questions were numerous, and worst of all, it quickly appeared none of them would be resolved in the story. She wondered whether there was a particular Jock Danger tale that addressed the Ne'er DuWells directly. It was strange (not to mention frustrating) to have them constantly mentioned, yet never explained. If there was such a story, she was desperate to read it.

Something else: the Nameless City had a name. That was... a bit odd. She did not know what this meant, or why it was so important it remained secret, but this only increased her curiosity further.

Accepting that she was unlikely to learn more, she read to the end of the book anyway, less for research than for enjoyment, and finishing was reminded of a familiar feeling; it was like coming out of a trance, all sense of time had been lost and it took a moment for Aurora to remember where she was.

It was late, gone midnight. She didn't mind. She found herself unable to stop picturing Jock Danger, the exciting places he'd visited, the perils he had overcome or the spoils he had gained. Moreover, she wondered what the Nameless City was, and why it was so special.

Surfacing from under her covers, Aurora took a moment to gaze at the gallery of posters on her wall that tempted her to a world of excitement. The promise of a life free from her mundane existence somehow felt closer when she realised she was related to someone who had lived that life.

She caught herself. That wasn't true. Jim Hayhoe hadn't led that life, *Jock Danger* had. Her grandfather was clearly well travelled – she had seen that from his pictures – but he wasn't an adventurer.

Climbing out of bed, she peered out of her window and into the darkness below. Barely visible in the trees that lay at the end of the garden, eyes glinted in the dark. The Wolf was watching. For a moment she wondered if Jock Danger had ever encountered a creature like this.

Once again, she held up her hand in a motionless wave that was not acknowledged.

Within a few minutes of climbing into bed, she had started to drift off, and it was then that she experienced a sensation she had never felt before.

Or maybe I had experienced before, maybe a hundred times over, but I had forgotten every time. Completely disorientated, I had no sense of what was up or down, but I didn't seem to care. Lying under my bed covers was like treading water, the duvet around my chin the sea resting under and around me.

Unable to break free, I sank, taking a deep breath without realising it. My feet stuck out the end of the bed as I pulled the duvet up, and was sure I felt heat on my toes, as if sunlight was warming them. How? There's no sun at the bottom of the ocean, I thought to myself. In the split second before I awoke – if I really was asleep – a strange feeling kicked through my body, as if I had stumbled even though I was lying down. In that instant, clear as day and illuminated in an ethereal glow, I saw something I would never forget.

The moment was as brief as a passing thought, but I remembered everything with such clarity I could have been there forever. I felt the breeze on my face, smelled the salt in the air and heard waves gently lapping on an unseen shore.

And towering over me on a mountaintop ahead was the Nameless City, its spires of crystal reaching into the sky with an otherworldly majesty.

Whatever Aurora was experiencing ended as soon as it began, and she snapped awake, legs flailing. Sitting up, she was oddly breathless. Everything was as it was, but with a sharper focus than she had ever known. She must have read too much, her brain was overactive, she told herself as she lay down once more. She pulled the duvet up around her neck as she tried to relax.

Which was when she noticed.

The top of her bedcovers were moist and cold, as if they had been left out in the rain. She pressed her nose to the duvet and noticed an aroma of salt water, like when her clothes had been dampened by sea spray.

She lay there a while, unsure what to think. Gradually she calmed and sleep claimed her once more, but she knew one thing had changed: she was ready to believe.

She had to see her grandfather again, tomorrow.

For Aurora, the adventure had already started.

Chapter 11
Rags and Tatters

As she lay in wait early on Sunday morning, ready for her parents to fall into her trap, Aurora allowed herself to mull over a theory she had been nurturing for some time.

On the rare moments that her parents showed each other affection, they had been known to tell the story of how they met. Specifics changed, but Aurora knew it was to do with a pub quiz, a hotly debated question in the football round, and an impressive display of knowledge that prevented a fight breaking out. What she didn't know was which of them displayed the knowledge, and which of them was ready to fight over it. Neither combination would have surprised her, and Aurora liked to mix it up; sometimes her Mum would amaze Red with a knowledge of football he thought no woman had, other times she was the one preparing to crack some skulls.

Her theory was this: her parents did not care for football anywhere near as much as they claimed. She was sure that they certainly used to, and still liked it a lot, but not half as much as they once had. In all likelihood, they would be content to just spend the day together, watching TV or going out, whatever took their fancy. Aurora liked to think the reason behind their fanatical pretence was fear. Fear that one would stop loving the other if they no longer shared this obsession. So they kept up the charade, unaware of their rather ironic predicament.

Aurora listened carefully to the sounds of the house waking up. She heard Red go into Eric and Ryan's room, and she heard them moan as he forced them out of bed. Red would be heading her way next, but she was ready for him.

"Get up," he ordered, stretching his long neck round the door.

"Sick," Aurora mumbled, keeping the covers drawn up to her chin, "Not going."

"Don't be pathetic," he said, "It's an important game. We need a linesman."

"If you put me in that car, I will plaster the inside of it with vomit," Aurora threatened, careful not to appear too alert.

"It's an important game," Red offered, unused to having to negotiate rather than order.

"I don't *care*," she moaned. "I just want to sleep."

"You must be sick," Red mused. "No one in their right mind would say that."

Aurora retched for effect, signifying the conversation was over.

It did the job. Red backed out the door and shortly after Joan had taken his place.

"You feel warm," her mum said, feeling her brow and setting down the essentials (water, bucket, loo roll) before adding reluctantly, "Would you rather I stayed home?"

On any other day Aurora would have found this touching. It was the nicest thing her mum had said in a long time, but today it would completely ruin her plan. "I'm just gonna sleep," Aurora said feebly.

"Okay," her mum said, relieved. "Feel better."

Aurora waited. From her bed, she heard the door slam and the car start, unwilling to move until her family had reached the end of the road in case she jinxed anything. Only once she was convinced they were gone did she throw her covers off.

Wearing her clothes under the duvet had done a great job of raising her temperature, and fetching her bag from under her bed, she left her parents a note saying she was feeling better and had gone to visit friends for the rest of the weekend. She didn't know how long she was going to be, but in case anything happened this would explain where she was.

The note was probably unnecessary; it was unlikely they would realise she was gone.

When Aurora and her family had driven back from St Elmo's, she had noticed that Northwood tube station was nearby, so at least she knew the route there. She had been on the underground before, but never alone, and it made her nervous. Northwood was only a few stops away with no changes, she discovered to her relief.

Watford station was busy due to a match at Wembley further down the line. The people moved around her with such speed and selfish purpose that she felt slightly intimidated by the fact she didn't know which platform to head to. Buying a ticket, she passed through the gates and headed towards the escalators.

Aurora had read somewhere that human traffic was like a current that was hard to escape, but she had never known how accurate that statement was until now.

It's a bit like walking through a living maze, she thought without pleasure. The people around her – most of them taller – seemed to be unaware of her presence, and in the hustle and bustle she was jolted and bumped without acknowledgement or apology.

More than their selfishness, she was taken aback at how the people moved without thought, as if the herding instinct to become part of a mob of bodies waiting to get somewhere was overpowering. Whenever she saw one of these clusters of people queuing to get through the barriers or get on the escalators, from a distance there seemed to be a strange mist hanging around them. Stranger still, whenever she got closer, she would see it wasn't a mist at all, but something a little bit like loose strands of spider web.

No one else seemed to notice – or perhaps they did, and were used to it – so she decided to ignore it too. Still, this was easier said than done. The strands seemed to be everywhere, and they inspired a strange feeling in Aurora. Whenever she saw the wolf she experienced a sense of unconditional trust. This was the opposite; a profound distrust and worry over something she could not define.

Stepping onto the escalator, she clung to the right hand side so she wouldn't get in anyone's way and composed herself. Commuters in a hurry overtook her, but she paid them no notice until a dark shape flashed by.

No one else seemed to react, but there was no denying what she saw. Whatever it was, it certainly wasn't a person.

Leaning left to get a better view, but mindful of others walking down the escalator, she saw the shape. It was hard to define; the closest description was that it resembled a large bundle of rags, its features concealed as it overtook other people, nipping in and out without being seen.

Aurora looked around, wondering how no one else could have seen it. The shape reached the bottom of the escalator, and disappeared down a foot tunnel. She was ready to dismiss the sight until another appeared.

And another.

Then another.

Aurora had never seen anything like it. A knot of fear rose in the pit of her stomach as the escalator neared the bottom and she came closer.

The blurred, dark shapes moved in abrupt twitches as if animated in poorly captured stop motion. It was only in the fleeting moments when they were still that she could get a good look at them.

Slightly smaller than a man, they wore rags and tatters that concealed most of their bodies. This could not hide their hunched shape, or their limbs, which were clawed or malformed. Their faces, perhaps mercifully, were concealed by hoods.

Aurora was aware of a feeling of such fundamental *wrongness* when she saw them; the first comparison she could imagine was of a shattered mirror, the reflection distorted and unrecognisable. Or she was reminded of something broken, put back together wrong.

She stepped off the escalator and carefully made her way towards her platform, mindful to avoid going anywhere near the creatures, yet keeping them in sight. So far they had not noticed her, and she wanted to keep it that way.

Looking around, it seemed she was the only one who could see them, but why? Were they mistaken for other commuters? It seemed preposterous, but the only other explanation was that they were invisible. Maybe, somehow, it was both, she did not know.

While they navigated between the commuters, drifting between them with ease, Aurora noticed by watching one shape in particular some subtle details betray its presence. Every now and then it would brush past a commuter, and when that happened the person it touched would shiver, unconsciously.

In what Aurora was sure would get a reaction, it passed close to a happy toddler in its pushchair, pausing momentarily to watch the infant. The little boy saw it and immediately burst into tears, terrified. Aurora noticed that the creature was not scared off by the toddler's reaction, it knew it had been seen, but had decided there was no threat here, and moved on at its own pace.

But that was not the most common effect. Every now and then, the creature seemed to pick someone, as if sizing them up, and rather than brushing past, it would calmly place a hand on them. When this happened, their prey would lose their concentration; their eyes glassed over, their sentences trailed off.

Aurora waited for her train feeling trapped and claustrophobic. With all the people on the platform there was little room to move, and the creatures seemed uncomfortably close. They moved around the platform like insects; seemingly random at first glance, yet something coordinated their movements with a greater perspective, lending them efficiency. It was only a matter of time before one of the creatures passed her way, and more than anything Aurora wished her tube would arrive immediately. A few metres away, one of the creatures, less active than the others, sat slumped against the wall, perhaps mistaken by commuters for a beggar, perhaps entirely invisible, she wasn't sure.

Aurora stared, unable to tear her gaze away. She could not make out its face from beneath the hood, only the steaming breath bursting from its salivating jaw when –

It looked at her –

staring her straight in the eye. It knew she was watching and it was not used to being seen. All the other creatures within view stopped at the same moment and turned to face her. They seemed to share one mind; if one knew something, they all knew.

The slumped creature rose, forcing itself up in small, hateful twitches, like a wind-up toy coming to life.

It started towards her.

Aurora was paralysed with fear as it shuffled closer. It gained speed and raised itself to a height greater than hers yet remained hunched over, a needle-like red glow coming from the eyes under its hood.

Somehow, everything got quieter; the platform was stripped of noise. All she could hear was the creature's breathing, which grew louder as it got closer. Even from a distance, she thought she could smell its breath; it reeked of rancid, dead things.

It was less than five metres away when the tube arrived, the doors opening behind Aurora. The rush of people coming off startled the creature, forcing it to withdraw from the clamour of bodies, and Aurora snapped to and climbed aboard.

Like a broken dam of silence, the sound rushed back.

The doors closed with the creature less than a metre away. The train hovered on the platform for a few moments, giving it time to shuffle up to the glass.

Standing mere inches from Aurora's face, its breath steamed up the window. It stared at her, unmoving, until the train started to pull away. Others creatures joined it, their eyes all fixed on the train, as Aurora sat shaken, gasping in ragged lungfuls of air.

Chapter 12
Something Rotten

Terror was a new sensation to Aurora. Like anyone her age she had watched a few scary movies or walked home in the dark, but the sensation of pure fear, knowing that something could physically harm you, was something she had not encountered before. The creatures, whatever they were, terrified her, and she hoped to never see them again.

Even so, as alternatives went, St Elmo's was not a preferable one. Aurora kept her wits about her as she approached the home, knowing she would have to remain out of sight after last time.

Out in the sunlight, touched by the crisp autumn breeze and away from the stagnant air and shapes of the underground, it was as if the whole thing hadn't happened, a bad dream, and she felt her head clear instantly.

Underground monsters though. It was a lot to accept. Something else she had seen, to join the wolf, or her vision of the City. Something to give her parents cause to truly freak out, should they know. She couldn't begin to imagine what they would say if they could see her now.

Perhaps now wasn't the time to dwell on this.

Wolf. Creatures. The City. Granddad.

There had to be a link.

*

Her grandfather was sitting in his chair as before and Aurora wondered if this was all he ever did. Trapped in a tiny room, haunted by past triumphs, knowing nothing amazing will ever happen to you again. Aurora couldn't think of anything more depressing.

She snuck in, gently pulling the door to behind her. Her grandfather's eyes lifted; he knew she was there.

"Hello Granddad," she whispered. His faint smile returned, marred with the usual pain. The radio was back on, Aurora noticed, making her head throb immediately.

"Awe…rora," he muttered. He seemed to be doing better, managing all three syllables.

"I need to talk to you," she told him. "I've been reading your books. I like them a lot."

The old man smiled, but he couldn't concentrate on her. His eyes wandered, as if he wasn't strong enough to maintain focus on any one thing. "Sorry, can't…" he muttered. "Radio…"

"It's horrid," she mused. "I thought I turned it off."

"Would you?" he pleaded. "Only way I can… talk…"

"I… I'm not sure," she said hesitantly. "The last time I did it ended badly."

The fight left him and he slumped back in his seat.

"I'm sorry Granddad," she told him, "but you saw what happened. If I turn it off and you start shouting and everything, you'll get restrained again and I'll be in trouble. I really don't want either of those things to happen."

"They… won't," the old man managed. "I promise." There was something about the way he said it that made Aurora believe him.

I shouldn't be doing this, Aurora thought, but somehow the word "Okay" emerged from her lips.

I am going to get into so much trouble.

She took the radio down. There was something about it she found unsettling, but she couldn't put her finger on it. She read the brand name: *Good 4.0*, engraved in the wooden base.

Good four point zero.

Good four point oh.

Good four oh.

Good for nothing?

"Good for nothing… why did I think this?" she wondered, mostly talking to herself. She had heard the term before, but couldn't place where.

"Good for nothing… means Ne'er Do Well," her grandfather whispered.

"Oh."

Aurora stopped dead. In that moment, everything seemed to change.

Until then it still hadn't seemed quite real. Even those things on the underground, now she was away from them, could be somehow forgotten, pushed out of sight and mind.

But this was different. Suddenly Aurora felt very aware of her surroundings. She was here, alone and unprotected, and maybe being told off was not the worst thing that could happen to her.

The cynicism her parents had tried to install in her since birth fought back in vain. It was a radio; that was all. It was just another story, and she was being silly. Fiction did not blur into reality. The name was a coincidence. They couldn't be real.

Could they?

"You read the books… You know…" the old man whispered.

Wolf. Creatures. The City. Granddad. If they could exist, couldn't the Ne'er DuWells?

What if everything she'd seen being real was the only way it could all make sense?

She turned the radio off and set it down as quickly as possible, not wanting to touch it any longer than necessary. The red light flashed with maddening frequency in its death throes, then faded to black.

She turned round to her grandfather and braced herself, waiting for a response. The old man visibly relaxed, his breathing deepened, as if exhausted, but that was it.

Nothing else happened.

Aurora felt a wave of relief, but maybe a pang of disappointment too. "Are you okay?" she asked.

He nodded. "You wanted to… talk," he said, seemingly no longer in pain, but still lacking in energy. "I don't know you… but I'd like to. Tell me… about yourself."

She lit up. No one in her family had wanted to know anything about her before. Still, she didn't really have that much to tell, or at least she didn't think so at first. Once she got through the straightforward stuff – twelve years old, school, friends, don't get my family, they don't get me, read lots – she carefully steered the conversation into what she wanted to really talk about: him.

"Why doesn't Mum come see you?"

"My fault," he explained. "… Hardly saw her growing up. Why would she come to see me now? There's… no blame."

"The first time I heard of you was the other day when I went through her things. I just thought you were dead."

"Oh," he said, then coughed violently. "Not for a little while."

She mentioned his books and how much she enjoyed them, but held back about her vision of the City. She still didn't totally trust that at any moment he wouldn't spring into life and bring all the staff of St Elmo's down on them.

"There was something else though," she said, unsure whether she should bring it up or not, but deciding maybe he was the only person she could share this with. "On the underground. There were these… things. They were creatures, dark shapes, made all wrong. No one could see them but me. But they saw me –"

A sound cut her off. She heard footsteps down the hall, coming their way.

A moment later, the handle on the door started to turn.

"Hide," her grandfather hissed, urgency in his voice. "Now!"

She ducked behind his armchair. She was small enough that its wooden frame concealed her. Using what must have been every ounce of his strength, her grandfather pulled a sheet from his bed and across his lap, creating a screen for her to hide behind.

Crouching there, her heart in her throat, Aurora saw a figure enter the room. Behind the chair, her view obscured by the sheet, it was a struggle to see who it was, until the figure stepped in front of her grandfather. She knew who it was as soon as she saw those perfectly polished shoes.

"No more outbursts today," Dr Goode said, leaning in towards her grandfather. "Good. Let's keep it that way."

"Over eleven years here, and this was your first attempt," he continued, moving away from the old man. Aurora could only tell this from his feet; she couldn't see him without exposing herself. "I must say, I'm a little disappointed. Still, I don't think your young accomplice will be coming back here any time soon, do you? One incident the others will understand – it's *you* after all – but more than that? She'll have my head."

The others? She? Questions flashed through Aurora's mind. Dr Goode could be talking about his superiors, he hadn't said anything specific, but maybe… There was another *she* Aurora had heard mention of recently.

"Let's make sure this is set appropriately," Aurora heard Dr Goode say, "It's not playing the song you know so well, and I know you get fidgety if you don't get your music."

Then she realised; he was heading towards the radio. Was the 'song' his name for the nauseating sound it usually made, or did he really think it was meant to play music?

Either he was in on it, one of them, or he wasn't. How could she tell? And what would be worse, her accusing him of being involved in a conspiracy he knew nothing about – and the fallout that would mean with her parents – or letting him continue to keep her grandfather a prisoner of the Ne'er DuWells?

The answer was obvious.

"What are you doing?" she asked, stepping out from behind the armchair. Dr Goode jumped and Aurora thought she could detect guilt, or maybe she was imagining something that wasn't there. Regardless, he quickly composed himself and slipped on the calm exterior she found so unnerving like a coat of charm.

"Aurora," he smiled, but it seemed like his patience was tested too, "I didn't see you there." He glanced at the door, confused to see it closed. She could see him thinking. "Where's your mother?"

"She's not here," Aurora told him. "I came alone."

"I'm not sure that's a good idea," he said calmly. "Not after last time. I believe we agreed to leave it a while before you came here again."

"What are you doing with that radio?" she demanded.

"It's a coping mechanism," he explained. "People like your grandfather need routine in their advanced state. It's important they have things they're used to, like their favourite radio programmes. Little things to bring him comfort."

"I don't think it brings him any comfort," she said. "I think it only hurts him."

"Well, I'm sorry you feel that way," he said, shaking his head, "but as a qualified medical professional, you'll just have to trust me."

Unnoticed by either of them, the old man had begun to move. He sat up straighter than he had before.

"Have you heard it?" she asked. "It nearly drove me crazy, and I was only listening to it for a few minutes. He has to put up with that all day!"

"Well, for starters there's a fair chance his hearing's not what it was, and secondly, it was probably acting up when you heard it. It normally works perfectly fine. It plays those old songs he likes, the ballroom numbers."

"You're lying," she hissed.

"You know, I don't think I like your tone," Goode said, seemingly changing the subject. "I think it's time I called your mum. What would she say if she knew you were here now, throwing accusations around, acting like this?"

"She doesn't know. And if she's not going to stick up for him, someone ought to. Might as well be me."

Her grandfather's feet planted themselves firmly on the carpet. His ankles braced.

"Aurora, I'm afraid I've had just about enough of this," the doctor sighed, his patience frayed. "You shouldn't be here, your presence is disturbing, and you'll have to leave."

"Maybe things should be disturbed!" Aurora snapped. "They can't be much worse than they are right now!"

"You are meddling in affairs you don't understand. You can't *begin* to imagine the damage your being here could do. Go home."

"How much are they paying you?" she demanded.

"I don't see how my wage has anything to do with –"

"Not the home. *The Ne'er DuWells*. To keep him here captive, using the radio somehow."

"Oh damn," Goode sighed deeply, his fingertips rubbing his brow. "I really wish you hadn't said that."

The old man in the chair quietly moved the sheet off his lap. He gripped the arms of the chair.

"You are, aren't you?" Aurora gasped.

"You've convinced yourself. It doesn't matter what I say. I could tell you that the phrase is forbidden here. That it sets him off; part of his dementia. But you wouldn't believe me, would you?

"I tried to be nice, to do things the decent way. To keep you safe," Goode continued. "You have no idea how uncommon that is where I'm from, but you wouldn't have it."

By this point Aurora didn't really know what he was talking about. Nor did she notice the old man rising.

"Go!" Dr Goode snapped, grabbing Aurora roughly by the elbow and dragging her towards the door. "Forget about him. Don't come back. If you do, I'll inform your family, and if that doesn't make you see sense, I'll take things further, and you won't like that."

"What would my granddad have to say about that?" she argued, wrestling against his grip.

"Who cares?" All pretence of civility appeared to be gone now and Aurora struggled to see him as a doctor at all. Her suspicions seemed more likely by the second. "He's a sick old man. He won't even notice you've gone."

"He might," she smirked. "I turned the radio off as soon as I arrived."

"You did what?"

"That's why you didn't hear it playing his 'song'."

Jim Hayhoe now stood fully upright behind Dr Goode.

"You didn't… it's never been off for that long before –" the doctor began, dread in his voice. He turned –

– Right into Hayhoe's fist, which caught him square across his jaw. Goode was down in one. It was one hell of a punch.

"*Don't* talk to my granddaughter like that," Jim Hayhoe growled.

Chapter 13
Another Way of Looking

"I shouldn't feel good for doing that," said Aurora's grandfather, as he casually rubbed his knuckles and looked down at Dr Goode's unconscious form. "Still, circumstances being what they are, perhaps it was justified."

Unable to form any words, Aurora stared up at the old man, her mouth hanging open.

"Well, this is interesting," he observed, "You can talk to me when I'm at death's door, but as soon as I'm on my feet you can't think of anything to say." From anyone else it might have sounded short, but there was a playfulness in his voice he couldn't hide.

Say something, dammit.

"I..." A thousand questions burned in her mind, but she didn't have the first idea of where to begin. She started with the most obvious one: "What the hell happened?"

"Language, young lady," he warned, "There's a time and a place for it. It's like you told Goode: you turned the radio off, and that cursed thing has been making me sick for as long as I can remember. Without it, they'd have been unable to keep me here.

"Anyway," he said, changing the subject and turning his attention to her, his eyes like a pair of spotlights, "On to more important business: let's take a look at you."

"Um, shouldn't we be getting out of here?" Aurora suggested, indicating Dr Goode on the floor.

"Oh, don't worry about him," her grandfather said, reaching into his suit jacket and pulling out a thin pair of glasses. "I gave him the Jock Danger special. He'll be out for hours."

Balancing the glasses on the end of his long nose, he scrutinised her face for what felt like ages. "Mm-hmm," he mumbled. Aurora felt like she was being examined but didn't know what for. Her grandfather had nice eyes, she thought, as he looked at her, but she could imagine them serious too. She guessed he could be quite scary if he meant to be.

"You, young lady, are really very pretty," he concluded seriously, turning her face red. His smile broke out again and he held out a hand. "It's a pleasure to meet you, Aurora."

"You too," she said, feeling quite sheepish as she tried to control her blush. She took his hand and he shook it in an overly courteous manner, a gentleman to his core.

This is more like it.

"I'm Jim Hayhoe. You can call me Granddad. Shall we get out of here?"

*

Twelve year olds should not struggle to keep up with pensioners seven times their age, but Aurora was starting to feel that was exactly what was happening.

"We'll need this," he muttered, "and this. *Definitely* this…"

The old man was closely examining his shelves and bookcase, selecting items to take with them. He took the desired objects and handed them to Aurora, who struggled to hold on to everything as he loaded her up.

"You don't need to read this one," he muttered. "You've read that... ugh, I can't believe I wrote *that* one..."

For her part, Aurora was keeping herself together rather well, not that she had much choice. Her eyes kept straying to Dr Goode, who had still not regained consciousness. There were matters she urgently had to discuss with her grandfather, but his concentration span left a lot to be desired. She was about to mention the creatures from the underground again when her grandfather broke off from the task in hand and crept over to the door. He snuck a peek out to make sure there wasn't anyone coming, and gently closed it.

Watching the door close, he let out a yelp.

"What is it?" Aurora asked, afraid they had been seen.

"I've got... old!" he cried, examining his reflection in the mirror that hung from the back of the door. He moved his face from side to side, squeezing, poking and stretching it from every angle. "So they were right: the nose and ears *don't* stop growing," he moaned.

Aurora was losing patience. They didn't have time for this.

"Spit it out then," her grandfather said without turning around, still inspecting his wizened face. Aurora straightened up; how on earth could he tell she had something to say?

"Before Dr Goode came in, I was saying about the things I saw on the underground."

"Things? What things?"

"I'm not sure. I'd never seen them before. They weren't people and they weren't like animals, they were something else, like a creature or a monster. They seemed to feed on people's concentration, and no one could see them but me. There were loads of them, and they saw me looking."

"I'm not sure how I feel about this," the old man said gravely. "A story of this magnitude requires tea. Where's the kettle?"

"We don't have time!" she argued.

"There's always time for tea," he insisted. "I haven't had a brew in years, which quite frankly is a more brutal punishment than that radio."

"I don't *like* tea," she said, rolling her eyes at the old man, but he was having none of it. "You were the one who wanted to leave anyway."

"That's where you're going wrong, young lady," he continued, ignoring her point about escape. "A taste for tea is the first rule of being a British adventurer!"

Aurora made an exasperated sound, and her grandfather nodded patiently. "Fine," he said. "We'll go. It's probably for the best: I'm an Earl Grey man myself, but I'd wager the chances of finding any here would be slim to none."

"Okay," Aurora sighed, relieved. The old man turned from her, and continued sorting through the items he wanted to take. "You believe me, don't you?" she asked. "About the creatures?"

"Of course I do," he said seriously. "What sort of eccentric grandparent would I be if I didn't? Besides, you're not the only one to have seen these creatures before. Abominable things. They shouldn't exist in our world, certainly not in the numbers you describe, but it sounds like they've managed to come through."

"Come through from where?"

"Ah," the old man said, turning back to her. His eyes sparkled. "Where indeed? No place man can reach, that's for sure. Somewhere else entirely. You see, I've long believed that mankind's imagination is a very real thing – a place – a world that exists on its own. Our world is just one side of the coin and the two are intrinsically linked. Now, if this other world is based on imagination, and these creatures affect the imagination in people, then that can't be a coincidence; there has to be a link. It's all part of a bigger picture, just waiting to be revealed."

"And you think we can find it?" she asked, rapt, "The other world?"

"I don't know," he admitted, "There are clues out there. The biggest one has eluded me my entire life."

"The Nameless City," Aurora finished.

"Precisely."

"That's why I came to see you today," she told him. "I think I had a vision of it last night."

"Really?" There was a touch of reservation in the old man's voice.

"Really," Aurora insisted. "I'm not making it up. It's hard to remember, but I think it was like a castle on a mountain. I was watching it from by the sea. When I woke up, my pillow smelled of seawater. It felt like I was really there."

"I suppose if you're going to believe my stories, I'd better believe yours," her grandfather smiled.

"You'd better," she warned, and the growl in her voice made it clear she was used to people not believing her, and she was tired of it.

"Okay," he held his hands up in submission, "point made. But let me explain, because this is important: to see the Nameless City is almost impossible. No one knows where it is. Legends tell of sightings in the folds of the sky at sunrise and dusk, or in the arc of waves in the blackest of stormy waters. It exists between shadows and light, dreams and hopes, beyond reason and in madness. It's found through the imagination, rather than a certain location. Since I learned of it, the Nameless City has been all I have looked for: all my adventures were to find it. Even when I was looking for relics or treasure, they all had ties to the City. If it truly is the gateway to this other world, then it hides the secrets of the universe; what lies beyond life and death. Those creatures are just another part – a dangerous part – of that puzzle."

"But why me? Why was I the only one who could see them?"

"You have a talent, Aurora," he told her. "A rare one, that will become stronger over time, if you allow it to. You are able to see the world from another angle, and it's what enabled you to see those creatures. Anyone can do it, but most have conditioned themselves not to. Your willingness to see is what sets you apart, and it will be key to us finding the City."

Someone with Aurora's imagination had no chance of resisting a pitch like that. The old man spoke with such conviction that she could feel herself getting drawn in.

He *believed*.

It was then that the barriers of doubt her parents had installed in her decided to kick in, and she felt shame for what she knew she had to ask.

"It's true, isn't it?" she asked tentatively.

"What do you mean?"

"All this: the other world, the Nameless City, the Ne'er DuWells. I know I have an active imagination – Mum and Dad are always telling me – but you're not messing with me, are you?"

"I'm not, Aurora," he said with a sad smile. "Those parents of yours might want you to 'grow up' but there's two things they don't know: first, the real world has things in it beyond belief, regardless of whether their little minds can imagine them or not. Second, you're an explorer, just like me, and we can't sit idly by while there's an adventure to be had!"

Chapter 14

Jailbreak

And so, possibly Jim Hayhoe's greatest adventure began.

His new companion in tow, there would be no stopping his quest to find the Nameless City and elude the Ne'er DuWells.

Or so it seemed, until a well-spoken voice said four words that threatened to ruin everything:

"No one's going anywhere," Dr Goode said, standing next to the door. They had left it too long, he was awake and upright.

Aurora swallowed. With a shout, Goode could stop their adventure before it had even begun.

"Just you try and stop me," her grandfather growled. For him it wasn't just about the adventure; if Goode called for help, he would be trapped once again, and Aurora almost certainly wouldn't be able to save him.

"You've one hell of a hook," Goode conceded, rubbing his jaw.

"It should've kept you out till morning," Hayhoe said, "but I'm not as strong as I was. You've seen to that, haven't you?"

"*Time* has seen to that. Jim, I've no idea what you're –"

"I know you," her grandfather pressed. "I know all of you, despite your efforts to remain anonymous. You're almost one of them, but you're not quite there, are you? It's not just about the blood, it's the heart too, or lack of. Dress up however you like, it doesn't make any odds: you'll never be a true Ne'er DuWell."

A tremor of something unpleasant seemed to go through Goode, but he regained his composure. "This is really sad," he sighed, shaking his head. "You're worse than I feared. You're not well."

"Drop the act," the old man warned. "Tell *her* she should have killed me when she had the chance."

Hiding behind her grandfather as he faced Goode, Aurora made herself useful. She had found an old canvas backpack that could only have been owned by an adventurer like Jock Danger, and was discreetly loading all the items her grandfather had handed her into it. She hoisted it over her shoulder, surprised by its weight.

"Aurora, please," Goode pleaded, diverting his attempts from the old man to her. "I'm sorry I was short with you before, but you can see why when he ends up acting like this. Can't you reason with him? He's not a well man."

"He's better now," she told him. "The radio won't keep him here anymore."

"This is hopeless," he breathed, and seemed to decide something. He began to move.

What happened next seemed to take place very quickly, yet Aurora would only remember it in glimpses. Goode had one hand on the door, and was about to pull it open. At the same time, his free hand reached into the pocket of his jacket, for what, she would never know. It was then that Aurora made a decision she could never turn back from.

The radio was still on the shelf behind her, and she grabbed it, pitching it at Goode. Everything up until this point had been disobedience, but this was something far worse.

The radio was very heavy, and she was afraid it would do little more than drop at his feet. She clearly didn't know her own strength, because Goode had to step out of the way to stop the radio hitting him, and it struck the door, slamming it shut. The radio came apart, smashed to pieces.

Immediately, waves of energy emanated from the radio as it shattered. Aurora had time to think, *well, that's different*, before things stopped making sense.

She felt a colourless shimmer that reminded her of a heat haze wash over her, and immediately felt tired, nauseous, and confused.

She had to sit down.

She had to stay put.

She had to stop thinking.

Dr Goode absorbed the brunt of the energy and collapsed. Aurora would not be far behind. She lurched forward.

A hand grasped her wrist. The effect was immediately sobering; the will in that grip cutting through the confusion like torchlight through darkness. It was enough to get her legs moving. She allowed herself to be led out.

Her senses returned to her in the corridor and it took her a moment to remember where she was.

"That was most unpleasant," her grandfather remarked, standing over her. "Are you all right?"

"I'm better now." Away from the radio she felt herself recover. "How did you do that?"

"What you felt when the radio broke is what I've endured every day I've been here," he said. "Your safety was at stake. It was all the motivation I needed to get us out." He caught himself, suddenly embarrassed by his own boldness. "Wish I'd got my tea though," he added, trying to make light of it.

It was too late: for the first time, Aurora had seen a glimpse of Jock Danger in the old man, and she wasn't likely to forget it.

She smiled.

"So, um, what are we supposed to do now?"

Having visited her grandfather twice now, Aurora knew the way out of St Elmo's. The problem was, the way she was used to entering was incredibly public; they would pass by the communal room and reception desk and she had only managed it unseen due to her speed and small stature.

Neither of those worked now she had her grandfather in tow. They had to try another route.

They didn't know the corridors of St Elmo's, and they snuck along at an uncomfortable pace, torn between acting casual, sticking to the walls and creeping, or making a run for it. Despite her grandfather's newfound energy, Aurora doubted he would be much for running, and truthfully she still felt nauseous from the residual effects of the radio.

After a half dozen twists and turns, the corridors all started to look the same. The indistinguishable doors, walls and carpet were disorientating and Aurora worried they were running in circles. Should they fail to get out before Goode came to, the consequences would be disastrous. She could only begin to imagine the trouble they would be in.

Her grandfather led her down a few more turns, but despite his attempts to take charge it was clear he didn't know where he was going either.

"Where are we?" she hissed.

"I wish I knew," he admitted. "This place is bigger than I thought."

It was at that moment that a woman spotted them. They had been careful to remain hidden until now, watching unseen as staff pushed trolleys of bed sheets or food round the home, but they had failed to see her coming.

The lady was pretty in a sophisticated way. She was in her early forties, smartly dressed in a polo neck sweater with a long coat and gloves.

"Hello," she said, a warm smile spreading across her face as she laid eyes on Aurora.

"Hi," Aurora replied. Her grandfather had moved on already and she could sense his impatience. Scouting the route ahead he hadn't looked twice at the woman, but Aurora knew they would attract more attention if she didn't say anything.

"Are you lost?" the woman asked kindly. There was something about her smile Aurora couldn't place. It was captivating.

"Pretty much. Do you know how to get out?"

"Try the staircase behind me," she suggested. "It leads out into the gardens."

"That's perfect!" the old man cried, leading Aurora out by the wrist.

Aurora seemed unable to tear her eyes from the lady as her grandfather dragged her out. "Thanks!" she yelled.

The lady held up her hand in a motionless wave that was neither responded to nor acknowledged.

Aurora wasn't sure, but before the door to the stairwell closed behind her, she thought she heard her say, "You're welcome, Aurora."

*

Not too far away in Jim Hayhoe's room, Dr Goode came to. Face down on the antiquated carpet with pieces of the shattered radio scattered around him, he suddenly recalled what had happened and a shock ran through him as if he had been soaked in iced water.

He shot to his feet, and the world's worst head rush struck him.

He was out, Goode realised as soon as he saw the room was empty. *Free*. This was impossible. Worse, it was inexcusable. It was his duty, the one thing *they* had trusted him to do, and he had failed. His opportunity to prove himself worthy, detaining their greatest enemy, had ended in disaster.

Goode wanted desperately *not* to call it in. Provided they hadn't got too far and he was quick enough he could get Hayhoe back. Everything could be as it was.

But there was the girl to worry about now too, and that changed everything.

Pushy and disruptive, she was going to land him in big trouble, but she was clearly smart and loyal too. He admired that. She would be in danger, and worse, she would *be* dangerous; there was no telling what she might prompt Hayhoe to do. He had to find them.

With a feeling of dread, he made a call he knew he was going to regret.

"We might have a situation," he said gravely.

Chapter 15

On the Run

Of all the people to break out of prison each year, girls not yet in their teens and pensioners make up a very small percentage.

"We need to get organised; lay low for a bit," her grandfather decided as he peered from their hiding place in a large rhododendron bush. "Apparently I'm too old to just make a run for it anymore, and we need more information before we decide what we're going to do. Fortunately I know just the person to help on both counts."

"*If* he's still alive," Aurora muttered, unaware she had shared the thought out loud.

"Oh, he's alive," he said. "That I can guarantee. And no more age jokes from you, missy. We need to get to London."

As soon as the coast was clear they made a break for it. The grounds behind them, Aurora cast a final, fleeting glance back. The threat of St Elmo's seemed to diminish the further they got from it, until finally it submerged behind the treetops like a sea monster returning to the ocean.

Her grandfather didn't look back. Aurora reckoned he wouldn't ever want to look at St. Elmo's again.

"So, Dr Goode," she asked when they reached the nearest bus stop. "He's a Ne'er DuWell?"

"He is," he said. "They work hard to remain anonymous, but I never forget a face."

"But he's different. You said so in the room, or were you trying to mess with him?"

"He's not a blood relation, but he's still one of them."

"So they're a family?"

"The most evil family on the planet."

"Who's '*her*'?"

Her grandfather looked uneasy but said nothing.

"You mentioned a 'her' to Dr Goode," Aurora pressed, "and to the Ne'er DuWell in your book."

"Enough questions for now," he told her softly as a bus pulled up, "Wait 'til we're somewhere safe. You never know who's listening."

They climbed on board. Her grandfather rooted around in his pockets for his wallet, and Aurora saw from his face he realised he no longer had one. He was about to speak when the bus driver gave him a nod. "Forget your pass, mate?" he asked.

"It appears so," her grandfather admitted.

"On you get," smiled the driver, pointing a thumb behind him.

"Much obliged." He went past, and Aurora heard him mutter, "That's new…"

The double decker was equally busy and unclean. As they made their way to the last remaining seats, her grandfather's nose wrinkled and Aurora wondered how long it had been since he had last used public transport.

"You did really good, throwing that radio," her grandfather hissed once they had sat down. "Not to mention coming for me in the first place. I know you have a lot of questions, but their spies are everywhere, so we need to wait for now."

"I do have one question," Aurora said. "Aren't we supposed to be headed towards London?"

"Of course."

"Well, we're not." She pointed at the list of stops, and he saw they were heading towards Watford.

"Ah."

He pressed the button.

Ten minutes and one change of bus later, they were back on course.

The bus shot past a greyish blur, and Aurora was almost certain it was the Wolf watching them. One look behind her confirmed it; there it sat, head tilted slightly, as if puzzled. There was something different about the Wolf now. What had changed?

Their route led back past St Elmo's. Her grandfather kept his head down, but Aurora couldn't help stare as they passed the home.

Their bus sped past a familiar figure. A look of alarm struck Dr Goode as he recognised the fugitives. Aurora ran to the back of the bus to get a better look as Goode pursued them on foot. Unable to help herself, she stuck out her tongue at the shrinking figure. She noticed her grandfather roll his eyes and she shrugged, smirking.

Dr Goode gave chase. He ran, but to no avail. The bus turned a corner and soon disappeared from sight. With no hope of catching them, he slowly, abandoning the chase for now. There was no point exhausting himself in vain.

Calming his breathing, he removed his tie and starched white doctor's coat, abandoning them with all remnants of his assumed identity.

The doctor's identity had outlived its usefulness. He would not return to St Elmo's again.

He was Jack DuWell. And he had a very big problem.

Chapter 16

The Underground, Revisited

If Aurora thought her ignorance of the underground was bad, it was nothing compared to her grandfather's. She kept watch as the old man scoured the tube map, concentration knotting his brow.

"It's gotten… messy," he frowned, trying to will the information he required from the nine-zone display of multicoloured worms.

"We'll work it out when we get on the tube," he decided, grabbing a small paper copy. "As long as we head towards London we should be fine."

Aurora used her remaining money to buy travel cards for both of them. The old man apologised profusely, telling her it was a grandparent's duty to pay for everything on days out and promised to pay her back.

"We can talk now, can't we?" she asked moments later as they sat on a Metropolitan Line train trundling towards London.

"If we're careful," he said, "but keep your eyes open."

"So they kept you trapped like that, for all those years?"

"I've no idea how long it was. Judging from how big you've got, it must be over a decade. You can't begin to imagine how powerful they are. Or how much they hate me. To arrange something like that would be easy for them. But it doesn't matter right now. We've a more pressing issue to address. I've a lot I need to teach you, Aurora, and we haven't much time, so you'll have to pay attention."

She did, chiding herself for feeling a little disappointed; first day of her adventure and her classroom was on a rickety old tube train. Oh well, it couldn't all be dirigibles and mad scientist's lairs.

"Try to imagine that what you see in front of you isn't what's out there, but instead it's what you *choose* to see; what you've been trained to see. Our eyes see a thousand impossible sights every day, but our minds stop us believing they can be true. That strange shape lurking in the corner of your eye? The something you feel lurking behind you that's gone when you turn around? The shimmer that must be a trick of the light? These are signs of the world of imagination manifesting in our own.

"Throughout most of your childhood those around you encourage you to grow up and live in the real world." Aurora knew he was referring to her parents here. "They do this because they can't remember it for themselves, and one day the sight is gone, and all memory of it has passed into myth, until years later in your ignorance you try and purge your own children of it. I'm old, I have to fight against what I believe to be real, so it's a struggle for me to see, but for you it should be easy."

Placing a hand on each of her shoulders, he turned her towards the rest of the commuters in the tube carriage. "Places like this are perfect. Commuting is one of the few times when people's minds truly wander. It's boring; they've done it a thousand times. They have nothing to do but wait to arrive, so how do they choose to fill their minds? Pick someone, and begin."

Aurora's eyes roamed over the assembled commuters, unsure who would make for an obvious candidate. Her gaze settled on what she thought would be an easy target; slumped in his seat was a man in filthy overalls, staring out of the window.

"I've got someone," she said.

"Good. What do you see?"

"He's tired. He's slouching, staring off."

"You're only observing his body language. It's logic, and while it will point you in the right direction, you need to go beyond that. What do you *see*?"

"That's it. He's not paying attention. His eyes aren't focusing on anything outside the window."

"You're observing. You're not seeing." The old man's patience was infuriating. "Forget playing detective for a moment and see. What do you see, Aurora?"

Aurora bit her lip in frustration. There wasn't anything else to see! Why couldn't her grandfather understand that? Maybe he was wrong about her. Maybe it was too late for her after all.

"Nothing, I can't-"

But I could.

A growing veil of darkness grew around the man's head, spreading like ink in water, reminding me of when storm clouds form above angry cartoon character's heads.

"I can see!" *I said, turning towards my grandfather.* "I can-"

"Keep concentrating," he ordered. "Hold that thought. Now, look again."

102

Other commuters had drifted off like the man in overalls. They shared a similar haze of darkness around their heads, and I knew somehow that in that moment these people had no passion, interest or desire for anything. What I noticed most was how widespread this was, as if for the duration of that tube journey, they had chosen not to think or feel anything.

As I became more comfortable picking out the hazes, I began to detect the differences between them. A woman on her phone was having an argument with someone, her words generating small sparks of malice that sprayed from her lips onto the passengers beside her.

Behind me was a boy maybe Ryan's age looking at his phone. I didn't need the sight to tell me he had just been dumped, and as he looked at the phone I traced delicate, intricate shapes rising from him, only to wilt and die like dead flowers.

As our tube came to the next stop more passengers got on, as if it wasn't crowded enough. An old lady shakily made her way across the carriage, lines of distress rising from her. Before long, a young woman gave away her seat, and both women displayed swirling tendrils of warm colours that melded and illuminated everything around me for a moment, gratitude mixing with satisfaction.

"It's like pop art. That colour..." I whispered. My grandfather smiled, understanding but struggling to see. "I think I get it," I continued, "Not only are we affected by the things we can't see, but we create them too."

Reaching the next station a young couple parted ways, the woman kissing her boyfriend goodbye before getting off the train. Their auras, for want of a better word, were mixed together, and as the tube pulled off they disentangled, but although separated, his kept alight, only slightly dimmed without her.

No longer an over ground train, the tube disappeared into the darkness of the underground for the rest of the journey. If we didn't have lights it wouldn't have made much difference: I probably could have seen by the light of auras alone.

I watched the bright spheres and spirals play through the air... and then I saw it.

The creature pulled itself through a window connecting the tube carriages with the same contradictory effortless grace and jerking spasms it had the last time Aurora had seen it, apparently unfazed by the way the tube lurched in the tunnel.

It dropped from the window and landed on the ground with what should have been a sickening thud. Instead, it had once again become quiet; the creature had absorbed the loud rattling of the tube tearing along the old track; only a low din remained. It didn't seem to care about its own wellbeing, all it wanted to do was move forwards.

The creature was slightly different from the one that had gazed at her through the doors that morning, but it was just as terrifying nonetheless. Aurora's hands found her grandfather's arm, and she gripped it.

"What's wrong?" he asked.

"It's here," she hissed. As before, no one had seen the creature, and she did not want it to be aware that she could.

"I can't see it," her grandfather said, his eyes scouring the carriage. Aurora thought she saw him grimace in discomfort, but maybe he was just looking.

With her guidance the old man was just able to make out a dark shape, a bundle of rags that snaked through the commuters like dirty cloth dragged through water. Unless he paid close attention, the creature would soon vanish from his sight. Its presence was like trying to understand a difficult concept; lose concentration and risk losing it forever.

"I see something," he said, "but not clearly. Can you see it well?"

"Yeah." Aurora wished she couldn't. The creature was stooped, but occasionally straightened to get its bearings like an animal sniffing the air. It was then that Aurora could make out a lipless mouth under its hood, a row of teeth like black daggers, wet and unclean. No two creatures were exactly alike, she realised; some were beaked, others had drooling maws, but they all shared the same lifeless eyes.

The creature drifted past the man in overalls, acknowledging him with a small turn as a king would his subject. From under the creature's rags crawled a loosely coiled grey ball of tendrils and barbs that seemed so light it almost floated in the air.

It latched onto the man, surrounding and enveloping him. The dark shroud that hung over the man hardened, as if setting, but went further, obscuring his eyes, ears and mouth in a mask of darkness.

The creature and its parasite had won him, and harvested what little bitter satisfaction it could.

As the parasite fed, it seemed to extend, its coils loosening and stretching out. It was then that Aurora remembered the spider web like strands she had seen earlier that day when she first entered the tube.

The strands sought other prey.

"Did you see that?" Aurora whispered.

"I think so," her grandfather replied as the creature moved on.

"Something came off it," she hissed, "Another creature, like a hairball."

"It's feeding."

Finally, the dark shape approached the young man, sizing up its prey. The man's aura was still bright with his lover's memory and the creature hissed; both coveting and despising the light the man's aura generated.

Quite unaware of the creature that stood no higher than his chest, or the jeopardy he was in, the man took no notice as the creature slowly, almost gently, wrapped itself around him, its body distorted horribly like a nightmarish constrictor.

Climbing onto his back the creature laid its talons on his shoulders and with all the gentleness of a mosquito, descended its mouth towards the man's throat. It would not use its parasitic minion to harvest this man; his aura was too sweet to share.

The man shuddered. It was a tiny gesture, but from where he sat Jim Hayhoe noticed, not quite sure what he was seeing. Even if he couldn't really see, every fibre of his being knew it was something horrific and unnatural.

To his granddaughter, however...

It was a sledgehammer between the eyes. Rather than its teeth breaking the flesh, the creature's face distorted and stretched, so the two became one blurred thing, a distortion in a hall of mirrors.

But as bad as this was, the true horror was shown through his aura. The swirls stopped extending, the spheres diminished and the colours faded, darkening to a muddy grey. The creature was sapping something from this man, some indescribable force that could not be measured, and seeing this unnatural act happen made me feel sick.

Without realising it, I had stood up. The thing terrified me and all reason in my body screamed to sit down and ignore what I was seeing. The man wasn't being hurt, not really. There would be no wounds to show from this encounter, no bruises or broken bones. He would be utterly unaware.

But I would know.

I stepped forward.

Aurora's grandfather realised what was happening too late. "Aurora!" he hissed, urgently. He tried to grab the girl, but she was out of reach. He knew better than to retrieve her, it would only attract attention. So he waited, trying to focus all his energies on being able to see the creature on the man's back, knowing he would have to do something if it made a move on her.

Aurora waited for the tube to stop at the next station, and as it came to a halt, threw herself into the man, pretending to trip.

The man snapped out of his daze immediately, and for a moment, it seemed as if he was aware of what was happening and he recoiled, confused. The creature extricated itself from the man as if in pain, unable to feed, and landed on the floor in front of Aurora like a dead mass.

In one horrible, tiny moment that stretched forever, Aurora and the creature were eye to eye once again. It may not have been the exact same creature, but the hive mind remembered.

It knew her. And it hated her.

But it was too late. The creature knew it could do nothing here. Its focus broken, people were starting to come around from their respective dazes, and despite not understanding what they were seeing, were beginning to notice the creature. The parasite of strands, already stretched too thin, was forced to recede, and it left pieces of itself behind that scattered and dissipated in the carriage.

The creature hissed at Aurora, uttering a venomous, wordless curse before barging off the train through the mass of bodies that were in the midst of trying to get on. She overheard snatches of words from the people around her as the sound returned.

"– What was –"

"– Some kind of homeless –"

"– Something wrong with his face?"

The murmurs subsided as people rationalised it to themselves, the conditioning her grandfather had warned her about resuming control and returning them to the world they understood.

Aurora sat on the floor for a moment, panting. On reflection, that might not have been one of her brighter moves. Strong hands wrapped under her shoulders, and the man she had bumped into hoisted her to her feet.

"Thanks."

"No worries," he said. He looked tired, like something important had been lost, and it would be a while before it returned. A moment passed as he peered down at her curiously. "I don't know why, but I feel like I should be thanking you for something."

Aurora smiled, unsure what to say. With no idea how to explain it she was pleased he hadn't remembered. "Your girlfriend is very pretty," she offered, finally.

"Yeah," he agreed, his aura igniting, a small thing; muted, but with the potential to heal one day if correctly nurtured.

She smiled once more as they parted ways, feeling the proudest she could remember... until she turned and looked at her grandfather.

Chapter 17
The Stairwell of Perspective

Children shouldn't see their grandparents angry. That's not how it works. Parents tell you off, grandparents spoil you. This was a fundamental rule of the universe. And Aurora was about to watch her grandfather break it.

"Of all the stupid, irresponsible, foolish things I've ever seen, this is the worst," he began, "and I should know. I've angered Mayan tribesmen by stealing statues of their gods. I've fought ex-Nazis under tombs in Egypt. I even married your grandmother, but I never —"

"You're proud of me," Aurora interrupted, deciding she had better stop him before he got too carried away.

"Pardon?"

"You're proud. I can see your aura. You're trying to be angry but you're not. It's sweet."

"You can't expose yourself like that. There's no telling what that creature could've done to you. That was foolish and rash, and you scared the life out of me," he fumed. "And you're right, I am proud of you. I shouldn't be, but I am."

They sat in silence for a moment.

"What's the point of me having this ability if I can't use it?" she asked.

"Suppose that thing had killed you," he replied. "What then? You wouldn't be able to stop the rest of the creatures, which could be spreading like wildfire for all we know."

She considered this for a moment while her grandfather stewed.

"I lied, you know," she said.

"Pardon?"

"I couldn't see your aura. It switched off after the creature ran away. It broke my concentration."

Her grandfather smiled broadly. "Sly minx."

*

Within minutes they made it to Baker Street, navigating the crisscross of tube lines until they reached Covent Garden. Aurora was wary of seeing more creatures, but either there were none to be seen or they were avoiding her.

As she approached the lift to exit the station, her grandfather took her arm.

"We're taking the stairs," he told her.

"There are 193 of them," she replied, reading the sign on the wall. "Can you make it?"

"I don't really have much choice. Count them as you go, would you?"

*

As per her instructions, Aurora counted the stairs out loud, feeling patronised. Upon reaching the ninety-sixth step on the tightly spiralled case, her grandfather wheezed, "Stop!"

They took a minute. In the silence of the staircase Aurora heard the rasp of his breathing and wondered how healthy the old man really was. He seemed to read her thoughts and looked up at her with a wink.

"I'm fine," he said. "Bengal tiger took out a chunk of my thigh in Nepal back in the seventies. I've not been good with tall staircases since. We're here, anyway. This is it."

Aurora looked around. *This is what?* "Granddad, there's nothing here."

"Go up five stairs," he replied, "then look back at me."

Doing as she was told his orders suddenly made sense.

From the hundred and first step, the wall beside the ninety-sixth took on a whole new perspective. Hidden from view was a door, designed to match the walls from every angle except that precise step. She took a step up to one hundred and two and it disappeared. The same happened on one hundred.

"Impressive, isn't it?" he beamed.

It was pretty cool.

Passing through the door they went down a narrow corridor, lit by a few sickly spotlights that created a moody glow. The corridor ended with a rickety old service elevator. Her grandfather moved the mesh gates to one side and they got in. The elevator had only one button, and they pressed it, the ancient device lurching to life, the metal apparently resenting them as it moved. They travelled up for what seemed like an age. As it rattled and shook Aurora felt quite queasy, and it made her painfully aware of how long the journey upwards was taking.

As they slowed to a halt, the old man turned to Aurora.

"I'm taking you to see a friend who's... a little unconventional." He said, "You should probably know, Norm is immortal."

"Immortal. And he's called Norm?"

"He's gone by a few names, I think, but he likes Norm the best."

"It's so... ordinary."

"The name is, but the man really is not, believe me. He's traditional, but he doesn't believe in formality. It's complicated. Just keep quiet and try to keep up."

Aurora frowned, trying to understand.

"Don't worry if he ignores you," Hayhoe continued, "He's very old, far older even than me, although he doesn't look it. He's seen a lot of things, and neither one of us are particularly remarkable to him."

"How old is he, exactly?"

"I don't think he knows," her grandfather smiled.

The elevator doors opened onto an entrance hallway, vast and dark. Aurora stole a glance out of the hallway's slim windows as they walked through. They were high in the city, and she could see the sunset descend upon London, the tall buildings draping shadows silently over the streets.

In between the windows was an array of mounted paintings; the last and most prominent of them a seventeenth century portrait of a well-dressed man with flowing dark locks, pointed trim beard, high cheekbones, bright eyes and a healthy complexion. He was every inch what an immortal should be, she thought, staring up at the handsome aristocrat, when a sophisticated voice drawled, "I hate that picture, doesn't it make me look like a Charles Spaniel?"

She spun round, and her heart sank.

Norm bore a vague resemblance to the man in the portrait, in that they both had two eyes, a mouth and skin. It ended there. The man standing before them looked more like a skeleton; grey skin was draped over his bones, with dark eyes and shabby hair that had been shaved all over and grown out for too long.

"How's it going, lad?" he asked her grandfather. Raising his eyebrows, he added, "You got old."

"Don't I know it," Hayhoe replied mournfully, and they shook hands. Aurora wondered if he did know it. "Damn DuWells had me trapped for over a decade. Aurora here busted me out."

"Is that right?" Norm said, addressing her for the first time. She watched him with intrigue and supressed revulsion. It wasn't really her fault; he was pretty disgusting.

"You'd let yourself go too if you were as old as I am," Norm told her. She tried to deny this was exactly what she had been thinking, but he cut her off.

"Come on then," he sighed. "In."

Chapter 18

Beyond the Norm

Norm's place was something to see. It quickly became apparent that the hallway with the pictures was more like a massive porch. Inside, the actual entrance hallway was like a manor's; ceiling medallions and chandeliers, lavishly carpeted floors, and wood panelled walls covered in artworks and artefacts from forgotten times. Her eyes scoured the place, excitedly.

"You'd better show her round," her grandfather smiled, "Otherwise she's only going to wonder."

"I'm not a tour guide, *James*," Norm grumbled.

"Very well. How about some tea? Maybe a bite to eat? Or is that out of the question?"

"…Fine."

Aurora caught a sly grin off her grandfather as the grumpy immortal led them to a Napoleonic era sitting room, an immense painting of a battleground dominating the wall.

"Any chance you've got Earl Grey?" the old man asked.

"Pah," Norm sniffed. "Potpourri. No chance."

"Had to ask," Hayhoe shrugged, taking a seat. "You're probably wondering why we're here."

"You're looking for the Nameless City," Norm purred. "Still."

"I'm not going to stop until I've found it."

"You've said that your entire life and got nowhere," Norm said, "and in five times that I couldn't either. Look at you Jim; you're in no shape to be running around looking for things like this. You should retire; now's your chance to live out your life in peace."

"Peace," the old man scoffed. "They'd never let me have that. *She* never would. My only hope is to keep looking for the City."

"And what makes things different this time around?"

"We've got her," he said, indicating Aurora, who blushed.

"It's wasted both our lives, son," Norm said, ignoring her, "There's no point squandering a child's life too."

Aurora wanted to object, but a nudge from her grandfather silenced her. She opted to pout instead.

Norm served tea from an ornate pot which had some pretty unwholesome images painted on it. He went to pour Aurora a mug, but her grandfather stopped him. "Don't bother giving her any, she doesn't like it."

"Where'd you get that idea?" Aurora snorted. "'Course I do!"

"All right," he shrugged, giving Norm the go ahead and helping himself to a ginger biscuit.

"Whatever," the Immortal sighed, pouring her a mug.

Aurora took the hot drink and took a tentative sip. It was bitter, and she instantly went to add sugar. As she stirred the drink she wondered why she had protested. She *didn't* like tea. Maybe she just wanted to fit in with the two old men.

"Look, Jim, no disrespect to you and your girl, but you're not going to find anything. The City's a phantom. Every lead we've had has led nowhere. The closest we've come is the Avalites, and they can't prove anything. All we've ever had to go on is the words of shamans, opium fiends and near death experiences."

"Well, I can see which of the three you fit into," Hayhoe frowned, "Look at the state of you!"

"So?" Norm smirked, "It's not like it's going to kill me. What's the point of me keeping in shape? Health doesn't matter if you can't die. Vanity doesn't matter when you live forever. After all this time, I've worked it out. I just had to stop caring."

Aurora took another sip of her tea and decided to add a second sugar. She knew it was best to keep quiet and observe as the two men continued to talk.

"Look, just stop being so stubborn for once," her grandfather pleaded, "We're on the run, the Ne'er DuWells are after us, and the only chance we've got is if we find the city. After all we've been through, after all I've done for you –"

"What's that supposed to mean?"

"You know exactly what that means!"

Aurora could see that despite her grandfather's best efforts, Norm was not interested. An idea came to her while she watched them argue.

I tried to remember what Granddad said on the tube. What else? That was what I had to keep asking. What else? Norm was old, obviously, and bitter about something, but I needed to see more.

Come on, I scolded myself; you could do this earlier. What else?

Something came to me. It was different from before, and it took me a while to realise that it was an aura at all. Grey and muted, it hinted of something extraordinary underneath, owing, I guessed, to his years of experience. Shapes moved around him discreetly, creating bizarre patterns I could barely understand.

As I watched, fascinated, I looked at Norm's face. He was holding something back. I was so engrossed in his aura, I was shocked to see him look right at me, breaking my –

"I don't stare at your vibes, missy," Norm sneered.

Aurora stopped immediately, breaking eye contact and busied herself with her tea, adding a third sugar.

"She can do it, Norm," her grandfather noted, helping himself to a second biscuit. "Not a lot of people can."

"Why do you think it's a hidden city, Jim?" Norm sighed, "It's not supposed to be found by people like you or me."

The old man groaned in frustration and leant back in his seat, miserably chewing on the biscuit. They sulked in silence, neither one prepared to budge an inch. *This is ridiculous,* Aurora decided. If this was the most they were prepared to discuss matters, they weren't going to get very far at all.

"Norm," she found herself asking, nervously, "How are those creatures getting through to our world? The ones in the underground." The question had been bugging her for a while, and he seemed like someone who could answer it.

Norm looked at her suspiciously. "They say the Umbra is the darkest part of the shadow," he said. "That's what they're called, Umbra. Or so they say. Perhaps the nastiest of all Riftrot."

"Riftrot?"

"It's the name given to anything that comes through the Rift. There are others too, but the Umbra are the worst."

"The one we saw on the tube had something with it. It looked like a cloud, but made of wires and string."

"That's another one. They're called the Hayes. They're aggressive and dangerous too, but they're not smart like the Umbra. I've only encountered them a few times, nasty blighters. My guess would have to be that in the last few decades something important has changed. Don't ask me what, but something must have broken down the walls between realities normally maintained by the City. Without the barriers, the creatures are becoming bolder, coming through to our world unchecked, and with the exception of people like you, unseen."

"And if this continues, what would happen?" She added another sugar to her tea, completing its metamorphosis from brew to syrup.

"I'd imagine the Umbra would prey on everyone they can find. Eventually they'll get brave enough to leave the underground, and when that happens, man will become the mindless cattle they've risked becoming for so long."

Aurora was stricken. "And you're okay with this?"

"Live as long as I do, you struggle to see the good in people any more. This planet used to be *beautiful*. People changed all that. I've seen it. The whole world's gone from green to grey. The masses are pretty mindless already," he muttered. "I doubt I'd notice the difference, and I don't think they would either. The only thing I find interesting about all this is who or what let this happen."

"Maybe it was the Ne'er DuWells?"

"Could be anyone," Norm shrugged, his gaze straying to Aurora's grandfather, "They're certainly evil enough, and powerful. They did sink the Titanic, after all."

"What?" Aurora cried, shooting forwards.

"I'm joking," Norm explained. "Sorry. The amount of things they have been involved in, it's almost ridiculous. So Jim and I made it a joke: the Ne'er DuWells are so evil they… and then you would insert an example."

"Half of them were true though," her grandfather growled, clearly finding no humour in the joke anymore.

"The Ne'er DuWells are so evil, they invented global warming?" Aurora suggested.

"You got it," Norm grinned.

"Don't encourage her," Hayhoe warned Norm. "They're not to be joked about."

The silence resumed: Aurora awkward, her grandfather moody, and the immortal plain bored. Aurora winced as she sipped her tea, practically feeling her teeth erode as she drank it.

"Well," her grandfather said to Norm after a lengthy pause. "If age has made *me* stubborn, god knows how thick headed it's made you. Shouldn't have bothered in the first place, just thought you were a better man that that. You could have at least come looking for me."

Aurora gave her grandfather a look of despair, but a quick glance back from him abated her fears. He had a plan, she was sure of it.

"We're staying the night," he declared.

"Be my guest," Norm grunted, not making eye contact with his old friend, "No one will find you here."

"I'll be in the Edwardian lounge if you need me. I always liked that room. Might get a bite to eat first. Bloody biscuits aren't filling me up one bit."

He left Norm and Aurora alone.

She gave him a polite smile, still a little uncertain how to act; she had run out of tea and had nothing else to busy herself with.

"You want to explore, don't you?" the Immortal said. A wry grin slowly started to spread across his face.

Aurora's face lit up.

"Come on then."

Chapter 19

The Loft

From Zone 1 to Zone 8, all the way out of London, Jack DuWell was becoming desperate.

His phone rang, and as he answered it he noticed with a sense of gloomy inevitability that the sun was setting, his eyes squinting in the receding light.

"Where have you been?" asked a voice on the other end of the line. It reeked of self-indulgence. "I've been calling for ages."

"Getting nowhere," Jack replied honestly. "Do you know where they are?"

"Sources indicate they were London bound but we lost them. Interesting note: we spoke to Tundra. They said it's highly likely she interfered with an Umbra. Sent their readings into a spin. Apparently they've never seen anything like it. They're sending some people over."

"Brave girl."

"Stupid girl," the voice corrected him.

"I'll head into London," he said. "See if we can pick up the trail." He neglected to add that he might have a shower and change of clothes first.

"You should know," the voice added with reservation, "there's interest in this."

"I can handle it."

"That's debateable. But you must have known there would be. It's *him*. Remember what happened to Michael."

"You don't need to remind me," Jack said. He could feel himself getting angry and added, "What sort of interest?" He pictured the ever-growing collection of assassins, undesirables and honest to God lunatics on the DuWell payroll. "Razor Bill? Mr 43? The Three Evils? Not Fred the Needle!"

"It's from the top," the voice warned. "Drake. He's flying in. He'll be in touch."

"There's no need –" Jack began, sweating immediately.

"Drake disagrees. But then, he's disagreeable. I thought you'd like a heads up. You know how he is."

"How can this day get any worse?"

"*She's* not happy."

Jack swallowed audibly.

"You asked."

The line went dead. Jack sighed, looked around him, and headed for the nearest pub.

*

"The Ne'er DuWells are so evil, they tricked the world into believing Brussel Sprouts are good for you, when actually they're worse than chocolate?"

"That *is* evil."

As evening turned to night Norm showed Aurora the Loft. It was massive; each room decorated in the style of different periods, with the artefacts to match. The less well-presented rooms contained masses of items organised in no particular order, and Aurora noticed a stuffed hammerhead shark, a Penny-farthing bicycle and some sort of early Twentieth Century flying contraption thrown in with a collection of junk that would put even the worst hoarder to shame.

But despite the treasures in the Loft, Aurora was much more interested in the man who had collected them all. Norm was turning out to be both surprisingly entertaining and somewhat endearing.

"But I don't get why you find everything so boring," she told him. "If I could live forever I'd find so many cool things to do!"

"I thought that too, at first," he replied as they walked through a dining room. "Thing is, I've wandered the earth for longer than anyone has ever known, and tried everything it has to offer. And in all that time, you know what the one truth I've learnt is? There's not much to do."

"Tudor?" Aurora guessed as they walked through the dining room. She wasn't too adept at historical periods, but liked having a go. Norm nodded, feeling somewhat like a history teacher and oddly not minding.

"But to be that bored with the things you've seen…" she continued. "Just how old are you?"

"I don't remember."

"Do you remember where you're from?"

"Nope."

"What about your parents? Your family."

He shook his head.

"I'm sorry."

"It's fine," Norm shrugged, "It's been so long that the concept seems abstract to me, if you know what I mean."

Aurora did not. All her time spent dreaming and imagining other worlds had never once included her family, but now she was on an adventure of her own, she found her thoughts were straying to them frequently. Were they missing her? Did they even know she was gone? The note she had left would buy her a night, maybe two. After that, who knew what would happen? Her grandfather hadn't said. For some reason, she had assumed he would take care of getting her home; grandparents were meant to do things like that, but now it dawned on her; *he wasn't like most grandparents*. He seemed unused to having people to be responsible for, and he certainly wasn't used to being old.

Passing another room Aurora realised with surprise that it was coloured in yellows and blues, decked out with obelisks and scarabs like Ancient Egypt.

"Is that...?" she trailed off, indicating the Egyptian room.

"Oh that," he chuckled, waving a hand dismissively, "I was going for Vegas casino from my Rat Pack days and got a little confused. I like it better that way."

"What's Rat Pack?"

"You know," he grinned, "Frank Sinatra? Suits, big bands, greased hair and whisky?"

"Like Private Eyes?"

"Uh, sure," he frowned, "Just without the detective work and more singing. Give or take a decade."

125

"Oh. Okay."

"Still," Norm considered, "If I had been alive back then – in Ancient Egypt – I probably wouldn't remember it. You never know."

Aurora gave a little nervous laugh until she realised Norm was smiling at her.

"You're messing with me," she said.

"A little," he teased.

They walked on, passing through an ornate eighteenth century bedroom with a four-poster bed, drawing table and chandelier.

"Napoleonic?"

"Close. Hanoverian, apparently."

"What's Hanoverian?"

"You got me," he admitted, "When you live through different periods they kind of blur into one. I just picked bits I liked and got a guy to sort it for me."

"That must have been one confused guy."

"It's amazing how eccentrics choose to decorate. I'm just one of many."

"So, are you one of those immortals who just lives for ever, or are you unkillable too?"

"How many immortals do you know, exactly?"

"You know what I mean."

"Oh, well, I'm pretty damn unkillable," he said with pride, "I've tried almost everything to finish myself off."

"Norm, that's dreadful!" Aurora cried, appalled. Finally, her curiosity got the better of her. "Well, what did you try?"

"It was more like putting myself in situations where the probability of survival was low. Really, really, low. I fought in both Wars. They were horrific, the first one in particular, and although it became clear quite quickly that nothing there would be the end of me, by that point I had become too invested in the guys I was with to leave them. In the fifties I found some atomic test sites, but I grew back too fast. When you see that flash…" he drifted off. "Anyway, my best and last attempt was a couple of decades ago. I hitched a lift on a boat up to the North Pole and threw myself into the ocean with a car chained to my ankle."

Aurora gasped. She couldn't think of anything more horrific.

"Jim'd kill me if he heard me telling you this," Norm said, seeing the look on her face. Aurora smiled, giving a look that read 'I won't tell.'

"That was something though," he continued, "Utter blackness. You don't know cold until you go somewhere like that. I really thought that one would do it. Drowning, the cold, that pressure. The Abyss. What I saw in myself. There are monsters in those depths that defy description. True horrors; old, angry and forgotten. Gods might have left this earth, but they're hiding in the seas. But even they couldn't kill me."

"Wow," said Aurora, amazed.

"Yeah. It's… good to have someone to talk about it with," he said wistfully.

Aurora was flattered to be a confidant to such an amazing being, but she tried to be cool. They left the bedroom and quickly passed through a small sitting room straight out of Second World War England.

"Seems to me you just haven't found the right way to do it," she suggested. "You know what could work?"

"No, but I get the feeling you're going to tell me."

"You should train to be an astronaut," she told him. "Then, when you get into space, you shoot yourself out of the ship and throw yourself into the sun."

Norm's eyes lit up, "That sounds like a plan. I've never been into space."

"There you go, see. A new experience, and most likely a very permanent death."

"I like you," he chuckled. "Most little girls are just nice. Nice and boring. You've got a little mean in you, haven't you?"

"Maybe," she grinned. "I've one other suggestion too."

Norm raised an eyebrow.

"From what you and my granddad were saying, it's pretty obvious that neither of you know that much about the Nameless City, or this world it's meant to lead to. Isn't it possible you may not be immortal there?"

"You could be right," Norm said, and took a moment to consider her suggestion. Aurora watched him mull it over and allowed hope to grow in her heart.

"Look, I'm not promising anything, but I'll think about it, all right? If nothing else, I'll try and stop you from getting killed. You might be the first interesting person I've met since Jim."

Aurora smiled. It was a start.

Finally, Aurora and Norm came to the Edwardian lounge where her grandfather was snoozing in an armchair, his feet up and a hat he had found over his eyes like a cowboy pensioner. A small collection of empty plates was stacked in an uneven pile next to the chair.

"It's his first meal as a free man in a decade," Norm shrugged. "He can eat whatever he likes."

Aurora stretched herself out next to the fire on an antique chair, (Norm went to great pains to tell her it was an Edwardian chaise longue, whatever that was,) and it dawned on her she was incredibly tired.

"There's one other thing you should know," Norm added, perching on the end of the chair, "Has anyone ever told you how you got your name?"

No one had.

"Your parents were expecting a boy, and had plenty of football players' names ready for you. But when a girl arrived instead they were flummoxed. When your grandfather first laid eyes on you he told me he couldn't believe how beautiful you were, sleeping peacefully and quite unaware of everything around you. He asked your parents your name, and they told him they had no idea. He was the one that suggested Aurora."

"After the Northern Lights?"

"After the princess from Sleeping Beauty. You were the real thing. He told me afterwards that it was probably the only time he ever really felt like he got on with your parents. It was the last thing he told me, before he vanished."

Aurora had never heard this before, and she felt a great well of emotion growing inside her. It sent chills over her skin. Lying there on the chair in front of the fire, the excitement of the day suddenly caught up with her and a wave of tiredness overcame her.

"He's lovely," Aurora yawned, touched yet sleepy. "No one in my family's ever really made me feel like they care. Not like he has, and he's done it in no time at all."

"He does care for you," Norm stressed. "Whatever happens, regardless of what you learn about him and who he is, you need to know that."

If she was less drowsy, Aurora might have picked up on the immortal's words. Her eyes closed for a moment, and the comment passed her by; all she knew was that sleep would claim her soon. There was one thing she remembered to ask before that happened.

"Norm," she asked, her eyes staying shut, "Do you ever… see wolves?"

"Wolves?" his brow furrowed.

"Yeah. I know a big blue one. Followed me since I was little. Not doing anythin' wrong… just… hanging around…"

Sleep overtook her and she drifted off. Norm rose from the chair and went over to where Aurora's grandfather was sleeping. He tapped the old man a couple of times with no reaction. He shook him harder and the old man awoke, snorting and spluttering.

"You really fell asleep," Norm sniffed. "You wouldn't have done that back in the day, son. Guess time's catching up with you."

"Give an old man a break," he grumbled. "Did she win you over?"

"Of course she did. She's a smart one. Dunno how she can be related to you."

"Beats me," Hayhoe said. He got up, saw the girl sleeping on the chair and pulled a blanket over her, carefully moving the hair from her face.

"She adores you though," Norm added.

"That goes both ways. I never would have believed she'd come for me. After all this time."

"I didn't know where they were keeping you," Norm admitted. "I should've tried harder. I guess I thought you were dead, but you know how I struggle to keep track of things."

"Forget about it," the old man shrugged. "I'm out now."

"She's got a wolf friend," Norm mentioned, moving things along. "Torrid are nearby."

"Good. Provided we stay on the right side of them, maybe they can help us out."

"From the sound of it, this one has been following her for a long time."

The old man smiled sadly. "That does not surprise me in the slightest."

The Immortal took another look at the sleeping girl and asked, "You sure you want to go through with this? She's only young. Younger than you were when we met."

"She's strong. She'll make it, and if she learns the truth along the way, maybe it's for the best. Everything about this has been unnatural from the start. Anyway, I don't have a choice, do I? They put me in this position, I have to follow it through."

"They might have, but you started it in the first place. Don't forget about Thomas."

"I know, I know," Hayhoe said. "Something had to give. If finding the Nameless City is the only way to sort this out, then so be it. Even if it means the death of me."

"Heh. Maybe me too," Norm said, and a smile tugged at his lips.

Chapter 20

A Wolf at the Door

For the second day running Jack awoke with a stinking headache. This one was his fault. Leaving the hotel room where he had spent the night, he went to find coffee in the hope of purging his hangover. Twenty minutes later he stood clutching the hot beverage against his freezing palms. He brought the collar of his coat up to retain what warmth he could as steam rose from his drink.

He waited, watching the street.

*

The same cool breeze, waves breaking softly on the beach. This was a place of calm. All was well, yet excitement coursed through me. Anything was possible here.

I became aware of a bright light, and turned to see where it came from.

I was wrong last time; the City wasn't on a mountain, it was a mountain. It grew from the rock itself, grown and trained into something habitable and majestic. My mind couldn't begin to comprehend its size.

Remember, I told myself. Remember, as the mist around the mountain's base revealed an even larger secret.

*

When Aurora awoke the City's secret escaped her. Within moments she had forgotten that she had forgotten, and soon all that remained was a feeling of unfulfilled curiosity.

The Loft was silent. She assumed the others were still asleep and, despite wanting to explore Norm's home further, decided her time would be better spent researching, which meant reading more of her grandfather's books.

Rummaging through her bag, she pulled out a thinner volume she had grabbed from his shelves. The cover was plain black without an image; its title simply read 'Other Lives.' Rather than a Jock Danger adventure it was an anthology of short stories. Each tale was brief, a few pages at best, the subject always different. She skimmed through until she found one tale in particular that interested her.

The Lament of the Forgotten Scientist

Maybe it's the fate of someone born into an evil family to do evil things, even if they don't intend to. When I'm at my weakest, this is how I justify it to myself.

Countless generations have dedicated themselves single-mindedly to the acquisition of power. Between wealth, determination and ruthlessness, they have succeeded admirably. No one stops them, because no one really knows who they are. It's been their first rule for ten generations.

The Machine was my chance to stop all that. I built it to find and to explore realms previously undiscovered but longed for. If I could prove we were all one, maybe it would end our pattern of self-destruction.

It has been perverted. *They* have it, and they use it for their own ends. I don't know why I thought it would be different, but I guess I had to try.

The Machine is now about influence. It taps into my very hopes as its source of power, and does damage I can't begin to understand. So much for exploring.

It can subdue and stupefy.

It can make you forget, or be forgotten, and therein lies my hope.

They *will* forget me. I will see the world, and live the life I wanted, and they will be none the wiser for it. But this isn't why I'm doing it. If I can't make a change from the inside, I will *make* them change from the outside, even if they despise me for it.

It's the only thing I can do. The corruption has spread to my children, as I knew it would. They are as selfish as my ancestors, and as ambitious as any who came before me. They should never have been brought into it.

She should never have brought them into it.

Things are going to change.

The story ended abruptly at the bottom of the page, and Aurora had to check overleaf to make sure it wasn't unfinished. That was all there was.

She found she was quite unsettled by this story's tone compared to the lightweight Jock Danger tales. Presumably it was a tale with a moral, although what that moral was meant to be escaped her.

Hearing movement she quickly stuffed the book back in the bag, although she wasn't sure why she did this. Norm entered the room, wearing a pink apron over a tatty green dressing gown.

"Nice look," Aurora teased as she stretched.

"I'm making breakfast," he replied. "Only way to start an adventure. Tea?"

"Sure. Does that mean you're coming?"

"It means I'll get you on your way, and we'll see from there."

Getting up, Aurora realised her grandfather wasn't in the chair he had slept in the night before and wondered where he was until she heard him shout at Norm.

"What do you mean you don't have any black pudding?" he cried with disbelief. "Tell me you at least have hash browns, or has your drug addled brain forgotten the art of a good breakfast too?"

She made a mental note to ask her grandfather about the short story at the right moment. Right now there was a more pressing issue: breakfast.

"This coming from the man who once thought white pudding came from chickens!" came Norm's retort. "Remember who taught you how to fry an egg!"

Aurora rolled her eyes. They sounded like an old married couple.

*

"Good morning, Mr DuWell," said the lead of three identically dressed individuals; a woman accompanied by two men. In addition to their black suits, their posture was immaculate. They all shared the same icy exterior.

"You're from Tundra, I take it?" Jack asked. It was meant to be a joke. Anyone who had encountered Tundra before knew this was exactly what their representatives were like. The quip was met with the exact amount of indifference he had expected, and they observed him without response.

This day promised to be even more humourless than the ones that had preceded it.

"I thought Torrid did the leg work," Jack observed.

"We're undergoing... differences," she answered, to Jack's surprise. "For the time being, you'll find we're up to the challenge. However, we've still not been told why you desire the man and the girl. If you're withholding information we'd rather you told us. It inhibits our ability to make a full prognosis."

"Surely you should know," Jack said, laying on the charm, "that the old man is incredibly dangerous. The girl has potential too, and if Hayhoe gets her to realise it, there's no telling the damage she could do."

"The Avalites have never perceived Jim Hayhoe as a threat," she answered. "He has a history with our tribe that goes back years. Any feud the two of you share is of no consequence to us."

"Look," Jack sighed, "you'll just have to trust me. Everything will be explained in time, but for now we need you to *acquire* them. Unharmed, if that makes you feel any better."

"As you wish. But an explanation will be sought in due course."

"Just try and sort this out before my brother arrives. He'll want results."

"That depends on them. Everything will happen as it is supposed to."

Jack's urge to roll his eyes was nearly overpowering. He did not have time for Zen observations.

Frustratingly, they did have a point though. No one knew precisely where the old man and his granddaughter were; they just knew it was somewhere nearby. Right now all they could do was sit tight and wait for the fugitives to reveal themselves.

*

Leaving Norm's loft was like waking from a dream, or at least departing from a museum you could sleep in. Aurora was sorry to go, she had barely scratched the surface of discovering what treasures the Loft held, but there was adventuring ahead of them, and it could not wait.

It was a cold, clear morning with a bite in the air; autumn was beginning to succumb to winter.

"You okay, Granddad?" she asked, seeing her grandfather pull his collar up, trying to get warm.

"Old bones," he said, forcing a reassuring smile. "I'm still not used to them."

"Right," Norm declared, "Let's get going. I have a few leads left. Should get us moving in the right direction. Who fancies a trip to Soho?"

"We stay above ground," advised her grandfather. "Steer clear of the tube for the time being. With the Umbra's presence down there it's too risky, especially if they know Aurora can see them."

It was agreed, and they set off. Aurora was filled with a sense of promise; they had survived the first obstacle and having regrouped, were off again.

This time the adventure would start properly. They were going places.

As they headed towards Soho the streets were already starting to fill up. Aurora struggled to avoid people who failed to notice her, and she was jostled a couple of times as she tried to keep pace with Norm and her grandfather. She would not have been surprised to see strands of Hayes on the busy pavement.

A hand tapped her shoulder as she passed yet another figure, but it was a deliberate gesture trying to get her attention. Aurora spun round and saw a familiar face. It was the woman from St Elmo's; the pretty lady with the posh voice who had helped them escape. The lady who knew her name.

She looked at Aurora with compassion, but there was urgency there too.

"Watch out, Aurora," she warned. Then, just before she merged into the crowd, she added, "you're in danger."

Chapter 21
Not the Start They Were Looking For

It was Aurora who spotted the suited figures first. It was only when her grandfather and Norm saw her stiffen that they knew there was trouble. There was something about the three approaching them that she had never felt before.

"Miss Card, Mister Hayhoe," the lead suit said. "We would like you to come with us please. There is no cause for alarm."

There definitely was cause for alarm. My sight, my ability to look at auras, had flared up immediately, and without me willing it to do so. The first time had been a struggle; the second had been hard. This time I didn't know if I could even switch it off if I wanted to.
All three gave off a feeling of intense cold, and I saw patterns and shapes unlike any other orbiting them with a calculated slowness.
The three were linked somehow, from the same place.
But under their skin was an undercurrent of something hard: willpower maybe, or passion. It burned like a cold fire. It was when I looked deeper that all three suits looked straight at me, and I forced myself to switch the sight off.
They knew what I could do.

"We're not going anywhere," Aurora's grandfather told them, manoeuvring himself in front of her, quite oblivious to her struggle with her vision.

"Mr. Hayhoe, we haven't time to argue with you. We require both of you to come with us, immediately. It's a very important matter."

"You didn't hear him the first time?" Norm growled, unimpressed.

The suits looked down at him, "This isn't any concern of yours, sir."

Aurora watched, unsure what to do. The tension was mounting. Any moment now, something bad was going to happen, she could feel it, and two old men and a girl was no match for these three. She did not know who they were, but it seemed likely they were involved with the Ne'er DuWells somehow.

"These chaps remind me of that time in Burma," Norm said, eyeing Aurora's grandfather.

"Are you sure?" the old man asked with some apprehension.

"I said I'd help," Norm replied, and Aurora realised they were talking in some kind of code.

"Stop!" a voice shouted, and with dread Aurora saw the supposed Dr Goode running towards them. Except he really didn't look like a doctor anymore.

"Jim, Aurora, please listen to them," Jack blurted out, "No one needs to get hurt. If you come with us now you'll be safe. I won't be able to guarantee that later."

The lead Tundra turned to Jack, "We told you to wait –"

"Now!" Norm yelled, and using the moment of indecision, he threw himself at Jack and the suits. For such a scrawny man, he spread himself quite wide. "Run!" he shouted as he knocked them back.

It was a successful move. For a moment, the Tundra were taken aback, and it was all the opportunity Aurora's grandfather needed to grab her wrist and flee.

Aurora looked back when she heard the shot and stopped running. Time seemed to stand still. The suits pushed Norm off them, a large red mess spreading across his chest.

In slow motion, she saw Jack shout "No!" at the Tundra, forcing them to lower their guns.

Norm collapsed to his knees, facing towards his friends. He winked at Aurora.

"Run," he whispered, and collapsed face first onto the pavement.

They ran.

Aurora's grandfather led them blindly through the back streets and alleyways of Covent Garden. They struggled to make any speed. He was no longer built for running, and she was in shock, her eyes brimming with tears that threatened to wash down her cheeks at any moment.

He played it smart, dodging and mingling with crowds until they merged with a crush of people headed towards the underground. There was nowhere else for them to go, and with great reluctance he led her into an empty and waiting lift headed downwards, praying he hadn't leapt from a frying pan into a volcano.

The lift opened onto a corridor that led to a deserted platform. They had missed a train by only a few seconds and the signs warned there wouldn't be another for several minutes, maybe more owing to a delay on the line.

There was something wrong with the lights; they flickered on and off with ominous irregularity.

The old man looked around; they were safe, for now. He turned to Aurora, who stared at an invisible point ahead of her.

Very gently, he took her face in his hands and turned it towards him.

"It's okay to be scared," he told her kindly.

"They shot Norm," she mumbled, a tear rolling down her cheek.

"I know," he replied, wiping the tear away. "They shot Norm. Norm the Immortal, remember?"

Aurora blinked. It was one thing to hear it, another to believe it.

"They shot him, but that won't kill him," her grandfather continued, "I promise. I've seen him survive much worse."

"You have?"

"Course I have," the old man snorted, "He used to collapse all the time: oldest trick in the book. He was doing us a favour. We did it in Burma, thirty years ago. That's what he was talking about."

Aurora released a sound that was either a sob or a laugh, her grandfather couldn't tell. "I know you said he was... but it's still hard to believe..."

"Trust me. Norm is fine."

Aurora took a deep breath. Norm had to be okay; it was a leap of faith but she had to trust everything she had seen in the last few days was true. If she could believe in mind controlling radios, blue wolves, auras of imagination and criminal families, she could believe in him.

"What are we going to do now?" she asked, wiping her eyes.

A hissing sound stopped her grandfather from replying. He winced, clutching his bad leg. They fell silent.

"We're underground, aren't we?" she realised, only just noticing in all the chaos where they were.

A sense of horror dawned upon her. There was no echo to that hiss, or to her words. There was no noise of any type.

From the darkness of the tunnel at the platform's end, something stirred.

The lights continued to flicker off, and each time they came back the shape had advanced. Even though her grandfather could see it less clearly than she could, they both knew exactly what it was.

The Umbra was coming for them.

"Run!" Aurora yelled. Her grandfather needed no encouragement.

They ran to the end of the platform and turned the corner. This station, like the one at Norm's, had lifts and a long flight of winding steps, but no escalators. Aurora mashed the button furiously, but the lift refused to arrive.

Seconds crept by. She ran to the stairs and looked up; the sign on the wall warned that the stairs were to be taken only in an emergency. Although this certainly qualified, she knew there was no way her grandfather could outrun the Umbra with his old wound, nor climb the stairs.

The Umbra staggered closer, she could almost smell it. Desperately looking for a weapon, Aurora spotted an abandoned half full can of coke by the moulded plastic seats. Snatching it from the ground, she hurled it at the creature, an arc of brown liquid tracking its path.

The Umbra was ready, its deformed claw struck out, cleaving the can in two. Aurora gulped.

"Well," she told her grandfather, "I'm out of ideas."

"I have one," he said, grabbing the girl by the wrist. He pulled her towards the edge of the platform.

"What're you doing?" she cried, trying not to shriek.

"Do you have a better idea?" he snapped, stepping off the platform and onto the tracks. "The signs said delays. Trust me."

Aurora fought the urge to fight him; this went again every sensible instinct in her. People died doing this. "This is not cool," she warned.

The darkness engulfed them.

Chapter 22

Unlikely Saviours

They walked as carefully as their haste would allow, gingerly stepping in between the tracks, unaware of what was electrified and what was safe but taking no chances. Aurora glanced behind her, trying to spot the Umbra. The creature wasted no time in following them, dropping from the platform onto the tracks with all the grace of a corpse.

"It's following," she said, trembling.

Her grandfather said nothing, but clutched her wrist tighter and picked up the pace.

Walking through the tube tunnel was like nothing Aurora had ever experienced. The threats that surrounded them were numerous; from the Umbra, to the trains themselves, to being electrocuted on the tracks. As if that wasn't enough, she thought she could hear rats.

Or worse, she couldn't.

She couldn't hear the panting she had come to expect from her grandfather.

She couldn't hear her trainers scuffing against the ground.

She couldn't hear her own breath.

This was clearly the Umbra's doing. It was absorbing the sound around them. It could be anywhere.

"Faster," her grandfather ordered, as if reading her mind.

Aurora took a step forwards, but her foot refused to move. She tripped on the metal rail and she lost her grip on her grandfather's hand. The wind was knocked from her as she landed hard. She tried to call out, but no sound escaped her lips.

Get up, she told herself. *Keep moving.* The Umbra would be on them in moments, if it wasn't already. Forcing herself to her knees, she scrabbled forwards.

Keep moving.

She shuffled forwards on all fours for a few metres, until she bumped into something hard and warm. She clutched what must be her grandfather's ankle and sighed with relief.

"Aurora?" she heard her grandfather call out, from some way behind her. A moment of cold panic hit her and she realised: she had lost her bearings and turned around after her fall. She had been crawling the opposite way, and her grandfather's call came from behind her. This was not Jim Hayhoe.

Drool dripped around her. The Umbra hissed.

Leaping back, she heard the barely suppressed sounds of its claw swipe at where she had been mere seconds ago. She turned around and crawled as fast as she could, her panting muted by the Umbra's presence.

She wanted to cry; not caring if it was cowardly. She wanted to go home.

Something hit her back, knocking her on to her side. Something ripped; the Umbra had clawed at her, and only her backpack had saved her. If the Umbra hadn't been the one to do it, she would've heard the fabric tear, yet it continued to mute the sound in the tunnel.

The tears came freely now and she struggled to see. The Umbra was getting closer. Where the hell was her granddad?

Forcing herself to her feet, she noticed the tunnel was getting lighter. She must have been reaching the end, nearing the next station. It was quicker than she had expected, and she stumbled into the light, practically running, wanting this whole thing to be over.

The light grew brighter and as she wiped the tears from her eyes she realised it wasn't the next station.

The Umbra had killed the sound. This was a train!

From the side of the tunnel, her grandfather jumped out and snatched her from harm's way. There was just time to see the Umbra shriek horrifically before the train blocked her view. Whether the train had hit it, or it had dodged out of the way, she didn't know, and didn't really care. She just wanted to get out.

They waited in the tunnel as the train and its carriages shot by: the sound returned with a sudden and deafening roar. It seemed to take forever to pass.

As soon as the train had gone they were on the move again. The Umbra was nowhere to be seen, and within a few minutes light from the next platform started to dispel the darkness.

The platform was empty when they climbed up onto it. Aurora had never been so pleased to be in the light.

"Is it still…" her grandfather began to ask, but one look at her face confirmed his fears and he knew something was deeply wrong.

It was back.

There was no time to do anything; they were unprepared for the speed with which the Umbra leapt at Aurora.

Her grandfather tried to stand in the way, but was brushed aside with ease as the creature set upon Aurora with a murderous fury.

The old man fell badly and struggled to get up as the creature stooped over Aurora. Its claws pinned the girl down, and she was clearly able to see under its hood for the first time.

That every Umbra was different was irrelevant. She hadn't seen the first creature clearly, and the last one had had a lipless mouth. This one was beaked, a jagged bill once yellow, now black with filth and neglect. Once more she knew as it stared at her with its hateful red eyes that the hive mind knew her. It knew what she could do and needed to extinguish her before she could harm them.

"Fight, Aurora!" her grandfather bellowed, struggling to rise, "Keep concentrating!"

She was unable to resist as the creature's beak opened, starting to distort nightmarishly like a bent mirror. Her grandfather's voice came as if through water, and as her concentration waned, she wondered why he was making such a fuss.

A wave of indifference washed over her, making her cold and numb inside.

In what she felt to be her final moment, Aurora's last ember of resistance glowed once then flickered as she gave in.

Jim Hayhoe crawled forwards with tears in his eyes, shouting and cursing at the creature. He had managed to get to his knees, determined to reach Aurora before she was lost forever, when he heard a growl behind him.

For a moment, he thought it was another Umbra, and prepared himself for the worst. He did not care about himself; Aurora had to be safe; that was all that mattered.

As he turned to face his fate, a large form leapt over him with ease. It collided with the Umbra, throwing it off Aurora. Her sense of self rushed back to her like a blast of cold air, and her ember of resistance flared to life. Her grandfather stumbled over and pulled the girl into his reach, holding her small form tightly in his arms. She held him too, grateful for the feeling of a warm body against her.

She looked over. The two shapes tumbled as one, locked in combat, their movements a blur as they set upon one another. The Umbra she knew, but the other she had never expected to see here.

Her Wolf, the beast Aurora had seen so many times before, blue and massive, attacked the Umbra with a relentless but calculated savagery, growling and snarling. The Umbra fought back, shrieking, clearly fearful of its attacker. It scratched the wolf's side, but rather than show pain, the animal clamped its jaws down on the Umbra's claw and tore it off.

The unholy wail from the Umbra filled the underground.

"Can you see that too?" Aurora whispered. The old man nodded, unable to speak.

The Umbra staggered back, clutching its ruined stump, black ooze spattering the tiles. The Wolf gathered itself and leapt onto the Umbra once more, angling its jaws around the creature's throat. The

Umbra knew what it was trying to do, and squealed and thrashed, desperately attempting to push the Wolf away.

Finally, its jaws in place, the Wolf twisted, snapping its prey's neck with a sickening crack.

Aurora looked away as it made the kill. As obscene as the Umbra was, she couldn't bear to see its fate.

The creature fell limp from the Wolf's jaws, tumbling from the platform onto the tracks, broken and dead. Impossibly, it slowly faded from sight. Within minutes it would be as if it had never existed.

The Wolf stood panting and proud only a few feet from them. Aurora got up, freeing herself from her grandfather's arms and approaching the beast, fascinated and fearful. It lowered itself onto its haunches and watched her coolly.

The beast was definitely blue, which was strange enough. It was also very large, over six feet in length. But most remarkable of all was under its fur; a series of symbols and patterns tattooed to the flesh beneath; designs collected from a dozen different races and cultures, many unfamiliar altogether. The patterns ran from its head down to the tips of its paws. The fur stood on end; it was still wound up from the fight. As it calmed, its coat settled and the symbols soon disappeared from view.

Aurora held up her hand in the motionless wave she always gave to her saviour and then gently lowered it on its muzzle. The wolf's mouth was stained with the Umbra's blood, a foul smelling dark slime that was starting to fade like its body had and she was tentative to touch it.

Aurora's heart pounded in her chest; should she touch the wolf? It seemed like the natural thing to do.

Her grandfather watched her, fixated, unable to say anything.

"Blue doggie," Aurora smiled, remembering the phrase from her childhood. A lump caught in her throat: it was real. She was right, and had been all along.

Nothing would be the same from now on.

A clamour of footsteps rang on the platform, and the adventurers turned to see a small group of men approaching. They were dressed for the outdoors; work boots, jeans and tattered sweaters.

The Wolf rose and sauntered over to the group. The men didn't seem in the least bit surprised to see it. It was one of them, somehow.

"Please come with us," one of the men urged.

"What do you think?" Aurora asked her grandfather, still a little shaken. They had heard that before, and it had ended with Norm getting shot.

"Let's go," he said, and guided her in their direction.

If the Wolf was one of them, she supposed that was enough to earn them a chance. They didn't have much choice.

*

The Tundra and Jack watched unseen as the men led Aurora and her grandfather out of the underground and into an unmarked van.

"Aren't they –" Jack began.

"Yes," the lead Tundra confirmed.

"And the odds they'll be bringing them to me are…?"

"Slim."

Jack sighed, frustrated, and once again reached for his phone. "*She's not going to like this*," he muttered.

Chapter 23

Avalites

Barely adhering to the speed limit, the unmarked black van tore away from London. Aurora had no way of knowing where they were going, or in which direction. All she knew was that she was grateful to be alive.

Six humans and one wolf filled the van. Two of the men sat in the front while the other two were in the back opposite Aurora and her grandfather. The Wolf lay between Aurora and the door like a massive blue draft excluder, apparently asleep.

It was reassuring to have it nearby. Aurora knew from the Wolf's aloof demeanour it would not want her to be dependent on it, but it was hard not to be after the Umbra.

Despite all this, or maybe because of it, it was an awkward journey, maybe the most awkward Aurora had experienced, and she'd been in the car when Red's team had lost eleven-nil.

To a team in a younger league.

Who were at the bottom of that league.

And were girls.

Whether they wanted to or not, their saviours had given something away: Aurora's sight flashed on in the same way as when the suits had approached them. But this was different.

The suits in suits had been cold with something strong burning underneath. For whatever reason they had concealed it with willpower and discipline. There was no underneath here. For the men in the van, the same fire was on the surface, and burned brightly and without shame.

I didn't mind. After the Umbra, it was like sitting in front of a fire having climbed out of a frozen lake.

"We're sorry about your friend," said the one who appeared to be the leader of the men, a note of regret in his voice. He was well built with a Belfast accent and an explosion of red hair. "We saw what happened, but it was far too late for us to do anything."

Aurora's grandfather laid a hand on her shoulder and she took this as a sign to play along, so she lowered her eyes.

"Thank you," the old man said soberly. "He'd led an eventful life."

The uncomfortable silence resumed. To Aurora it seemed like the men were waiting for something. If they weren't going to be the ones to make the first move, she might as well.

"Well, who are you then?" she asked. She was defiant, but quieter than usual, still not quite herself yet. If she had thought the men had been truly dangerous she would have held her tongue, but they didn't seem menacing.

The truth was, Aurora was fed up. This was meant to be *their* adventure, but it wasn't going that way at all. Every step they took got them no closer to the Nameless City.

The men looked at each other, unsure what to say.

"Maybe I can help," her grandfather suggested. "You're Avalites. Torrid, to be precise. I've dealt with your tribe a long time ago, but it's clear I'm out of the loop."

The name rang a bell. It took her a moment but Aurora remembered; Avalites were mentioned fleetingly at the start of *Jock Danger and the Phantom Oilrig*. Their chief, Ragnar, had been the man who wagered the name of the Nameless City as a bet.

"That's right, we're Torrid," said the red haired man, who resembled a slimmer, younger version of what she had expected Ragnar to look like. "I'm Rory."

"I'm a Rory too," Aurora offered, oddly self-conscious.

"Are you?" her grandfather asked, curiously.

"When people are fed up with me."

"I never knew that," the old man smiled, then, to Rory-the-Avalite, "You've been following us."

"We've been following Tundra," Rory corrected him. "They were the people who shot your friend."

"They're like you," Aurora said, struggling to articulate herself, "but they're different somehow. You're warm, they're cold."

"We're both tribes of Avalites," he told her. "You won't have heard of us. We keep under the radar. Makes life easier that way."

"*She's* been following me," Aurora said, indicating the Wolf, who opened one eye lazily. She didn't know how, but Aurora knew it was female. She had always known it, but she had never thought to say it out loud.

It had never been real until now, she remembered.

"The Wolf was keeping an eye on you for us," Rory agreed, "but as soon as we knew Tundra were after you we had the same purpose."

"But why were the Tundra after us?" her grandfather asked.

"We don't know," admitted the man sitting next to Rory, who introduced himself as Pete. Of Asian origin, he was slimmer than Rory with shaved black hair and a beard.

"But you're both Avalites, surely you would know why."

"We'll explain more when we arrive," Rory said. "Things are very complicated right now."

Aurora's grandfather sat back and folded his arms. Apparently this was enough for him for the time being. It wasn't for Aurora though.

"But I still don't get any of this!" she cried, feeling more alert and desperately wanting to understand. "What are Avalites? How can you have a wolf just sitting in the van? They're not exactly domesticated!" She looked down at the Wolf and quickly added, "No offence."

The Wolf opened one eye, emitted a low sigh through its nostrils and the eye closed once more, clearly not fussed.

"This should be fun," Rory smiled. "I've never had to explain who we are before. The Avalites are a tribe that have existed in one form or another for as far back as anyone can remember. There are things out there that mankind can't understand, or can't protect themselves against. That's where we come in. The creature that attacked you, for instance, that's one of our specialities."

"So you train wolves to fight them?" she asked, still not getting it.

"The Wolf *is* one of us. Believe it or not, that's a person in there. This is how we hunt the Umbra."

"You're werewolves?"

"We're not werewolves!" Rory protested. "That's ridiculous." He turned to Pete. "*This* is why we never tell anyone who we are."

"I can't really tell the difference," Aurora shrugged, a little put out by Rory's reaction. "You turn into wolves, but you're not werewolves. What am I missing?"

"It's whatever the ideal hunter is perceived to be for that area," he said. "If we were in Africa, we might be lions or hyenas. In the Arctic, polar bears maybe. But wolves tend to be the most common, especially in England. It's probably a folk tale thing. But all that werewolf gibberish; full moons, silver bullets, the way they lose control and all that," he paused to look at the wolf sleeping next to Aurora, "Doesn't apply."

"Okay, so you're not werewolves," Aurora said, suddenly feeling very aware that the sleeping beast next to her was a human being. "But why are there two tribes?"

"Well, it's all to do with perspective," Rory explained, "Torrid believe that the wolf is about harnessing emotion. We embrace life. We're happy, and loud and opinionated. Too opinionated, some might say. Tundra are the opposite; they believe the wolf is used to vent their emotion. You saw what they were like. It doesn't take a genius to realise that different philosophies means we don't always get on so well. I mean, some of us do. There's this one Tundra, Victoria," he whistled, "She's got the whole ice queen thing going on for her. I mean, damn –"

"Rory," Pete said quietly.

"Right," Rory nodded. "Sorry. Where was I? Oh yeah. Anyway, Tundra have their uses though. They might be no fun at parties but they're very smart. They're the ones who enable us to hunt down the Umbra."

"I hate to say it," Aurora said, "but they're not doing a very good job of it. Have you used the underground recently? There's hundreds of them down there!"

Rory started to reply, but Pete cut him off. "This is where it would be best to wait until we arrive," he suggested.

"Fair enough," her grandfather said, deciding to chip in, "but I take it you'll also be able to explain why Tundra were out to get us? And why they were working with the Ne'er DuWells?"

The Torrid said nothing, and remained looking uncomfortable.

The Wolf stirred, then settled again. Aurora and her grandfather exchanged glances; they both felt they were quickly getting out of their depth.

Chapter 24
Torrid

"What I don't get," the voice on the phone told Jack, "is why you didn't shoot him yourself. He wasn't anyone important."

"I can't believe you," Jack sighed, exasperated. "We're supposed to be anonymous: that's what we've always been told. The only way we've built up all this power is by no one knowing who we are. Do you just not get that?"

"You want to make it in this family, you have to kill someone."

"And how many people have you killed exactly, Marcus?" Jack snapped.

"I never leave any witnesses, so you'll never know." A rustling crackled out of the microphone and Jack knew his brother was smoking and giggling at the same time. He had always been a terrible liar.

"What are you even doing while I'm out here?"

"It's the Baron's ball tonight. The feud between him and the Viscount is developing nicely. I think Vivian might have had something to do with it. I thought I'd do what I could to push it a little more."

"So you're sipping champagne in a tux while I'm out here, that's what you're trying to tell me, is it?"

"Breeding, Jackie, it's all in the breeding. It's probably why you're having such trouble," he paused to take another drag before adding cruelly, "I love you like a brother, but, you know, you're not. A real one, that is."

The insult washed over Jack with minimal damage. It was the family's way; whenever things were going well he was acknowledged as one of them, but at the first sign of trouble his adoption was quickly remembered.

There were times when he wondered why his father had brought him to join the family. It was too late to ask now.

"We're getting off topic," Jack said. "The point is I can't work with these Tundra idiots."

Jack had made the call out of earshot, but he still saw the suits look over when he said it. Their hearing was impeccable.

"Don't upset them. We put in a lot of work getting them to trust us. People have died – literally – so we can get this opportunity."

"Really?"

"Yeah, but only because we were the ones to kill them. You didn't hear that from me. The point is, don't worry about their little dead friend. He's nobody we care about. We've covered up things like that before, I'm sure we will again."

"How's she supposed to trust us now?"

"Who cares?" Marcus scoffed, "It would've been nice if everything had gone to plan, but in truth it doesn't matter one way or another. Cooperation's not mandatory."

"It's going to make things harder."

"It doesn't matter anyway. It's out of your hands."

"No –"

"Yes. His plane touched down about an hour ago. Drake's looking forward to hearing all about your misfortunes."

"You know how much he hates Hayhoe," Jack realised he was sweating. "He'll kill –"

"*Her* orders: Hayhoe's not to be killed. Yet."

"We're pushing it too much," warned Jack. "We're risking hundreds of years of progress and power unnecessarily. Father wouldn't have approved."

"Father's dead." Marcus reminded him.

Jack was silent. That was that.

"Jack?"

"What?"

"You failed. Come home."

Jack hung up, and considered his next move.

*

After what felt like hours the van came to a halt, its tyres crunching noisily on the ground. The back doors burst open and light flooded in.

As her vision cleared, Aurora saw they were in a wooded clearing. Tall trees surrounded them, as wide and as deep as the eye could see, and for maybe the first time she was unable to hear the murmur of traffic. A cool breeze picked at the fallen leaves, tracing the paths of swirling currents of air. Rory, Pete and the others jumped out and escorted them from the van.

The Wolf stretched and sauntered away, leaving the group without looking back. Aurora couldn't help but feel disappointed as it disappeared into the trees.

"Where's she going?" she asked.

"She doesn't live with us," Rory explained, "She lives on the edge of our settlement"

Aurora's grandfather watched the Wolf with a thoughtful expression. He leant in towards Rory and whispered something Aurora could not hear. Rory nodded his head in the direction the Wolf had gone and grinned, "That's her."

"Good lord," her grandfather muttered, looking both amazed and impressed. Aware his granddaughter was watching him curiously, he added, "I suppose you should take us to see Ragnar now."

"I'm afraid that's not possible," said Rory grimly, "He's dead."

"I'm so sorry," the old man replied, "I had no idea. When did it happen?"

"Six years ago. I'm sorry, I thought you knew."

"He was an amazing man. Truly unique."

"Thank you," Rory nodded, "He always spoke very highly of you. He was my dad."

"I thought there was a resemblance. You've big shoes to fill."

"Well I guess it's fortunate for me that responsibility isn't mine yet," Rory said with a casual air. "Torrid has a new chief, and he's very much looking forward to meeting you."

Dotted throughout the forest were log cabins and huge tepees concealed and sheltered by towering pines and oaks. As they crossed the settlement, faces emerged to get a glimpse of the new arrivals.

The only consistent feature of the Torrid that Aurora noticed was their auras. Race, age or gender, it did not seem to matter.

Her talent was growing.

As the shade from the trees darkened the forest, it was easier to see them by auras than by sight alone.

The woods practically glowed with orange beacons as I picked them out, all sharing the warmth and strength Rory and the others had.

I felt Granddad's hand on my shoulder, and I knew he understood what I was doing. "There's so many of them," I whispered. He didn't say anything.

People approached us. I could see they warmed to us both immediately, but something about my grandfather made them keep their distance.

I wondered what it could be. Maybe he intimidated them. He was Jock Danger, after all.

As the light grew dimmer under the thickening cover of trees, Aurora realised they were being led to the very centre of the forest, towards the largest cabin of all. It seemed very old, and natural, almost growing from the side of a mound. It was surrounded by fallen trees and felled branches. They passed through the massive oak door of the cabin and went inside.

Its interior was spartan, the opposite of the homely cottage Aurora had expected. Rory showed them into a modest sitting room and excused himself, leaving the room. Moments later a booming voice carried through the wall and made them jump.

"They're *here*?" the voice thundered. "Marvellous!"

"An Avalite chief is very proud and powerful," her grandfather whispered, "So for pity's sake watch your mouth around him."

He had barely time to utter these words before the door flew open, and a mountain of a man filled the room. He dwarfed even Rory and looked more like a Viking warrior than a modern day man; coarse blond hair fell around his shoulders framing a face that harboured beaming eyes and a savage smile.

He locked in on them immediately, giving Rory only a second to introduce him as Bjorn, their Chief.

"Ha!" he bellowed, grabbing Hayhoe's hand and shaking it vigorously. The grip was so strong that the bones in the old man's hand cracked. "Jock Danger!" he exclaimed, "The explorer! The adventurer! The lunatic! Fantastic!"

"Well," Aurora's grandfather exclaimed, flustered, "It's been a long time since anyone's called me that. I was beginning to think my back catalogue was completely forgotten."

"Not here. *Jock Danger and the Toy Makers' Crypt* was one of my all-time favourite stories, growing up," the chief grinned, displaying a set of gleaming sharp teeth. "And you," he said, turning to Aurora, "Let's get a look at you."

Aurora was expecting him to squat to her level, but to her surprise he picked her off the ground as if she was a toddler. Her embarrassment was cemented when she let out an inadvertent squeal as he lifted her.

His face was fascinating; a weathered tapestry of scars and lines forged over years of combat. His eyes were the deepest blue she had ever seen; she could get lost in them, she thought as they bore into her soul.

"You have a warrior's spirit, pretty girl," he said, and she realised he was reading her aura. If his was any brighter she'd need sunglasses.

"You can see my aura?"

"As bright as searchlights," he beamed, "I could see you in the dark."

"What about my granddad?" She hadn't tried it on him yet; it had never struck her to do so.

Bjorn's smile faltered, and both Aurora and her grandfather noticed. Seemingly sobered, he put the girl down and patted her shoulder as if to reassure her.

Aurora's brow furrowed.

I didn't like this one bit, and decided to see for myself. It was Granddad, this was important. If there was something wrong I should know.

It was harder than it had been before. Seeing auras had become easier, mainly because, I suspected, the most recent people I had tried it on were Avalites. Somehow they were more in tune with the unseen world than normal people.

My vision blurred, and I saw Granddad frown as he recognised the strain on my face. I pushed through and hit a wall, invisible and cold. I recoiled, knowing exactly what this sensation was: it was the same feeling I felt around the Umbra.

"I don't get it," I said, panting, "I can't see it."

"You may have noticed some of our people were a bit hesitant when they saw you," Bjorn told Aurora's grandfather, "This is why."

"What are you talking about?" the old man asked, failing to understand.

"I can't see your aura, Granddad," Aurora explained, feeling she sounded a bit like a hippy, "It's… there's…" she struggled to find the words, and found the only comparison unsatisfying. "It's like… if you didn't have a shadow."

"There's something unique about you, Mr Danger," Bjorn observed, "It's also quite familiar. To my people, it's most unsettling. Somehow, it seems to share echoes of the Rift."

"The Rift? That's not my fault," the old man huffed, "It's probably the Ne'er DuWells' doing. I've been their prisoner for over a decade, chances are the machine they used on me had that effect. I'm sure my *aura*, or whatever you call it, will grow back in no time now I'm free. Anyway, I'd rather you didn't invite the comparison of me to the Umbra, thank you very much."

"Please calm down, Mr Hayhoe," Rory said, trying to keep the peace. "We're not trying to offend you, but it is of concern. We brought you because you're both too valuable and too dangerous to be left out there unsupervised."

"Well, that's charming," her grandfather guffawed, clearly offended. "I don't really think that's for you to say."

"Mr Danger, with respect to your past experiences – which are impressive – the fact is we're the experts when it comes to the

Riftrot, and our business with the Tundra is our own," Bjorn said, asserting himself, "All you two have done is expose yourselves at every turn without realising it, and to make matters worse, you don't have a clue how to defend yourselves; it was only our intervention that saved you in the Underground. Without our protection, you might as well hand yourselves over to Tundra now."

"So there is a division between Torrid and Tundra then?" the old man asked indignantly. "What would you suggest we do?"

"You stay here until we figure out what Tundra are up to."

"What about the Nameless City?" Aurora put in, feeling that their goals were being forgotten with whatever else was going on.

"What about it?" Bjorn asked.

"That's where we're going."

The chief let out a short laugh that was so loud Aurora nearly jumped off the floor. "Don't be ridiculous!"

"Won't you help us?" she pleaded, remembering the extract from *Jock Danger and the Phantom Oilrig*. The Torrid clearly knew something about the Nameless City, and maybe their knowledge would be crucial in finding it.

"Our job is to hunt the Riftrot," Bjorn said, becoming serious. "It doesn't matter how dangerous they are. Hunting them is what we do."

"And the City?"

"We have no time for searching for things that have not been seen in hundreds of years. The world has moved on. The Seen and the

Unseen are worlds apart, and we and the Riftrot are the only things in the middle. The creatures are our fate, not mythical worlds."

"Maybe it doesn't need to be like that," she suggested. "Perhaps if we worked together, we could –"

"No one can remember a time when things were any different," the chief interrupted. "We do as our ancestors did, and try to do them proud. Who are you to try and change things?"

Chapter 25

Drake's Accusation

Brothers fight. This is a common occurrence. Eric and Ryan went at it all the time. Sometimes it got pretty nasty, but it never normally meant anything. But pressed up against a wall with a knife's edge against his throat, Jack gave serious consideration to the idea that Drake might *actually* kill him.

"It would be so easy," Drake hissed, and Jack's concern increased when a tiny part of his brain noticed that his brother had not blinked for around a minute. "It doesn't matter that you're family, that's what DuWells do. Ignatius killed Silus, a hundred and fifty years ago, and he got away with it."

With his tailored suit and malicious sneer, Drake was the embodiment of imperial aristocracy. He had the build of a leopard, lean without an inch of fat, with a small vertical scar on his right cheek that had healed but never faded, wild eyes and short, black hair, a comma of which fell on his forehead.

A lifetime ago as a young man he had threatened Jock Danger over a game of cards. He may have aged, but time had not cooled his temper.

Jack wanted nothing more than to push Drake off him, but his brother's nature was so unpredictable that he didn't know what this could provoke. Instead he gasped, "This isn't… helping any…"

"You had one job to do," Drake said coolly, tilting his head from one side to the other like a cobra about to strike. "Keep him in the home.

How hard could that be? You even had the radio to keep him pacified. The *radio*, Jack: Father's masterpiece. What happened? Did he make friends with you?"

"Of course he didn't," Jack replied, fighting the voice in his head that screamed: *punch him. Punch him now.* "You don't have to remind me what he's done to our family. I never forgot how dangerous he was. But we never knew about the girl."

"Oh yes," a chuckle bubbled from Drake's throat. He relaxed the blade and stepped back. "The girl. A twelve year old. Looks like you've met your nemesis at last."

"We knew he had a family," said Jack, ignoring him, reflexively checking his throat, "Why didn't we move on them after what he'd done to ours?"

"I don't know," Drake admitted, pocketing the knife and straightening his suit jacket. "That was *her* decision. It doesn't matter though. He's out. That means he's mine to hunt down."

"Speaking of her decisions, she's the one who said they're both to be delivered unharmed."

"It's weaknesses like that which remind me you're not a blood relation," Drake sighed resentfully. "Why Father adopted you I'll never know."

"If you think you can do a better job than me, be my guest," Jack said, refusing to acknowledge the insult. "Talk to Tundra. See if you've any better luck trying to get them to cooperate."

"Very well then," his brother snorted, buttoning up his suit and adjusting his tie.

"Things are changing," Jack warned as Drake left him, "We never would have been so hands-on in the past. If you push them too much you'll stretch the old alliances with the Avalites to breaking point. They'll learn the truth."

"Let them try and stop us," Drake hissed, keeping his voice low. "*If* they find out."

And with that, he loped off in the direction of the Tundra.

"Idiot," Jack growled.

*

Aurora and her grandfather had reached the point where they were talking to a human shaped brick wall. It was a familiar experience; she had endured it for years with her father. The sad fact remained, as impressive a character as he was, Bjorn was not the best listener, and was clearly incapable of taking criticism.

Rory and a couple of the others moved around them, placing food on the table. They stopped every now and then to watch the debate.

"It seems to me that you have a problem with the Umbra because you're not strong enough to kill them," Bjorn snapped.

"Of course I have a problem, they're dangerous!" Aurora replied, her blood rising. "If you're meant to be keeping their numbers down, how come this is happening? Aren't you meant to be protecting people?"

"We saved *your* skin, little girl," the chief boomed, towering over Aurora.

"That's different!" she yelled, refusing to back down. "You were watching me. What about the people who aren't that lucky?"

Aurora's grandfather observed the shouts bounce back and forwards as if watching a tennis match. As inappropriate as her behaviour was, he couldn't help but respect his granddaughter's grit. Rory paused for a moment and glanced over at Hayhoe, who threw him a look. *Best not get involved*, it said.

Too right. You didn't need to be able to read auras to understand that.

"You should be grateful –"

"I am, but others would be too, if you were doing your job! It shouldn't be me who has to save people for you!"

"We can't save people," the chief thundered, silencing everything, "Because we can't find the bloody creatures!"

The room was suddenly silent, almost quivering in the aftermath of Bjorn's booming voice. Aurora opened her mouth to say something, realised she had no words, and closed it again.

"What?" she squeaked.

"That's Tundra's purpose," Bjorn sighed, his eyes lowered, suddenly quieter. "They track them, we kill them. Always have done. But we've been having… problems working together. Since then we haven't been able to find them like we used to."

Bjorn sat down on a bench next to the table, with a bump. The fight had left him. The bench wobbled momentarily, as if contemplating whether to collapse, but held together. Rory appeared and discreetly placed a flagon of ale in front of his chief. The large man took it in sullen silence.

Aurora's grandfather stepped forwards. "Well," he suggested, his tone carefully unthreatening. "Don't you think that's rather important?"

"Of course it is," came Bjorn's curt reply. "That's obvious. We've been striking blindly, lashing out. We're at our peak as hunters and for what?"

"So you can't track them at all?" asked Aurora, who took a page out of her grandfather's book and tried to remain as unthreatening as possible. She approached the chief, who was still far taller sitting than she was standing.

"Not like Tundra. They're experts at it. Their skills mean they can track them nationwide."

"There's one place you know where they are. What about sending your people into the Underground?"

"You've seen it: it's overrun. An Avalite strike of that size would attract massive public attention, and even if it didn't, the filth are too well established. The risk is too great."

"You said earlier it didn't matter about the risk –"

"There's a difference between a strike and a suicide mission."

Bjorn's tone was getting terse again, and Aurora backed off rather than risking angering him.

"So how did it used to work?" her grandfather asked, "Tundra would find them, they'd send you out, you turn into wolves and take care of them?"

"Once Tundra got a lead on one, we'd be off," Rory stepped in while Bjorn noisily gulped down his beer. "They gathered it from trances, meditation, that sort of thing. I don't have the concentration span for it all, to be honest with you, but that's why we had them. Their information was always reliable. We would hunt for days if necessary. There's nothing like a good hunt."

"So what changed?" Hayhoe asked.

"They got weird." Bjorn murmured, draining the last dregs from his pint.

"Meaning?"

"It was shortly after my father died," said Rory, "They added computers and satellite tracking to their methods, but then they relocated to London and went corporate, for want of a better word."

"Creepy bastards," Bjorn hissed. "Obsessed with the Rift. *Obsessed.* They've always been distant, it's how they are, but their fixation with monitoring the Umbra was becoming unhealthy. Anyone could see that. Some say they have these *theories...* they don't bear thinking about. Word got to us that it was corrupting them; and they weren't interested in helping us anymore. They had moved on from observing the Umbra to becoming fanatical about them, possibly even capturing them in order to breed them, if you can believe that. Things declined from there. One tribe became two."

"Who told you this?" Aurora's grandfather pressed, and she knew he suspected the answer.

"We have sources."

"And did you ask Tundra rather than believing these rumours?"

"The information was solid," grumbled Bjorn. "They denied nothing."

"It can't be as simple as that."

"I've had enough of your questions," Bjorn's eyes met theirs as he growled with disdain, and Aurora felt a very small indeed. "We brought you here because you were in danger, not for you to judge me."

"Chief," her grandfather begun, "We mean no disrespect –"

"This conversation is over," he snapped. They had pushed him too far. "It's time we put you somewhere for your own safety."

*

"I never said they *were* using the girl to help the Umbra," Drake purred, casually spreading butter over his bread roll with a silver knife, "But the question remains, what *are* they doing with her?"

They had taken Tundra to dinner. It was a cheap move, Jack thought, trying to impress them with prestige. The Savoy was a nice choice though. He had to respect that. But maybe hiring the whole restaurant for the night was a little much. Every table but theirs was empty.

Jack watched the Tundra curiously. All three had chosen vegetarian meals, and none of them drank. In comparison Drake had ordered a rare steak and an exceedingly expensive bottle of red wine, which he was leisurely working his way through. Jack knew he didn't have to worry about his brother getting drunk; between his high tolerance and how frequently he drank, it would take more than that to affect him.

"We can't say," one of the Tundra admitted.

"Because you don't know," Drake said, apparently without malice. "What did you say your name was?"

"Victoria," the Tundra said coldly.

"Well, Victoria," Drake smiled sweetly, light gleaming off his knife and, Jack thought, maybe his teeth too. "It would be better to know, don't you think?"

"We have accepted that Torrid have a different approach," another Tundra said. "This is why we no longer operate together. However, what you are proposing is ridiculous. Inconclusive assumptions based on little to no evidence."

"I thought so too, at first," Drake agreed, "but think about it: you stopped working with Torrid because they don't appreciate the big picture. You know they're resentful of this, and this means you are unable to trust them anymore. For reasons unknown to you, they then acquire the girl and the old man out from under your noses. We know the girl and the old man are very dangerous, so I ask you again: what *are* they doing with them?"

Jack tried not to smile: the Tundra were playing right into his brother's hands.

"You might not know Hayhoe, but I do, only too well," Drake sighed. "He is quite possibly the most dangerous man alive. He killed my twin brother Michael in cold blood, and most likely murdered my father as well. My dear little brother," he rested a hand on Jack's shoulder and pulled him near, "worked tirelessly to keep him restrained for the last decade, but even in his old age Hayhoe is not to be underestimated. Jack is smart: he did all he could, but still the old man escaped. He's resourceful, isn't he, Jack? You didn't see the escape coming, did you?"

"What can I say?" Jack said. He looked at his brother, expecting the nod of approval that he should contribute to the ruse, but Drake's eyes were in stark contrast to the benevolent smile he wore, and Jack's throat went dry.

To the Tundra, Drake continued, "The Card girl has talents no one can understand yet, and a madman like Hayhoe would relish the opportunity to create some anarchy. The Torrid care only for their hunting and would welcome more sport. You can't rule out the possibility that they're going to use her to tear open the Rift, or maybe seal it altogether. The possibilities are endless. You have to intervene."

The gravity of Drake's words seemed to sink in, and the Tundra conferred quietly amongst themselves for a moment. One of them left the table briefly to make a phone call. Jack held his breath while Drake calmly polished off his wine. The Tundra finished his phone call and returned to the table. He nodded his head.

"Your argument has some merit," they agreed.

"Then we reclaim the girl and the old man. By force, if necessary."

"Relations between our clans have not been so hostile. This would declare open war."

"You have no choice," Drake pressed. "If they realise what the girl is capable of, let alone her grandfather, they risk everything. You know this."

"You may be right. This course is undesirable, but retrieval is the only option."

"Well then," Drake purred. "Where would they take them?"

Chapter 26
Never Do Well

According to Bjorn it transpired that somewhere safe meant a holding cell.

"I think you hit a nerve," Aurora's grandfather told her, pacing up and down. "Silly man. You wouldn't think someone so big would be so touchy. Ragnar never took criticism personally."

"I don't suppose you know how to pick a lock?" Aurora asked him.

"Not like these," he said, examining the door. "Funny, isn't it," he mused. "I came this far only to be a prisoner again. At least I have a cellmate this time."

"Do you think Norm's okay?"

"He'll be fine. I'm more concerned about us for the time being."

"I suppose. Getting shot's not like drowning in the Arctic."

"Norm told you that?" the old man asked, raising an eyebrow. "That man. He has no sense of the appropriate."

"Something I've been thinking about," Aurora said, mindful to keep Norm out of trouble. "If the Avalites are as old and traditional as they say, they wouldn't risk everything like this over a feud."

"I smell a rat too," he agreed, "and I think we both know who could engineer something like this."

"Could they really do that?"

"No question. Ragnar knew that the Ne'er DuWells were no good, and he was always smart enough to keep them at arm's length whenever they started sniffing around."

"Do you think they killed him?"

"I wouldn't be surprised. There'll be no proof, there never is. Bjorn is no stooge, but he isn't wise enough to see what's going on. He's a warrior, not a politician, and if they did it ten years later, Rory would most likely be in charge. His cooler temper might have avoided this. It's possible they killed Ragnar, then without him to oppose them, lured Tundra away. Torrid wouldn't be able to do anything, they'd be too busy struggling to deal with the Umbra they couldn't find."

Aurora's brow knotted. "But why? I don't understand what they would get out of it."

"I don't know Tundra, I've only ever dealt with Torrid," her grandfather confessed, "but it must be their skills they're after. Talents like theirs would be incredibly useful for finding the Nameless City. They've been hunting it for generations. You deal with the Ne'er DuWells for long enough, you try to think the way they do."

"Which is something I've been wanting to talk to you about for a while now," Aurora said, finally getting to a question that had been on her mind for too long, "Who are they? You keep changing the subject or avoiding the question, but don't you think I should know?"

"I didn't want to put you at risk –"

"A bit late for that," she smiled.

Her grandfather nodded in agreement and sat down. He was silent for some time, and when his eyes met hers Aurora thought that with the exception of when he was under the radio's influence, he looked older and more tired than she had ever seen before.

He took a deep breath and recounted.

"The Ne'er DuWells are a family whose criminal activities stretch back at least ten generations, maybe more," he began. "They're enormously wealthy – they come from old money – but their only concern is the acquisition of more power. They've eliminated everyone and everything that's ever stood in their way, either through murder or financial ruin. I first encountered them in the Congo, or maybe it was Peru, when I crossed paths with some mercenaries they'd hired to steal native idols. From then on, it seemed like any time I ran into trouble they were behind it, either directly, or funding it somehow. Their involvement runs so deep into everything that you hardly notice them because they're everywhere. They have no idea of the value of human life, to them everything has monetary value, nothing else."

Aurora listened patiently. She suddenly felt very cold and exposed.

"The more I travelled, the more I saw their influence. Once you know what you're looking for, it's almost overwhelming when it's revealed. A toxic spill in India, a mining disaster in South Africa… an outbreak of cholera in Haiti, each had DuWell fingerprints all over them. They have torn entire families apart, orphaned hundreds of children, and they do so without care or regret.

"I learnt what I could about them but it was almost impossible given how secretive they are. Then I hit a breakthrough."

"What was it?"

"Not what, who. Thomas DuWell: the head of the DuWell family, superficially at least, and father to the upcoming generation. He disappeared shortly after I met him, but he told me everything he could about them. He was trying to escape his family, he was sick of the evil that had polluted his life, and had affected his children. He was a broken man, desperate. I think he wanted someone to understand him.

"You've already met Jack DuWell, the man who claimed to be Dr Goode. Thomas adopted him when he was a boy. Apparently he's a good sort, loyal to his family, but they've conditioned him to no longer understand what's right and wrong," he paused and smiled grimly. "Given that he kept me captive in St Elmo's, I think we can assume that's true.

"The two youngest children – who must both be nearly forty by now, are Marcus and Vivian. They're both selfish and cruel, no surprises there. They love the power and luxury that being a part of the family brings them, but, at least back then, they didn't get too involved in the family business unless they had to."

Her grandfather paused, and Aurora knew he was saving the worst for later.

"Then there were the twins. Michael and Drake. Michael…" He swallowed. "He died, over ten years ago and they blame me for his death."

"Is that true?"

"I didn't kill him, but I am responsible."

He was silent, and Aurora realised that he was reliving something very painful from a long time ago. His eyes met hers and it was almost as if he was looking at her apologetically.

"What about Drake?" she asked, feeling very uncomfortable.

"You read *The Phantom Oilrig*. That's him, at the start."

"Oh," she said. "He's nasty."

"He is. He's the embodiment of everything the Ne'er DuWells are meant to be; he has the mean streak in him that made their family so strong in the first place. He leads the family's day-to-day operations, but in many ways he's still a pawn, subject to the focus and guidance of *her*. Thomas's wife."

Here it comes, Aurora thought. *Her*.

"The really terrifying thing about Catherine DuWell is that she's only a Ne'er DuWell through marriage. Being evil just comes naturally to her I guess. She is the cruellest and most malicious person I have ever encountered."

He stopped talking. Aurora wasn't sure, but she thought she saw him shudder.

"She is poison," he continued. "The DuWells were manipulative and treacherous, but she pushed them in ways they never expected. They're more public and aggressive than they ever were," he paused and added. "According to Thomas, that is."

"They know about the Nameless City, don't they?"

"Thomas said they've been looking for it for centuries, ever since one of his ancestors stumbled upon it briefly. It's been an essential part of their heritage ever since.

"The Ne'er DuWells are very real, Aurora," he finished, the gravity of his words chilling her to the bone, "and you should be scared of them."

Apparently, this concluded the matter. An uneasy silence descended, and after a few minutes Aurora realised her grandfather had somehow gone to sleep.

She wasn't sure how anyone could. His words had profoundly disturbed her, and the situation they were in brought little comfort.

There was no way she was going to get any sleep that night. The bed in the cell was like a rock. However she wasn't going to do much else: she was in no mood to read, and there wasn't anyone around for her to practice reading auras. She assumed it wouldn't work on her sleeping grandfather, and didn't want to try it after last time.

It was one of the longest nights of her life.

Chapter 27

A Torrid Way of Life

As it turned out the two adventurers would spend nearly a week with Torrid. They were not prisoners, Rory told them as he unlocked their cell during the first morning but they weren't allowed to leave either. He admitted it wasn't an ideal situation.

"So what are we to do?" Hayhoe scowled.

"You're to stick around here for a while, stay out of trouble until we work out what to do with you."

"People will know we're missing, you know."

"No, they won't."

He was right. Aside from Aurora, not a soul in the world cared about, or even knew of Jim Hayhoe.

Aurora did not know whether any steps had been taken to hide her own disappearance, Bjorn never said. She imagined that a well-placed phone call to her family informing them that Aurora was going to spend some time with a friend in her parent's caravan would be well within Torrid's power, but maybe it wasn't needed. Maybe they simply didn't know she was gone.

Was it so easy for them to live without her?

Aurora and her grandfather's days were filled working with the Avalites. Rory told them it was to abate boredom as much as to understand how the Torrid lived, and that Bjorn insisted they earn their keep. "Actually, he wanted to keep you locked up," the younger Avalite explained, "But I talked him out of it."

Of the chief, they saw little. His ego had been significantly bruised in their last encounter, and Aurora for one was relieved; she had no desire to repeat the same argument again.

The chores they had to do effectively meant working on the land. The old man struggled with the work as his back punished him constantly, but he revelled in the fresh air after his years of captivity. He refused to try less strenuous work, still in denial of his advanced years.

Aurora loved it.

The Torrid lifestyle was fascinating, a web of little contradictions and intricacies. The most obvious theme was that they seemed to lead a lifestyle any eco-warrior would be envious of. Everything was recycled. Despite its rustic appearance, there were signs of modern living everywhere, carefully incorporated into the rural design. Solar panels were tactfully placed on thatched roofs. TVs and computers were present in most households, albeit seldom used. Their watchtower in the centre of the camp, which was as high as the pine trees that loomed over the clearing, had wind turbines fitted. Every available surface that was exposed to the sun grew food, herbs or flowers.

The most obvious contradiction (and the most unwelcome, to Aurora anyway,) was that the Avalites were vegetarian.

Vegetarian wolves. Lunacy. For a girl raised on burgers, hotdogs and chicken nuggets from football stadiums, this took some getting used to, to say the least. Her grandfather took to it easily enough, he was well travelled and used to a varying diet, but it was not entirely welcome to him either.

When she asked Rory about it he told them that it wasn't just humans that gave off auras, animals did too. When you can see that, he said, it rather puts you off killing them for food.

Although they appeared self-sustained, trucks regularly went to town for supplies. Aurora and her grandfather were of course not allowed to go as they posed a substantial flight risk.

Despite the threat of the Ne'er DuWells, the concern about her family, the worries she had about Norm, or even the threat of the Umbra, the time with Torrid proved to be a happy one and would provide Aurora with hope in the harder times that followed.

The tribe warmed to her quickly and she made many friends among them, but they were still hesitant of her grandfather. They would tell his stories round the campfire, or even ask him to share them, but Aurora could tell, even if he couldn't, that they remained wary of him.

Ironically, the main thing that bonded Aurora to the children of Torrid was football. They simply did not stand a chance against her. Red would have been astounded to see arguments break out amongst the children over which team Aurora should play for.

It was when Aurora was playing with the other children that her grandfather was left to his own devices, and she saw him going for long walks by himself. She figured he would want some private time, yet it was now, when they had the time and space to think without having to keep running, that a lot of questions that she wanted to ask came to the surface.

Where to begin though? It was a strange thing, to have someone so essential to your life around for the first time, and to have unfettered access to them. The old man was a vital and untapped resource, and she didn't know how to ask him all about his life, or her mother's, for that matter. Aurora did not know how this entire affair was going to end, but if there was one thing she hoped, it was that her grandfather could reconnect with her mother somehow. If he could do that, then maybe her mum would be closer to her, too.

It was when her grandfather came back from one of his amblings that Aurora realised he was returning from the direction the Wolf had taken. She remembered the odd exchange her grandfather had had with Rory when they first arrived, and realised the old man knew something about the Wolf he was not telling her.

Whatever it was, she wanted to know it too. More than that, she wanted to know the Wolf. She had saved her life, and had been around her as long as she could remember.

But why though? Surely it wasn't just because she was Jim Hayhoe's granddaughter, there had to be more to it than that. Her ignorance was a constant source of irritation, and Aurora was continually distracted at even the slightest mention of her by other Avalites. What was she like as a human? Why had she not come to see her since they had arrived?

Of course, the most straightforward way to get answers was to ask her grandfather, and Aurora was not surprised when he fobbed her off and changed the subject. She had learnt enough about her grandfather to know that if he wanted her to know something, he would share it when he was ready. It was clear that he was not.

So with that in mind, she set off to find the Wolf for herself.

*

The only cabin in the Wolf's direction lay at the top of the hill. It overlooked the camp from one side, and on the other side a path ran down to a crystal lake. The path was bordered on both sides by apple trees, and at its end was a jetty with a single rowing boat.

The cabin seemed normal enough. It was homely in design, more like a cottage than the others they had seen; it even had a thin plume of smoke coming from a chimney. Aurora wasn't sure what to expect, and decided against knocking on the door, opting instead to find a window to catch a glimpse through. She found one towards the cabin's rear, and balancing on an unstable pile of logs to get a better look, pressed her nose to the glass.

At first glance the cabin appeared to be empty, but soon Aurora saw signs of life: the fire crackling gently on the hearth, steam rising from a freshly brewed mug of tea. Then a woman walked into view.

She wore a dressing gown that left most of her arms and legs exposed, and Aurora could clearly see the tattoos and markings she had noticed on her lupine saviour.

This was her Wolf, in human form.

The same collection of designs and patterns ran from the tops of her feet up to her neck, then down again to the tips of her fingers. But it was when she turned Aurora's way, brushing back her wet hair, that her face was clearly visible and Aurora was most amazed.

It was the lady. The sophisticated one she had seen in St Elmo's, the same one who had tried to warn her of the Tundra on the streets of London. Even dressed in little more than a robe, she carried herself with the same dignity and elegance as she had when Aurora had seen her last.

Aside from the way she was dressed (the coat and gloves seemed obvious now Aurora thought about it; the tattoos would be a dead giveaway) there was something different about her. The lady looked sad somehow, the weight of a great concern marking her otherwise beautiful features. Aurora wondered what it could be.

There wouldn't be the chance to find out. Her breath had steamed up the window, and as she gently tried to clear it the logs she balanced on shifted under her weight and she nearly fell. She managed to regain her balance, but when she looked up, the lady was staring straight at her.

The look on her face was terrifying, it was one of such surprise and rage that as she approached the window Aurora ran for it.

She sprinted back down the hill, almost tripping over her feet, tearing through the mounds of dead leaves, twigs and branches that made up the woodland floor. This wasn't the same fear that the Umbra inspired in her, but something different.

It was guilt; she had invaded the Wolf's privacy, and worse, her home. For perhaps the first time, she felt shame.

Chapter 28
Guilt and Grudges

Aurora spent the rest of the day by herself, sulking. From a distance she watched a group of young Torrid children playing a game similar to hopscotch, but from the rhyme they sang, it was clear it was of Avalite origin. They recited it as they skipped from point to point, unaware that Aurora was watching.

They sang:

"The Nameless City is not what it seems
Shaped by thoughts and crafted from dreams
Men have looked but it's in no place
All Worlds Unseen is its own space
It's by man's logic they're undone
Reason won't find –"

The final word was lost as the children abandoned the rhyme, looking her way and running off. Aurora turned, and saw her grandfather standing behind her.

"Spying is going to get you into a lot of trouble," he said sternly.

"It's only kids playing."

"Don't be coy, you know what I was talking about. I know you want answers to a lot of questions, but this time you're going to have to actually *listen* to me and be patient."

She knew he was right, but there was no way she could admit it, and found it best to stare at a really interesting stick near her foot that was shaped a bit like a thigh bone.

"Beth – that's her name – will talk to you when she's ready, not before."

"I'm sorry," Aurora said, the words struggling to come out. She didn't get told off often, her parents didn't care that much for discipline, so the process was an unpleasant, if novel, experience.

"That's okay," the old man said, and his frown finally gave way to his usual smile. "I wasn't brave enough to discipline my children, and it did no one any favours. Especially me."

"Children? I didn't think mum had any brothers or sisters."

"That's what I meant. Child. *Daughter*. I'm old; I can say what I want. Just promise me you'll not do it again."

"I promise."

"Good. You hungry?"

"I am," she smiled.

"Let's go do something about that then," he said, leading her back towards camp. "So we're agreed," he continued. "No more spying on wolf women who could eat your face if they wanted to. Just on people who are evil or incredibly stupid…"

*

It was on the fourth morning while feeding the chickens that Aurora asked Rory how the Torrid made money. She could see how inventive they were and how self-sufficient they aspired to be, but there was no way they could create enough food to support them all.

193

"Not the way I bet you're thinking," he grinned. "We work. You know what we're like now, we're a passionate bunch, so it tends to come out in what we do. We're all sorts; teachers, doctors, carers, musicians, sportsmen. A lot of us go into the world and send money back here, which sounds oddly cult-like, now I say it out loud. Still, there's always a source of income coming in. Did you picture us in carnivals or markets selling homemade jewellery then?"

Aurora ignored him; she had got used to his sense of humour. "So who owns this land?"

"We do. It was bought for us."

"Who bought it?"

"The DuWell family," he said without guilt, even when he saw the look on her face.

"The *Ne'er* DuWells?"

"I'm not getting involved in that one," he said, holding up his hands, a knowing smile working its way across his face. "I'm not having the same arguments your granddad and my dad always had."

"They're evil though!" she insisted, "You should have seen what they did to my granddad! They kept him prisoner for over a decade!"

"That's the first I've heard about that. It's news to us. The only thing we have against them is your granddad's word and a gut feeling. A gut feeling, which, I might add, isn't shared by too many of us. Regardless, the DuWells don't seem too interested in us now Tundra have left. We hardly hear from them at all now…"

"What did they want from you though?"

"At a guess? What we know about the Umbra, the Rift, and the City. All of that stuff is really Tundra's area. The DuWells probably see it as a great investment, but it's not gonna bring them anything. Some things just don't exist for profit, and the Nameless City is one of them. Let them try I say, they won't be the first."

"Your dad knew better."

Rory paused for a second. He was clearly trying to find the best way to choose what he wanted to say. "My dad... knew they weren't what they said they were, and he never let them get too close. But he could recognise a good resource when he saw one. He just made sure he didn't let them have anything valuable, so to speak."

"Like the name of the Nameless City?" she suggested.

"Yeah. Like that."

"What's the deal with that, anyway?"

"Wouldn't you like to know? Avalite secret. We only share it with members of the tribe. Knowing the name of the City is the first step to reaching it, or so they say. Not that any of us have ever made it there. No one has."

Aurora contemplated this for a moment. "Why aren't you chief, Rory?"

"It's not an inherited thing," he told her. "We did vote, after Dad died, but I didn't get Chief. How are you supposed to compete with a character like Bjorn? He's more alpha male than anyone I've ever seen, and I think the tribe wanted someone with a very Torrid personality, especially as things with Tundra were getting strained.

I'm too chilled out, I reckon. Puts me on the Tundra end of the Torrid spectrum, if you get me."

"Doesn't it annoy you? I mean, Bjorn's a bit of an idiot, isn't he?"

"He's all right," Rory chuckled. "He just wants what's best for Torrid, and he's always been good to me. He did make me his number two guy, which he didn't need to do. Says I level him out."

"I dread to see what he's like when he's not levelled out."

"Ha," Rory said. He scattered a final fistful of chickenfeed on the ground. The fowl gobbled it up greedily. "Anyway. Getting back to it, Jim's grudge against the DuWell family won't make him very popular round here," Rory continued. "The only one of us who really has anything against them is your Wolf."

"Beth?"

"Can't stand them. Won't say why, but there's some hate there. Old wounds. You should ask her about them if you get the chance. You met her yet?"

Aurora didn't know how to answer that. "Not properly," she mumbled. It was close enough.

"I'm sure you will," he grinned. "From one Rory to another, she's amazing. The single most badass woman I've ever met. And I'm a Torrid. That makes me an expert on all things badass."

*

The nights were the strangest for them. After a day of work and an evening of interaction, Aurora always found it odd to be returned to their cell, isolated from the tribe once more. She still struggled to sleep, and every night she kept her grandfather awake asking questions.

"Where's Norm?" Aurora asked him on the fourth night, "What do you think he's up to?"

"He's either on his way, or he's looking for us," he assured her sleepily. "Or he's reverted back to his old habits and he's out of his mind back in the Loft."

Aurora didn't believe that and she told him so. He should have more faith in people, especially his friends.

"I'm just cranky," her grandfather said, adjusting his pillow. "We're being treated well enough, but we're still not free."

"We'll get out. Soon as Bjorn comes to his senses."

"Hmm," he grumbled. Minutes later he was asleep.

Aurora lay on the hard bunk and listened to her grandfather snore. The days tired the old man out, and she couldn't help but worry about him.

The nights were still hard, and she started to doubt everything. What was she doing here? Why was she in the woods, hanging out with a bunch of strange people, locked in a cold cell, miles away from her family? Why was she worried about a family of crooks that had never bothered her before she'd even learnt of Jock Danger or Jim Hayhoe?

"Can't sleep?" a voice asked. She started, and as her eyes scoured the darkness she realised Bjorn was sat on a bench facing them. His voice, usually loud and booming, was controlled and hushed.

"I'm not sure I like you watching me," she scowled. Bjorn still wasn't in her good books. A sliver of white broke the gloom and she knew he was grinning.

"We're going out," he told her, unlocking the cell door. He did it softly, careful not to disturb the sleeping old man.

Aurora frowned as she fastened her coat. "Where are we going?"

"You'll see."

Chapter 29
The Hunt

Aurora had never seen stars like this.

Without London's light pollution to conceal them the starlight created an incandescent aura that described every detail of the Milky Way. The moon washed everything in a silver glow and she could see almost as clear as day. Despite the fact that the air was bitingly cold, she had never felt so connected to the universe.

"Are you going to tell me what we're doing here?" she pressed. After a half hour of walking the two of them were deep in the woods. He hushed her. He was looking for something.

A familiar silhouette was waiting for them as they passed into the clearing, and Aurora felt a concoction of conflicting emotions jostling inside her when she saw who it was.

"Hello Aurora," the lady said, that familiar smile of utter delight crossing her handsome features. "I'm Beth. I would like to apologise for how we met."

"You don't have to," Aurora said too eagerly. "It was my –"

"You've nothing to be sorry for," Beth interrupted, somehow without sounding rude. "The only thing you were guilty of is a little curiosity. I think we can all understand that. The truth is, I've been looking forward to meeting you for a long, long time, and I was so taken aback when I saw you watching me that I rather forgot myself. I would like to start again."

"Me too."

"Good. I was trying to work out the best way to get to know one another, and then it hit me: let's go kill something."

"What?" Aurora blurted out, but Beth had already started to move into the woods. Aurora looked at Bjorn, who was not the ideal person to find assurance in.

"Go on, girl!" he urged impatiently.

She followed the older woman with Bjorn bringing up the rear after a while. He seemed to want to leave the two of them to it, but at the same time obviously wanted to see what would happen.

It only took her a few moments to catch Beth up; she was standing at the top of a hill, watching something like a hunter who had found her quarry.

"There!" she hissed, pointing.

Aurora followed her direction, and saw an unnatural shape shuddering downhill against the blackness.

"Look familiar?" Beth asked.

"Of course," Aurora answered, recognising the Umbra immediately.

"Come on."

She approached, Aurora following reluctantly. Beth moved expertly, utterly silent, stalking her prey with ease. Aurora tried her best to follow her example, her jaw clenching every time she broke a twig or brushed against a branch.

She didn't even hear Bjorn behind her; the chief was an absolute master of stealth despite his size.

"What's wrong with it?" she whispered. The Umbra moved sluggishly, one arm almost useless.

"We wounded this one in a hunt," Beth explained. "We're here to tie off a loose end. Well," she grinned. "You are."

Aurora's eyes widened. "What are you –?"

"Hey!" the Avalite yelled at the Umbra, cutting her off.

"What the hell are you doing?"

The Umbra turned, startled. To Aurora's surprise, Beth drew a pistol from her coat and casually squeezed off a few rounds at the creature. Aurora jumped as the shots shattered the silence. The bullets hit the Umbra, but with little effect, small black shards flying off like sawdust chipped from a block of wood.

"Weapons of this world cannot harm them," she explained. Aurora could see that. It was unhurt but scared, and a little angry.

"Okay, so what does?"

"This," she said, pocketing the pistol and holding out a wooden knife handle. Handle, no blade.

"And this would be…?"

"A training weapon."

The handle was ugly, modest and plain, not the ornamental weapon she would have expected. "The Torrid have used this for generations," she said, "You should be honoured."

"It doesn't even have a blade!"

"It does, you just have to imagine it. You work up from this, until you imagine your whole body is a weapon. That's when you can change shape like I do."

"That's nice in theory…" she trailed off, glancing back at Bjorn, who lurked some way away, almost invisible and utterly still.

"The Umbra, at their purest form, are bad thoughts. What kills bad thoughts?"

"Sleep?"

"Stronger thoughts!" Bjorn yelled, exasperated, from a distance.

"We've got this!" Beth shouted back, rolling her eyes, then to Aurora, "He's right though. Stronger thoughts."

"So, what, I'm supposed to wish it away?" she scoffed.

"No," the Avalite smiled with a glint of mischief in her eye, "You're supposed to take that knife, imagine a blade so sharp it can slice through diamond, and cut that filthy thing's heart out with it!"

"Oh-kay…" Aurora said, rather surprised as her bloodthirstiness.

Beth stepped back and gestured towards the Umbra.

Aurora swallowed. She had never killed anything before. She'd even pulled wasps out of swimming pools on holiday to stop them drowning.

"It's not a living thing," Beth said, as if she knew what she was thinking. She seemed to possess her grandfather's knack for reading her thoughts. "It's an idea."

"I don't know if I can."

"You have to," she said firmly. "The Umbra know you're out there. For whatever reason they see you as a threat, and that means they'll come for you. You must be ready."

The handle was thrust into her palm. Aurora took it reluctantly and peered towards the mangy creature. The Umbra had started towards them, stumbling in her direction.

"It will be weakened and slow, but don't underestimate it," Beth said, backing away from her, heading towards Bjorn.

"You're not staying?" she pleaded.

"The Umbra is the darkest part of the shadow," she smiled, "but no shadow can stand the light."

"That's beautiful," Aurora mocked, trying to put her nerves at rest.

"It's our mantra," Beth told her. "Just keep saying it and you'll be fine."

Beth backed away further, almost merging into the darkness.

The Umbra grew closer.

Aurora looked around. No one was going to help her.

"The Umbra is the darkest part of the shadow," she said, "but no shadow can stand the light." She repeated it again, and again.

The Umbra scrambled uphill, hissing.

"The Umbra is the darkest part of the shadow, but no shadow can stand the light."

Despite her fear, she was starting to realise how stupid the mantra sounded. That didn't stop her repeating it though.

Closer. She clutched the handle. Still no blade.

The Umbra broke into a shambolic run towards her. As it got within striking distance Aurora lost her composure. Forgetting the mantra she dived, skinning her elbow and forearm as she hit the forest floor.

The Umbra glanced back at her and ran for it.

She looked up. Beth stood over her, unimpressed.

"You forgot the mantra."

"It's a *stupid* mantra."

"Come on."

They chased after it. Aurora reverted to form and sulked, unsure why they were bothering. She was not a warrior. She was an adventurer.

"You have to do this," Beth warned. "So get angry, fast."

"I'm trying!" she snapped.

"No, you're not!"

Aurora fumed. She knew Beth was trying to get her riled, and it was working, but she did not like it one bit.

The Umbra was struggling further uphill, but it stopped when Bjorn blocked its path, sneering. The chief's motive was to contain, not kill, but the Umbra could not know that.

Choosing the easier option, it turned to Aurora. If it was going to get away, it had to be through her.

"The Umbra is the darkest part of the shadow," Beth reminded her, backing away.

"But no shadow can stand the light?" Aurora finished.

The Umbra approached. She started to recite the mantra, but it quickly got annoying.

This isn't going to work, she decided; *if I'm going to do this, I have to do it my way.*

Aurora thought about the Umbra and how they scared her. She remembered when it attacked her on the underground, and what the attack made her afraid of losing. Turning the tables, she thought about what they hated and what scared *them*.

It came to her.

"Don't stop thinking," she whispered, "Don't stop thinking."

She repeated it over and over; it became part of her breathing.

"Don't stop thinking."

As before, the Umbra came for her. This time however its intention wasn't escape, it wanted *her*.

They attacked at the same time, Aurora diving and swiping with the handle as the creature clawed at her.

Once again, Aurora fell to the ground. A smattering of black blood had sprayed her, and it slowly faded from sight.

More importantly, she was alive and holding a bladed weapon.

She had expected something exciting; a katana blade maybe. Instead, her weapon was little more than a dull blade, maybe six inches in length. But it was there.

A horrible sound filled the woods. The Umbra was screaming. It held its clawed hand, and Aurora could see she had slashed off two of its digits just above the joint.

From the wounds came black light.

When she reflected on the experience, she felt black light was not an accurate enough term; *anti light* would be closer. They were rays of darkness that covered anything they touched in heavy shadow, blocking off the moonlight's silvery glow.

The Umbra was scared now; she could hurt it. The girl was dangerous.

Aurora felt this was enough. She could defend herself. She knew killing the thing in cold blood was a response of fear, and she didn't want that.

"If you don't kill it, that shadow will haunt you for the rest of your life," Beth warned her.

Aurora had no choice. She had to remember what Beth had said earlier; this thing wasn't alive. It was a bad thought, whose only purpose was to bring harm, misery, and grey to the world.

Aurora approached the creature, which shrank back, terrified. She raised the knife, but her nerves got the better of her and she hesitated. The Umbra wasted no time in knocking her to one side and scrabbling away. It was afraid to stay and fight. She dropped the knife, and the blade had vanished before it hit the floor.

"You shouldn't –" Beth started.

"Yeah, I know!" Aurora snapped. She was running after the Umbra before she'd even finished the sentence. It was moving downhill now, almost falling over itself, weak from its injuries.

Aurora looked around for the perfect weapon, and found it; a felled tree branch, the approximate size of a javelin. She snatched it from the ground and tested the weight. Perfect.

"Don't stop thinking. Don't stop thinking."

She built up speed as she tore down the hill. The Umbra saw her coming, and stood hissing, ready to fight.

"Don't stop thinking."

She ran and leapt, clutching the branch in her hands.

Except it wasn't a branch anymore, it was a spear.

Unlike the knife it wasn't dull, this was sharp and bright, sculpted from white marble and emitting a cool purple glow.

The spear pierced the Umbra through the chest, and it shrieked horrifically. She twisted the spear, and it wailed once more. They locked eyes, only a foot or two away from one another. She had stopped reciting her mantra, and she wasn't thinking anything. This was the part she had dreaded; the creature was fatally wounded, but still alive. What happened next?

She knew she had to end it. Even if this thing was little more than a bad thought, she didn't want it to suffer any more than necessary.

"Finish it," Beth ordered from behind her, passing her the knife handle. The blade appeared as soon as it entered her grip, sharp and gleaming now.

She locked eyes with her prey. Aurora had expected to see something in the creature's gaze; fear maybe. But the same hate fuelled glare came through, and it only made the task easier.

Aurora knew; this wasn't an animal, this wasn't anything.

She swept the knife across in a fluid motion.

The Umbra's body fell limp to the ground. She stood over it, observing her kill. No thoughts filled her head, not glee, or remorse. It was fact, and that was all.

Bjorn emerged from the shadows and joined them, and the three of them formed a triangle around the felled creature. She no longer felt like an outsider to them now, she shared in a secret only they could understand.

The huge man knelt over the Umbra and dipped his fingertips into its wound. It was invasive, as if he was defiling the dead thing. The creature's body started to fade like the one Beth had killed in the underground.

Bjorn rose, towering over the girl. She raised her eyes to his.

Delicately, Bjorn traced a pattern over Aurora's face with the Umbra's blood. It was warm and smelled rank, yet she remained still. This was sacred somehow; she felt this was as much part of the tradition as the knife handle was.

Already the blood was fading from her face as Bjorn finished the design. Within moments it would be like it was never there.

"Your first kill," he murmured, "And a good one too. Remember tonight, Aurora Card. You have achieved something no one outside the Avalites has. If the Riftrot did not have cause to fear you before, they do now."

Their journey back through the darkness was silent, and even as she was returned to her cell they said nothing. Her Grandfather was asleep.

Bjorn locked the cell behind her and nodded as he left. She returned the nod with a flush of pride. Beth lingered for a moment after the chief left. It was clear she wanted to say something, but couldn't bring herself to do it.

Finally, as if resolving her frustrations, she held her hand up in a mirror of the motionless wave Aurora used to give her as the Wolf, and then let it settle briefly on the girls' hand. Aurora didn't know precisely what this meant, but she knew how it made her feel. Beth smiled and left soon after.

Aurora sat down on the bunk and reflected on the hunt. She was both exhausted and exhilarated at the same time. She had never, in her whole life, felt as alive as that.

"Did you have a good time?" asked her grandfather, his eyes still closed.

"It was… pretty interesting," she said as the old man sat up. For once, she was the one with an exciting story to share.

But before she could tell it the lights in their cell went out. From the corridor she heard noises of a struggle.

"Granddad?"

Her grandfather called her name, and she groped blindly for him in the blackness.

"Granddad!"

There was a rough grip on her arm, and knew instinctively it was not her grandfather's hand that clutched her. She cried out, trying to fight, until something sharp scratched her skin.

The world fell away.

Chapter 30
Doubt

Aurora came to. She felt awful; her thoughts sluggish and slow, as if her head was full of cotton wool.

She had trouble remembering what had happened, how she had come to be here. Where here was. She looked around.

She was sitting in what appeared to be a doctor's surgery, facing a desk. On the walls were various familiar posters with reminders for immunisation, how to recognise flu symptoms, when to call the doctor. Ugly steel filing cabinets filled every available space of the room.

Sat behind the desk was a doctor, who was busy looking through some files until he noticed she was awake.

There was something about his appearance that seemed familiar, although she had not seen him before. Her eyes scoured his face, until the memory lumbered to the surface like a floating corpse.

"A scar on his right cheek," she mumbled, only half aware she was reciting the description she had once studied so carefully. "A comma… falls on his forehead."

"Hello Aurora," the doctor said, "I am your psychologist, Dr Valentine. We've met before, several times, at your school."

Aurora did not understand. This wasn't right. She struggled to think. *Why was it so hard?*

"Psychologist?" she repeated, and her tongue felt like a dead weight in her mouth.

"I'm afraid so. Your parents requested I speak to you some time ago, they were very concerned about you."

A jolt of panic tried to cut through the fog. "Where's my granddad?"

"Ah," the doctor replied, the smile replaced with a look of concern. "There's no easy way to say this... The police found you and your grandfather yesterday, do you remember? You were both in a deserted cabin in the woods, freezing and starving. It was a good thing they found you when they did. Everyone has been very worried about you, your parents in particular."

Her arm itched. She looked down as she scratched it. There was a small mark.

"You were quite violent when we found you. The decision was made to sedate you for your own good," he told her. "No one wanted to do it. As a result, your thoughts may be quite foggy for a while."

"We weren't starving," she said, resisting. "We were captives."

Thoughts still a struggle. Like swimming through jelly.

"Aurora, it's clear you are a very smart young woman," Dr Valentine said, "but you also have a very overactive imagination. You have turned your humdrum life into a fantasy of excitement to escape from parents who don't understand you and a life that does not fulfil you.

"Since you were picked up yesterday, we have been paying close attention to what you've been saying." He held the file at arm's length and squinted at the documents it held. "There are no 'Ne'er DuWells.' I don't know where you came up with the phrase – maybe your grandfather mentioned it, maybe you read it somewhere.

Regardless, you have used the phrase to create a perfect nemesis. An unseen, absolutely powerful villain."

He lowered the file and looked her straight in the eye. "Psychologically speaking, they're your family, Aurora. The thuggish brothers, the parents you never see. Your grandfather can relate; your family, like these Ne'er DuWells, 'imprisoned' him, as he puts it. He has had to confront the fear everyone faces when they can't cope with the day-to-day world, and the sad fact is he couldn't do it. There's nothing wrong with that, it's just the way life is."

Aurora struggled. This made sense, she guessed. It wasn't hard to believe.

"Normally, the sort of behaviour you have been displaying would be fine," Dr Valentine continued, his voice slow and rhythmic, almost hypnotic. "It would go unnoticed, and eventually you might grow out of it. But you're dragging a very sick old man into your delusion, someone who can't tell the difference between reality and fantasy."

From the depths an idea came to me. It was so hard to think, but I remembered my talent, and tried to read his aura. This would reveal the truth.

The doctor saw my expression and a look of understanding crossed his face. "This was in your file too*," he said, sadly.* "In a fantasy, I'm sure a talent like reading another's thoughts would be a keen skill, the perfect way of knowing who's telling the truth or not, but as ideal as this would be, it can't happen in real life.*"*

Don't listen. Push through. Find it.

"It only goes to show your inability to cope with the complexities of the world," *he continued,* "and your need to see everything in black and white."

Releasing her strain, Aurora stopped trying. She couldn't do it. Either the sedative was making her slow or he was blocking her somehow, or... he was right, she thought, with a sense of growing panic.

"Aurora, I want you to pay close attention to me," Dr Valentine said, sincerely. "Your fantasies have moved further from reality as they have progressed. Your grandfather being held prisoner is one thing, fairly believable given his conviction. To go from that to meeting an "immortal" is further removed, but at least he resembles a human. But werewolves are something else entirely."

"Not werewolves," Aurora replied slowly but firmly, focusing on her words. "They're... Avalites."

"Of course they are," he patronised. "Regardless, if your fantasy takes you to another world altogether, there's a possibility you may stray from the world of the sane and never come back."

Panic struck her once more. *Did he know? Did he know about the Nameless City? Was that what he was talking about?* Aurora was quiet for a while as Valentine droned on. Finally he realised she was not listening and stopped talking.

"So what happens now?" she asked. She had managed to regain some composure, and sat staring at him with blank expectation.

The doctor smiled, as if pleased he had got through to her. "Well," he began "we may have to keep you here for a while to ensure you receive proper care. After that, we will be able to release you to your parents."

"And my granddad?"

"He's not a well man. He'll be returned to care. This whole event has furthered his decline significantly."

"Can I see him?"

"Not for a little while."

"Where is he?"

"He's safe. For now, that's all I'd like you to concern yourself with."

Aurora was stalling, and wondered if Valentine knew. Whether he knew it or not, he was striking at her most vulnerable spot: her doubt.

His argument was understandable; the adventure *had* become more elaborate. And they *were* headed for another world. How could he know these things, unless she had been ranting about them when she was caught? Maybe she was as disturbed as he suggested.

Unless, the thought struck her, *this was exactly what the Ne'er DuWells want me to think*. She couldn't decide. But she couldn't risk the Ne'er DuWells getting her if this was their doing.

Better to be insane and alone than in their custody.

"Can I see my file?" she asked.

"Whatever for?" Valentine's brow furrowed.

"I want to see my family," she said, latching onto the emotion. "Is there a photo? Do they really miss me?"

"Of course they do," he smiled. He removed the photo from the file and passed it to her. "It's good to see you take an interest in things that will help you reconnect."

Aurora stared at the picture, keeping one eye on Valentine. She felt him watching her and pretended to sob, waiting for him to get impatient. Finally it happened.

The doctor began to say something as he stood up, walking around the desk to her. She waited for him to get closer and made her move. Holding back until the last possible moment, she pushed him, channelling all her energy through her body, from her feet all the way to her fingers. He fell, awkward and uncoordinated, rolling over the back of the desk. A moment was wasted shoving everything on the surface of the desk onto him too: books, folders, and a laptop.

She made a break for it. Valentine would be a few seconds behind her at least. She ran from the office, slamming the door behind her. Turning to see where to go, she got the surprise of her life.

This was no doctor's surgery. She was in a corporate office, dozens of floors off the ground. Aurora ran to the end of the corridor and looked out at a spectacular view of Canary Wharf. It was night-time and they were back in the city again.

Another door opened, and she was surprised to see it was not Valentine, but half a dozen men and women approaching her, all dressed immaculately in suits. In no time they had her surrounded.

One man in particular stood out as he moved to their front. Very handsome, he was impeccably dressed in a midnight blue suit. He had closely shaven hair and the darkest skin Aurora had ever seen. Looking closely, she could see his face was adorned with intricate lines, subtly scarred into the flesh. The lines reminded her of Beth, and then it hit her.

"You're Tundra."

"Daniel Caliban," the leader nodded, extending a hand. "CEO of Tundra." Aurora glared at it, as furious as she was terrified.

Back down the corridor, the door to the fake doctor's office exploded open. Aurora jumped, backing off. She had nowhere to go.

Valentine stormed out the office. "Get back here!" he screamed, his eyes finding Aurora. He had changed utterly. The shift in character, from body language and mannerism to tone and even accent was drastically different. "I won't have this, you little –"

"That's enough, Mr DuWell," Daniel said firmly, stepping between him and Aurora.

The chilling realisation hit her; this was none other than Drake DuWell himself. She was in serious, serious trouble.

"The girl blindsided me," Drake protested. "I should've known better than to try a reasonable approach."

"Reasonable?" Aurora spat, trying to forget her fear. "You tried to convince me I was mad!"

"Aren't you?" he scoffed, "There must be something wrong with you to work with *him*! He's a murderer and a thief! Sending you home was for your own good!"

"Don't you dare say that about my granddad!" Aurora stepped forwards. "Not after everything your family did to him!"

Daniel placed a hand on Aurora's shoulder. It was meant to be a supportive move, but Aurora was angry all around and threw it off. This didn't seem to bother him.

"You had your chance, Drake," Daniel said, calmly. "Your motives were questionable when you suggested acquiring them, your methods more so. The girl is clearly not susceptible to your tactics. You are not to harm her."

"They're *mine*," Drake seethed. "If you won't help me, I'll take them with me."

"The purpose of extracting them was to assert that Torrid were not abusing their talents," Daniel explained, with a Zen cool. "We can do that without you. Given your emotional attachment to this matter, it's best that you leave. We'll let you know our findings."

"The old man, then." Drake was getting desperate. "Leave the girl if needs must, but Hayhoe and I have a history. What he's done to my family can never be forgiven."

"No!" Aurora cried. The threat of the Ne'er DuWells taking just her grandfather was almost worse than taking them both. Who knew what sort of fate he would come to without her to protect him?

She looked up at Daniel. She didn't much like him, but it was clear that he was in charge of the situation.

"You are to leave now, Drake," Daniel insisted. "Alone." Aurora felt a knot in her stomach unwind.

Drake cursed. He spat at the ground and stepped towards Daniel. "After all my family have done for your ridiculous tribe. Look at all you have! You would still be squatting in the woods with your barbarian tribesmen if it weren't for us, shaking your rain sticks and drawing patterns in the dirt!"

"We never accepted your money to become your research tool. You know that."

"You're making a huge mistake. I promise, you are going to regret this."

"The only thing I regret," Daniel said with the trademark Avalite will, squaring up to Drake, "is ever listening to you in the first place." His aura flashed to life momentarily and for an instant Aurora saw a will as strong as Bjorn's in the Tundra.

Drake backed off. He had pushed Tundra too far, and his temper had let him down. He shot a withering look that Aurora would remember forever.

"You watch yourself with the old man, little girl," he growled, nearing the door. "Ask yourself this: why don't the rest of your ignorant family want anything to do with him? I'm a brother short because of his actions."

"Whatever," Aurora replied, trying her best to act nonchalant.

"If you knew as much as I do, I wonder if you'd be as sure about him then," He gestured at the fake office. "Maybe you should take a look."

Daniel watched Drake leave, not taking his eyes off the aristocrat until he was out of sight.

"Make sure he leaves the building," he said, and two Tundra followed wordlessly.

Aurora shuddered. She knew Drake's words were meant to confuse her – that was the Ne'er DuWells' way – but they still left a mark in her mind. What did they know that she didn't?

She and Daniel exchanged glances. "Are you all right?" he asked her.

Aurora replied by aiming a kick at his shin. Daniel blocked the move without trying. "Calm down," he told her.

"No, I'm not all right!" yelled Aurora. "I feel sick from whatever crap you pumped into me. Not to mention I was just threatened by a man who tried to convince me I was insane!"

"I can only apologise," said Daniel. "The DuWells have never pushed this hard before. We didn't know he was capable of such a thing."

"Still think that?" Aurora replied. "You've ruined our –" she cut herself off. She was going to say 'adventure,' but the word seemed too childish. "You kidnapped us, shot Norm and drugged me. I'd rather be with Torrid," she ended, with a grumble.

"Your friend was a terrible mistake," said Daniel, and a trace of regret lingered in his voice. "We've been monitoring the emergency services since the incident, and there are reports that your friend is in care, and alive."

"He'd better be," Aurora said, trying her best to growl like a Torrid. She knew Norm would be okay, but she thought it best to keep the unimpressed routine going and see how much mileage she could get from it.

"I can't undo what's happened," Daniel admitted "but I can reunite you with someone that should help make things a bit better."

Chapter 31
Tundra

"Granddad!"

Aurora burst into the room, throwing herself into her grandfather's arms. He held her tight, then checked her over, inspecting her critically.

"I'm fine," she tried to reassure him.

"No, you're not," fussed the old man. "Look at the state of you. What did you do to her?" he barked at Daniel, who stood in the doorway, silent.

"It was Drake –"

"Drake DuWell?" her grandfather practically yelled. "What happened? Is he here?"

"No, he's gone now," she said. "He pretended to be a doctor and told me I was unwell, that I'd made this all up. I was so confused from the drugs I nearly believed him."

"But you didn't…"

"I was worried about you," she blushed. "I didn't really care if I was mad or not. Then when I got out of the room I saw where I was. That's when Daniel kicked him out."

"You idiots," her grandfather shouted at Daniel, ignoring the comments she had made in his favour. "What were you thinking? You can never trust those snakes! I can't believe you were stupid enough to let him even talk to her."

Daniel did not reply but seemed not to take offence.

"Are you sure you're okay?" the old man asked Aurora, smoothing the hair from her face. "This is why I never wanted you involved with the Ne'er DuWells. The mind games they play can be brutal. I know it doesn't seem like it, but you got away lightly."

"I'm fine," she sighed. "It's just... what if I'm not? What if I am crazy and always have been? What if he wasn't Drake but Dr Valentine, and when I ran out the room, I just went back into my fantasy again? What if we're both unstable, and I'm dragging you down further with my over-active imagination? What if –" she almost added: *what if my parents were right?*

The old man tried to find the words. Then it came to him, his troublemakers smile spreading across his face, and he shared with her a notion so absurd it could only make sense.

"Does it matter?"

"What?" she started, a smile breaking through her worries.

"Think about it," he said kindly, "I'm old enough to make my own choices, but not so old I don't know what I'm doing. And let's face it: what we've been through is far more interesting than anything either of us would normally be up to."

Aurora considered this. She hadn't looked at it that way.

He raised an eyebrow. Well?

"Okay," she smiled.

"That's my girl."

*

"Believe me, I'd rather not be making this call, but I thought you should know. There's only so much indecency a fellow can take before he's compelled to take action."

Drake was on the phone. On the other end of the line was Torrid.

"I don't care for Hayhoe," he said gravely. "Everyone knows that, but a child? What they were doing to her was too much for my conscience to allow. That's why I'm calling you."

He paused to let the voice on the end of the line reply.

"Well, I suppose you *could* describe it as torture…"

Drake smiled to himself. He wasn't the only one whose temper would get him into trouble. Let's see what the Torrid made of *that*.

*

Their reunion complete, Daniel decided this was the best time to clear his throat, and Aurora and her grandfather looked up at him.

"What do you think of this joker?" the old man asked her.

"He's okay," replied Aurora to Daniel's silent amusement. "He did stand up to Drake. His aura is almost identical to Bjorn's, only cold, if you know what I mean. He's on the level."

Daniel nodded, respectfully. "I hope that is enough for you, Mr Hayhoe," he said. "Or Mr Danger, as I'm sure Bjorn would have called you."

"You're a fan?" he sniffed.

"Your books are not without their charm," Daniel conceded. "Despite lacking an effective dramatic structure and adhering to some lazy stereotypes. Not to mention the numerous grammatical issues…"

"Everyone's a critic," her grandfather grumbled.

*

Tundra's office was a thing of beauty. If Aurora were to have to work in an office when she grew up, she would definitely want it to be this one. Cutting edge corporate aesthetics blended seamlessly with a Zen influence; offices were separated with elegant glass partitions, while long balconies and observation decks offered places to reflect and meet. Tall windows offered a spectacular view of the city, while plants, artworks and sculptures created a relaxed yet efficient atmosphere.

But it went further than that. In a way she couldn't quite articulate, it reminded Aurora of how the Torrid camp merged technology with nature, but re-imagined for the corporate world. It might not have made sense, but there it was.

The Avalite influence stretched beyond simply the way the office was decorated; they must have had a hand in influencing the building's architecture too. Aurora wondered: *if the Ne'er DuWells had got them this building, had they had it built for them too? Were they really that powerful?*

"Torrid do not appreciate what we are trying to achieve. They have no valid reason to distrust us," Daniel told them as he led them round the office. "But we can appreciate why the relationship is strained."

"Try telling them that," Aurora frowned.

"They're Luddites," Daniel said coolly. "Trapped in the past. The truth is, the Avalites need to move on. Torrid spend their time hiding in the woods. They no longer see the big picture."

"And what is the big picture?"

"The threats from the Rift are too numerous and cunning for them to be hunted down one by one and exterminated in the manner Torrid are accustomed. The reactive measure they provide is not a long-term solution when the Umbra grow by the day. Torrid fail to accept that."

"At least they hunt them," said Aurora, feeling oddly protective of her adopted tribe. "It's more than you can say."

"They do so for sport and tradition," Daniel said dismissively. "They have no desire to purge the menace."

"Do *you*?"

Daniel paused then, and Aurora found his hesitation chilling. "There is much we don't know," he said softly, "and much that needs to be learnt. We cannot learn these things if we are at Torrid's beck and call."

He was hiding something. Aurora let out a sound of utter frustration. This was driving her mad. Her grandfather did not disagree.

"This is ridiculous," she told the old man, ignoring the Tundra leader. "Why can't either of them see what's happening?"

"And what is happening?" Daniel asked.

"You and Torrid have been growing apart since Ragnar died," her grandfather interjected, noting that Aurora was becoming too frustrated to articulate herself. "And the influence of the Ne'er DuWells has pushed you even further still. They engineered this distance between the two tribes. Not only did they take you away from Torrid, they've been feeding you lies about everything.

Without the two of you working together, the Umbra are running riot." He left out the part where they believed the Ne'er DuWells killed Ragnar; that might be one accusation too far.

"Regardless," Daniel said. "We can't go on simply finding and stopping them one at a time. These are no simple fires we can put out. The rate they are increasing is exponential. We have the resources to research the Rift; we just need time to learn about it properly. Torrid won't allow us that time."

They had reached the surveillance equipment; a huge room that teemed with activity. A screen the size of the wall displayed a satellite view of Britain, while others displayed foreign countries.

"What's that?" her grandfather asked nodding at the map. Numerous hot spots glowed on it.

"The red spots represent a known Umbra manifestation," Daniel explained. "The purple areas indicate other Riftrot."

"There're hundreds of them!" Aurora cried, and she was right. The map was awash with red and purples blotches that seemed to be spreading like viruses. "How can the Torrid possibly find them on their own?"

Tundra moved around the office recording data and making calls. Aurora immediately recognised the cool green and blue glows of their auras, similar yet different to their Torrid counterparts as they moved round the room.

"They will do their best, I'm sure."

"So that's your alternative?" Aurora said, wrestling her temper under control. "You ignore Torrid until you come up with a solution? What about all the people you don't save while you're working it out?"

"The risk is... undesirable." Daniel seemed to steel himself. "But we have no other option. This must be done. We can't keep reacting, when with time we can fix this problem forever."

"Do you know that for sure?"

The Tundra said nothing, but led them out of the room to an elevator, and they got in. When the doors closed behind them, he pressed a button, and then two more. The three illuminated buttons made a triangle. *It's a code*, Aurora realised.

"Do you know what Torrid are saying about you?" her grandfather asked as the lift smoothly descended.

"I can't imagine it's favourable," Daniel mused, unperturbed.

"Their theories... obsession with the Umbra, rumours of worship, breeding them..." he trailed off. "Surely you can't allow such slander to remain unanswered."

"Mr. Hayhoe, if you're trying to rile me, I'm afraid it will be unsuccessful. What Torrid say does not concern me. In fact, some of their points are almost valid. What we do, we do in order to learn. There are things we need to know, and the questions go beyond your simple black and white morality."

"And what is it you need to know?"

"Everything," he said with cold intensity, and his eyes shone as he spoke.

"I'm not sure I like where this is going, Mr Caliban," her grandfather warned, as the elevator slowed to a halt.

"Well, I can't see you liking this much, either," Daniel said, as the doors opened.

Chapter 32
The Dark Secret

The elevator opened onto a large laboratory, as modern and sophisticated as the offices above it. The only difference in style was a large maroon tapestry, hung on the far wall, reaching all the way from the high ceilings to the floor. On the tapestry was a single image of an eye, which had flowered open, revealing light coming from within. There was something about the tapestry Aurora found familiar and unsettling, but she did not know why.

"No windows," her grandfather observed. "We're underground?"

"Very astute," Daniel said. "Keep those wits about you and your mind open. I don't think many would understand what we're trying to achieve here, but you might."

They walked to the other end of the lab, and as they passed through, many of those at work stopped to look at Aurora and her grandfather. They were all Tundra, she could tell at a glance.

As they came to the other end of the lab, they went through into a smaller room, and he gestured at the window ahead, which revealed an operating theatre below them.

"The Umbra are unlike the other Riftrot," Daniel explained. "The others are mindless, simple creatures that feed off man's concentration and imagination. But the Umbra are something else entirely. What we want to know is what, and why."

"*Why...?*" Aurora echoed.

They looked through the observatory's window at the operating theatre below, and saw a team of Tundra surgeons operating on a concealed shape. Even with a sheet obscuring it, there was no masking that dark form.

"Is that an Umbra?" Aurora gasped, horrified.

"It is," Daniel nodded.

"What are you doing to it?"

"We're looking for answers."

"Is it dead?"

"Riftrot aren't really dead or alive," he told them, "They're thoughts, made manifest."

"I know that. But if you kill one, they fade."

"Which is why we haven't killed it. Without feeding, this specimen would certainly have faded by now, but Tundra are determined to learn the truth."

"So?"

"Rory," her grandfather said grimly. "He means *they're* feeding it."

She didn't understand, and it annoyed her. "On what?"

"That's not important," Daniel began, but when he saw he would be unable to progress any further without explaining, he relented. "*We* are determined to find answers, whatever it takes. It only hurts the first time."

"It... It's you, isn't it?" Aurora was disgusted. She had felt the Umbra's embrace once, and she had no desire to ever feel it again. She had no idea how anyone could willingly volunteer for it.

230

"There are enough Tundra here to keep this creature alive without any serious cost to us. Look on it as donating blood."

"You can't be serious!"

"Daniel, you'd better be building to a point with this," her grandfather said, "because all we're seeing is something that looks like demon worship and monster autopsy."

"The point is," Daniel said, and for maybe the first time, a hint of frustration flickered across his face, "that the reason for the Umbra's superiority over the other Riftrot – and their increased success – is that they are designed this way."

"You mean like evolution?"

"I mean *intelligent* design. Despite their ragged appearance, there is a lethal and efficient design at work with these creatures. The Umbra share traits with all Riftrot, as if they were an amalgamation of their strongest traits, but if that was not enough, there is something else in there too; something we can see, but cannot contain."

He pressed a button on the wall, and it activated the intercom to the operating theatre. "We can learn no more from this one," he said. "Open it all the way."

The surgeons looked up at him, and then turned to work. Even from the observatory, Aurora could see them exchanging nervous glances.

"Watch closely," Daniel told them.

The chief surgeon leant behind the sheet and was concealed from view. Whatever he was doing, he was doing it very slowly and carefully.

"Avalite scalpels," Daniel whispered. "Real ones would not work on them."

One of the surgeons looked up at their leader to indicate they were ready.

"Do it," Daniel said.

For a moment there was silence, and nothing happened. Then, from behind the sheet came a flurried explosion of movement and confusion, and some of the surgeons fell back in the chaos.

Aurora wasn't sure what she was seeing. Something alive had exploded out of the Umbra's body.

It was a dark blur, at first small, but seeming to expand upon contact with the air, gaining in speed and strength as it grew. It rose, moving fast and violently, tearing free from gravity's chains as it headed towards the operating theatre's high ceiling. The thing was very dark and its presence made the lights flicker and the observatory window shake, meaning it was almost impossible to make out. Only one clear trait was determinable: this thing, whatever it was, had huge, black-feathered wings.

Then, in an explosion of light and dark, it was gone, leaving nothing, no trace that it had ever existed.

"Now do you see?" Daniel asked. While Aurora and her grandfather had leapt back, shielding themselves, he had stayed perfectly still. Clearly he had seen this before and he looked almost relieved, as if he expected them to now understand.

"What the devil was that?" the old man nearly yelled.

"We don't know," Daniel admitted, almost casually. It was as if, to him, all of Tundra's scientific prowess, and all their knowledge of the Unseen world had simply run out, and left them without an answer. This clearly amazed him. "Our best guess? Something of pure imagination."

"I don't understand," Aurora said. "That thing – whatever it was – was locked inside the Umbra? Is it in each one? How come it doesn't come out when Torrid kill them?"

"Because Torrid are going for the kill," Daniel said, "Their wish is to destroy the bad thought – or absence of thought – that the Umbra represent. We're not trying to do that. The tools we use are a cutting edge fusion of human precision and Avalite power.

"Can't you see? We're cutting through, finding the essence of what's inside the Umbra, the spark that makes them think and hunt and feed, that sets them apart from the other Riftrot and gives them their hive mind. And someone gave them that spark."

"But who would do that? Who could?"

Daniel's eyes widened, and Aurora could see that was the question he had been waiting for them to ask. "Nothing from *this* world. But we both know of another one. Don't you see? Someone sent the Umbra from the Unseen to us, and it's Tundra's responsibility to find out who."

Chapter 33

The Lion and the Unicorn

"Daniel, I agree, this is huge discovery," Jim Hayhoe said, "but if it comes at the cost of what is happening out there, then it's not right."

"We're on the cusp," Daniel told him. "We're too close to stop now."

"Surely some sort of compromise could be reached? Allocate some of your resources to helping Torrid hunt, while you continue to work on this. You never know: they might have some ideas about what we've just seen that you may have not considered."

"We've gone too far," Daniel said, shaking his head. "What we've done… Bjorn would never understand. The Avalites' history with the Nameless City has become something from folklore, but we know differently. It's there, and we have to find a way to get to it."

"So tell them!" he pleaded.

"They won't care," Daniel said. "Not like we do. Do you want to know the real difference between Torrid and Tundra? Once you get past the emotions and approach, the real thing that sets us apart is our belief in the other side. All Worlds Unseen, we call it. They say the Avalites dwelled in the Nameless City, hundreds of years ago. We could cross between both worlds, until something changed. What that was and why we left, no one knows. Torrid are content here, in the Seen World. But Tundra, we've always wanted to get back there. This could be our way!"

As they spoke, both men were quite unaware that Aurora suddenly staring at a corner of the ceiling with unnatural interest. Something had seized her attention, and she was trying to fathom what that was. "Daniel, old boy, I can't think of any other ways to tell you this," the old man sighed. "So I'm going to say it again: tell them."

"If they learn what we've done – feeding the Umbra, keeping them alive, experimenting with them – everything they've accused us of becoming will be proven correct."

"What if –" Hayhoe began, but Daniel cut him off as a Tundra marched up to them urgently. It was Victoria, the Tundra who had met Drake at the Savoy. She looked as troubled as a member of their tribe could look. "Yes?" Daniel asked, but before she could speak, Aurora calmly said: "They're here."

Daniel, Victoria and her grandfather looked at her.

"Who are?"

"Torrid." The word sounded unfocused, almost dream-like.

"She's right," Victoria confirmed. "A large group have entered the building by force. They're presently restricted to the lobby, but we don't know how long we can hold them there."

"Any casualties?"

"None yet. Only minimal property damage."

"Good," Daniel nodded. "Tell security not to engage, but to try to keep them in the lobby if they can. I'm on my way."

"How did you know that?" the old man asked his granddaughter, who was still staring at the ceiling.

"I can see them," I said, and I was staring so hard my eyes must have been as round as saucers. Sure enough, my talent to see auras had flared to life almost uncontrollably, and I could see the orange glow of a whole mass of Torrid warriors as if the ground between us and the lobby was not even there.

There was one aura in particular that seemed especially powerful. That wasn't right; it was as powerful as the others, but I could feel it looking for one thing only: me.

Beth.

I didn't know if it would work or not, but I tried to tell her I was okay. I thought it hard in her direction, and I hoped that like the weapons made to fight the Umbra, believing it would be enough.

I'm fine, I thought at her. Don't fight Tundra. There's been a huge misunderstanding. It's the Ne'er DuWells; they did it.

"That's remarkable," Daniel said, impressed. "You're only recently active. You shouldn't be able to do that yet."

"Sir," Victoria reminded him gently, but it wasn't needed. Daniel straightened and prepared to take his leave.

"What are you going to do?" Hayhoe asked him.

"I don't blame Torrid for behaving this way after we took you from them," he said, "It's the inevitable reaction to a rash decision we made in error. We should never have acted against other Avalites. And you're right; what matters now is ending the feud. Bjorn knows this as well as I. But there's something else: in person, our auras cannot conceal anything from one another. As soon as he sees me, he'll know what we've been doing. He won't understand. He'll react the only way he knows how, with force."

"You don't have to fight," Hayhoe pleaded, knowing all too well his words would be in vain.

"Compromise was never an option," he said sadly, "and we will not give up trying to find our way back to the City. Not now that we know how close we are."

"So, then what?"

"Bjorn will not want to see blood spilled any more than I do," Daniel considered, "but there is an old Avalite law that determines the leadership of a tribe through single combat. It is the only way to end the feud without more lives being lost. We will let the fates decide what the Avalites shall be: hunters in the Seen, or explorers of the Unseen." He sighed, and a sad, stern smile came to him. "Take care, both of you. It was an honour to meet you."

He left them in the observation room. Aurora was stunned; as much as she admired Daniel's conviction, she couldn't stand his inflexibility.

"They're not going to stop," she said with horror. "Are they?"

"It's their way," her grandfather told her. "The fight will probably be in animal form, most likely to the death."

"We've got to do something."

"That may be easier said than done."

*

"I told you they were tricky," Jack told his brother with a small twinge of satisfaction. It was a careful jibe; the thought of his brother's knife against his throat was as fresh in his memory as the scratch it had left on his skin and he had no wish to re-live it.

They were in the best place to share their mutual failure: the pub. Located in the financial district, the DuWell siblings appeared inconspicuous against the collection of bankers and accountants who were unwinding in the wood panelled saloon bar that was only one of dozens in the city. Drake had quickly discarded his Dr Valentine disguise and was once again in a tailored suit. It didn't help his mood.

They were actually in their second bar. Still fired up from his conflict with Tundra, Drake had got into a terrible row with the staff of the first pub they entered when he learned they didn't stock his brand of scotch. In their defence, only about eight locations in all of Britain did, and they all involved an exclusive membership.

Jack decided when they got to the second pub that it might be better if he were the one to order the drinks. His brother did not object.

"Whatever it is about that man I hate, his granddaughter's got it too," Drake muttered, grimacing as he sipped his inferior whisky. "That little witch is tricky."

"It must run in the family," Jack guessed, "What do you suggest? You know Mother's not going to accept failure."

"Like I care." Jack knew he was lying. Everyone cared, because if *she* was unhappy, heads tended to roll. In a few cases, this had happened literally. Jack took a deep swig of his pint and waited for Drake to continue.

"We know that call I made will bring Torrid down on them. I say we torch the building while they have it out," he sulked. "They'll be so distracted they'll all burn to death."

"That's not the most subtle idea you've ever had."

"I just want to get shot of them. This sort of work is below me. I'm the eldest. It should be left to Marcus."

"When have you ever heard of Marcus doing leg work? Or work of any kind?"

"He's pampered," mused Drake, "Vivian is too. Weakness and vanity isn't the DuWell way. This would never have been tolerated fifty years ago."

"You know," Jack began, "Aside from the fire, I don't think it's your worst idea."

"Meaning?"

"Well, things are going to get dramatic. The Avalites can't watch Hayhoe and the girl all the time. I say we wait, see, and grab them when the opportunity arises. We'll be gone before they notice."

Drake considered this, frowning.

"We could get that pub shut down too," Jack suggested with an encouraging smile.

"Abduction and financial ruin in one night?" Drake's cruel smile reappeared, "I like it." He clinked glasses with his sibling.

"Cheers."

*

The tension in the lobby was unbearable.

The two factions of Avalites had yet to engage in combat, and were reluctant to do so. Despite their many differences, they were a family, and no matter how much they had drifted apart in recent years, they would not fight unless there was no other choice.

The abduction of Aurora and her grandfather put this peace in jeopardy, but it could be explained by the manipulations of the Ne'er DuWells, as long as Aurora and her grandfather could convince them this was the truth.

But the revelation of the Tundra's activities was going to come to light very soon, and it threatened to push everything over the edge. It was hard for a non-Avalite to comprehend, but the Tundra's actions towards the Umbra were obscene in Torrid's eyes, regardless of their intentions.

The future of the Avalites hung in the balance.

Victoria escorted Aurora, and her grandfather to the lift, and together they ascended to the lobby. Aurora looked through the floors above them with her sight and saw the huge blur of colour that made up the Avalite forces growing ever closer; the two different sets of auras squaring up to – and then testing – one another like two giant, uneasy beasts of colour. The tendrils of emotion would reach out then leap back upon contact, surprised at their familiarity but shocked at their perceived betrayal, giving the effect of an orange and blue yin yang symbol in motion.

Torrid were beginning to understand what Tundra had done, and they expressed their reaction as shock, betrayal and rage.

"They're realising," Aurora said "We have to do something."

"I'm not sure what. They've both lost perspective, Torrid and Tundra alike," her grandfather said. "If neither of them are willing to compromise then perhaps the only option is what Daniel said."

"I wish you were wrong," Victoria said, behind them. She had remained silent until now, although Aurora sensed real remorse in her aura.

"What would you do?" Aurora asked her.

"I don't know."

"What about some sort of moderator, an impartial third party?" her grandfather suggested.

"Good luck finding them. I doubt there's no one alive with the sort of knowledge that would be required for the task," Victoria answered, shaking her head. "And even if there were, neither tribe would accept anyone with a preference for one tribe over the other, such as the two of you, nor defer to an outsider. I'm sorry."

Neither Aurora nor her grandfather had an answer to that. They concluded their journey in silence, dreading what would follow.

*

With its high ceiling, marble floor and pillars, the lobby already had a Roman, almost gladiatorial quality, and was now filled with actual warriors to complete the arena look. The moon could be seen through a skylight four floors above, illuminating the two chiefs, who prepared themselves for combat.

Or at least, Bjorn was *trying* to. Aurora watched him doing his best to ignore Beth, who was relentlessly attempting to capture his attention. She must have got Aurora's message and was trying to get the chief to stand down.

From their auras she could see that Beth was pushing her luck in challenging her chief, until finally he ended the conversation, and Beth turned away, furious.

When their eyes met Aurora saw relief in hers – she was pleased to see her unharmed – but mostly they showed hurt and frustration. There was nothing she could do.

No longer distracted by Beth, Bjorn paced back and forth along the lines of his men like a caged tiger, in contrast to Daniel, who sat on the floor, cross-legged, and meditated. He was of slimmer build to the chief, but he was still well built and strong. It would be a fair fight.

Bjorn looked relieved and he stopped pacing when he saw Aurora and her grandfather emerge through the Tundra's ranks. "Aurora! Mr Danger!" his voice boomed. "Are you all right?"

"We're fine," Aurora yelled. "Don't fight, please! There's been a terrible mistake!"

"The only mistake we made was waiting 'til now to do this," Bjorn growled. "If we had known what was going on earlier we would've put a stop to it. I wouldn't have believed it if we hadn't come. As soon as this is over the Avalites will be whole again. Things will be as they once were, and this... *abomination* will be at an end."

"You can't –" Aurora began, stepping forwards. Her grandfather grabbed her arm and held her back.

"Get off!" she snapped.

"Don't interfere, Rory," he ordered. "Once this begins, anyone caught in the middle will be torn to shreds!"

"This doesn't make any sense!" she wailed, her eyes filling with tears. "This can't be their only option. Don't they care? Don't *you* care?"

"Of course I do," he said, "but I care about you more. There's nothing anyone can do."

Daniel had been sitting still throughout the exchange, eyes closed, when suddenly they sprang open. They had changed from a soulful brown to pitch black. He seemed in a trance, unaware of his surroundings, and got to his feet. The crowd went silent.

The bravado left Bjorn, replaced by a deadly seriousness. Aurora and her grandfather knew what was coming; there was nothing they could do to stop it.

The two men were about twelve feet apart when they charged at one another. In the space of three steps they both leapt into the air and changed.

The only comparison that fit for Aurora was an exploding popcorn kernel. One minute it was two men flying towards each other, the next they twisted and distorted; replaced by something entirely different.

Aurora had expected them to both become wolves, but Daniel became a panther, with fur even darker than his skin. Bjorn chose a bear, brown and larger than his already considerable size. The sound of their roars as they collided was staggering.

The two warriors fought in bursts, charging at one another and fighting in short bouts before pulling away to regroup and circle one another. They were a blur of brown and black as teeth and claws struck, yet at no point did one fighter appear to press the advantage more than the other.

Aurora wondered just how much of the fighter's personalities remained in their animal form. For all his hot headedness, Bjorn's bear was remarkably patient, waiting for Daniel to strike before launching his own attack. This approach worked in his favour, utilising his formidable strength and reflexes.

He was far more manoeuvrable than Aurora had imagined, twisting to deliver a blow that she was sure had broken some of Daniel's ribs. But Daniel was not to be underestimated either. His tactical personality was still present, although the Tundra's normally cool persona had been dropped. Aurora remembered Rory saying that Tundra used the animal to vent their emotions. She could see this now. Daniel displayed a ferocity that must have surprised Bjorn. He struck at him with claws and teeth; scratching, biting and mauling. He went for exposed spots – the throat, the eyes; and Bjorn had to act quickly to prevent real damage, throwing the sleek black form off him with his mighty paws.

When they met for their third clash, Daniel's jaws found Bjorn's shoulder, working their way closer to his throat. Bjorn howled, and brought his paws down on Daniel's lithe form. Blow after blow rained down on his hide, but Daniel refused to relent, his claws raking the bear's brown fur.

Aurora could not bear to watch; yet neither could she turn away. Her eyes trailed across the watching crowd. From Beth to Rory, to Victoria, from Torrid to Tundra, their eyes showed the same expression. This was no sporting match; the Avalites were not cheering their leaders on. This was a solemn thing.

One of them was going to die. There was no cause for celebration.

Aurora looked up, anything not to have to watch the violence, and spotted something strange on the skylight; the silhouette of a man peering down at them. He was waving at her, trying to get her attention. He stamped his foot down on the glass skylight repeatedly. The glass cracked. As he brought his foot down a third time and the glass spiderwebbed Aurora realised with a dawning terror what he was doing.

"Get back!" she yelled, her voice carrying over the roar of the two fighting animals.

The Avalites heard her, and looked up to see the glass shatter. As the figure fell, Aurora heard him screaming swear words in a variety of languages.

With a rush of relief, she knew who it was.

Chapter 34
The Avalite King

Norm had not had a good week.

He had been shot, but that was nothing new: he had been shot before, many, many times. It had, however, been a long time since he had been shot protecting someone he cared for. He had planned to wait until Tundra had left, then sneak away and find his friends later. Unfortunately for him, a well-intentioned bystander had called an ambulance, and the paramedics had mistaken his resistance towards receiving medical care as a form of shock. They sedated him, and were halfway to the hospital when Norm came to and fled. He had made a mess of it; he wasn't prepared, and he hadn't exercised in years. Neither with the Tundra, nor with the paramedics was he ready.

Unlike now.

He angled his descent towards the Avalite leaders. His accuracy was good, although the sense in his plan was questionable.

This was going to hurt.

The fighting shapes of a brown bear and a black panther made the best crash mats available. He fell onto them, driving the two warriors apart.

Daniel fell away from the melee, but Norm was well entangled with Bjorn. The bear's blood was up, and he aimed a blow at Norm's scrawny form. Aurora flinched and waited for the blow to land.

It never did.

Aurora had never witnessed drunken martial arts before – she had never seen its peculiar and off balance style performed – but if she had, she would have known Norm was quite brilliant at them. He plucked Bjorn's speeding paw out of the air and twisted it, redirecting the massive creature's momentum and sending the bear flying.

He looked for his friends, and finding Aurora and her grandfather in the crowd, pointed at them.

"I've come to rescue you," he declared, proudly.

Before either could reply, Daniel leapt upon the immortal, the panther's jaws locking onto his arm.

Norm did not seem bothered. In fact, to the amazement of the gathered Avalites, he smiled. He brought an elbow down on the cat's solar plexus as it proceeded to maul him, which made Daniel screech and lose his grip.

By this point Bjorn had regrouped, and both Avalite chiefs combined their efforts to try and tear Norm limb from limb, furious at the outsider. Anyone else, even with his skill, would have been torn apart, but Norm's immortality meant he grew back quicker than they could destroy him.

He addressed their attacks with surgical precision. Thrown to the ground by Bjorn, he waited for the bear to tower over him, and quickly tapped five pressure points with his fingertips. The brown giant tumbled to the ground, roaring in confusion, half its body temporarily paralysed.

Daniel pounced onto Norm's back as he got to his feet. The immortal gasped as the panther's claws raked across his chest. He stumbled backwards, slamming the panther into one of the lobby's marble pillars. The cat fell, and Norm wasted no time removing his belt and binding its paws together. He struggled furiously, but was unable to break free.

"I wouldn't bother," he told both chiefs as he got his breath, "I can do this all day."

The two beasts seemed to listen and calmed.

Silence fell in the lobby. Both tribes of Avalites came to their senses and raised their weapons at the intruder, but quickly lowered them as Aurora burst through Tundra's lines.

"Norm!" she yelled, sprinting past the amassed warriors, into the bedraggled immortal's arms. It had been decades since he had embraced someone, but was quite happy to do so now.

"Hello young lady," Norm smiled, "Were you worried about me?"

Aurora took a look at his battered form. Already the scratches and bites were healing. Within minutes they would be gone altogether. The same could not be said about his clothes, which hung off him in rags and tatters.

"You look awful," she told him. She noticed something on his chest; where his clothes had been ripped there was a mark on his skin. It was obscured from being properly seen by the tatters, but looked like a scar or a tattoo. Norm straightened up and covered himself, oddly modest.

"So do you," he replied.

"I was worried. You did get shot."

"Pfft," he sniffed. "I've accumulated enough metal in me over the years to bring down an elephant. Can't even go through those things in airports any more. In fact, I made the bullets into a necklace for you when I pulled them out." He pulled a thin chain with two small metal lumps attached from his pocket and handed it over. "I got bored while I waited for you to turn up. Thought you'd like it."

Aurora took the necklace. It was incredibly ugly – the bullets still seemed to have blood on them – but the gesture was actually kind of sweet.

"How did you find us?"

"I recognised Tundra when they shot me. Cold auras, and all that jazz. I've been keeping an eye on them ever since; I figured, they tried to take you once, they might try it again," he looked over at them darkly. "They've got some explaining to do."

"It's not their fault," she warned him as her grandfather joined them. "The Ne'er DuWells got to them. That's what we have to explain."

"Not a bad show, old man," her grandfather grinned as he shook Norm's hand.

It quickly dawned on Aurora that along with her grandfather and Norm, she was suddenly the focus of the entire room. The Avalites were wary of Norm, and watched him apprehensively. Even Daniel and Bjorn, the fight gone out of them, watched him with a human fixation behind animal eyes as their tribesmen attended to them.

As her eyes scanned the amassed Avalites, Aurora was pleased to see that one of them displayed no fear, at least. Beth made her way to the front of the crowd of Torrid.

"You do keep some interesting company," she said, a wry smile on her face. It was clear that if Aurora trusted Norm, then that was good enough for her. The same might not be said of the others.

"You might want to introduce him," she suggested.

"This is Norm," Aurora said, casually adding, "He's immortal."

"We can see that," said Rory, who stood behind Beth.

"He also stopped you from making a huge mistake," Aurora continued. She paused, and turned to her grandfather. "I'm going to get worked up again," she told him. "I know it. Do you want to tell them?"

"Not a chance," he smiled, with a hand resting on her shoulder, "You've got this. They trust you. It's storytelling; just remember that."

An idea came to Aurora as she was about to speak. She pictured her aura opening as wide as it would go and hoped the Avalites would see she was telling the truth.

"You won't be able to see it," she began, "but Granddad and I have been in both camps now – because you both kidnapped us," she added with a scowl, "– and I think we have a pretty good idea what's happened. You've been lied to, by the Ne'er DuWells."

A ripple of discontent passed over the Avalites, and Aurora was afraid she was going to be shouted down or ignored. But as quickly as the murmur rose, it died down again soon after. From the Torrid camp, Beth, Rory and several others wanted to hear what she had to say, and hushed their comrades, while the Tundra sat in patient silence. Bjorn and Daniel, both slowly reverting to human form, observed wordlessly.

"I know you don't want to hear that you've been tricked," Aurora said once they had quietened down, "But it's true. The Ne'er DuWells must've wanted Tundra to help them find the Nameless City. They don't have any need for Torrid – their hunting was stopping the Tundra from researching, so they created this mess to get Tundra away from them and where they wanted."

"And they fell for it too," put in Pete, the Torrid who had been in the van with Aurora and her grandfather when they arrived at the Torrid camp. A murmur of assent went through Torrid.

"I've an ear necklace at home that's got a couple of gaps on it," Norm warned, sternly. "You interrupt the lady again and you'll help me complete it."

Pete turned ghostly pale. Aurora looked up at the immortal, who shrugged and gestured for her to continue.

"You didn't help matters," she told the Torrid, trying to prove that no one was to blame but the Ne'er DuWells. "You should know that the Umbra are more than sport and tradition. Do you think Ragnar would have allowed this to happen? Do you think he would've been too proud to make sure Tundra stayed?"

That shut them up.

"And their experiments… they had a purpose, no matter how grim they are. If you could just keep an open mind, listen to what Tundra are trying to achieve, you might begin to understand their goals."

That was not met so warmly, but no one spoke out in open opposition.

"So… what are we supposed to do now?" Rory asked.

"Well, I'd cut ties with the Ne'er DuWells to start with," offered Aurora glibly, although she knew she was going to struggle to come up with ideas beyond that. Public speaking was not her strongest suit. That tends to happen when you've been neglected by your family your entire life.

Then it came to her. The best idea she ever had.

"What would you do?" she asked Norm.

"Me?" the immortal did a double take. He mulled it over for a moment. "I dunno. It's a perspective thing, isn't it? They're both so pig headed and they need to realise they're not the centre of the universe. Don't think there's much to be done for either of them."

And for only a heartbeat did he think he had concluded the matter. One glare from Aurora confirmed he was not done. A nudge from her grandfather reinforced that.

"Hypothetically," the old man suggested.

Norm had a good, deep think. With the exception of trying to find Aurora and her grandfather, he had not thought hard about anything for a very long time.

"Well, the thing is, sport, hunting and studying aren't what the Avalites should be about," he thought out loud. "Everyone knows that. Avalites are meant to be about people, philosophically speaking."

He trailed off for a moment and smiled to himself. Aurora knew why: this was the same man who a week ago did not care if mankind ended in ruin. Funny how people change.

"You have everything you need already. Torrid understand the day-to-day, and Tundra see the big picture. It's just a matter of them listening to one another and relying on each other."

"What if they can't though? What then?"

"Well, then you would need someone to keep them on the right path."

"Like a mediator?"

"Precisely."

"And what would a mediator need to do? Or know?" Out of the corner of her eye, Aurora saw a smile of understanding break out on her grandfather's face.

"They'd need to know a hell of a lot, actually," Norm said. "All about the Avalites, obviously, and the Umbra. The Rift. Everything supernatural. Strategy. Politics. Diplomacy. Culture. They'd have to be respected too, maybe a little bit feared. Tough as nails."

Norm was rattling through the list of qualifications with abandon now, and didn't stop to think where Aurora might be headed with her line of questioning.

"Do you know all that, Norm?" she asked innocently.

"Not all of it, but I'd probably be a closer fit than anyone else alive, and," he paused momentarily and rolled his eyes. "You've just nominated me for this, haven't you?"

Norm looked around. Everyone was still staring at him, but this time he seemed to feel self-conscious.

"I think you just nominated yourself," Aurora said, before reminding him, "You need something to do."

"Gah," groaned Norm, shaking off the idea. "This is ridiculous. Not a chance."

"Well, hold on a minute," Beth said, stepping forwards. "This affects us. It's our future you're discussing. We don't want to fight one another, and should a mediator be the only way forwards, we would need the most qualified individual for the job. Can you do all that?"

Norm went to shrink away, but Aurora's grandfather caught his arm, turning him towards the amassed Avalites.

"This man," he said, putting his arm around Norm's shoulder, "Defeated both of your leaders in single combat, that should be proof of something. He cannot be killed. He is older than anyone alive, and has near limitless knowledge at his disposal." His tone dropped slightly, and he added, "When he's sober."

"I hate you," Norm muttered with a small grin.

"I hate you too."

"An outsider?" Rory asked, uncertain.

"Only an outsider can strike the balance between Torrid and Tundra. We're not suggesting he leads. We're suggesting he consults, and helps."

"He knows what's important," Aurora added for good measure, "and he knows what's right."

She saw the immortal look down at her with confusion. He was touched. It had been a while since anyone had made him feel that.

Murmurs ran through the crowd but quickly died down again. They parted in the middle, and Bjorn and Daniel approached, human once more.

"The Avalites are broken," Daniel declared. "No matter how much the DuWells have influenced matters, this is of our own doing. What we need to determine now is whether we can be made whole, whether we *want* to be made whole, and whether this… *Norm* should be the one who brings the perspective that enables it."

He turned to Bjorn, whose aura was awash with conflicting emotions.

"What you people have done, what you've allowed to happen…" Bjorn shook his head in denial. He was not taking to this idea one bit. "How can you possibly expect…"

"Bjorn," Rory stepped forward. He was apprehensive but would not be deterred. "Sir. We should hear them out."

"It's perverse," Bjorn spat.

"We have to think of the big picture. It's what my father would've wanted."

Bjorn swore. He hated this. "It won't work."

"This is encouraging," Norm said sarcastically.

"We have to try," Rory urged. He got it.

"Fine," Bjorn sulked, "but don't expect even the slightest bit of success. This will not work."

"But you will try?" Hayhoe asked.

"We will talk," Bjorn relented.

"As will we," Daniel offered.

"I don't get a say in this, do I?" Norm moaned. Aurora glared at him. He did not.

"What the hell," The straggly-haired, emaciated, dark eyed man straightened, trying to look as regal as he could. "But I'm going to need a good suit, a fancy car and a throne."

Aurora looked up at him. *Seriously?*

"I've never had one."

Chapter 35

Amends

In the few hours that had passed since Norm was appointed mediator, his first decision was to call an Avalite council to try and address some of the more immediate problems and ease some of the tension between the tribes. It was a remarkably proactive move on the immortal's part – Aurora had expected him to stall before doing anything, at best to have just arranged some drinks simply so he could have a beer – but he set to his duties with passion, granting both sides a bit of time to confer internally before anything began.

Aurora, her grandfather and Norm stood slightly away from the Avalites while they readied themselves, but that didn't stop several of their number from coming over and talking. Every time she looked over, Aurora saw Beth watching her, and wondered why she had yet to join them.

"Any ideas what you're going to do?" her grandfather asked Norm, "It's a big task."

"A few," he said, "Although they're a little vague so far. Trust is the main problem, and it'll take work to get past that. If they can come to an agreement, it makes the most sense to keep Tundra here – the technology's good – but we'll mix it up a bit. Keep some Torrid here too, to keep Tundra grounded; take some Tundra to the Torrid camp to help them hunt. If they'll allow it, of course. I've a few questions about the Avalites' international presence, and whether they have any political influence. Stuff like that."

"Impressive."

"I don't know what I'm going to do about these experiments," he added hesitantly. "The effect they've had on Torrid's trust is a real problem. It looks like a deal breaker for both sides. We'll see. I have an idea, but I've only talked to Daniel briefly about it. Anyway…" he trailed off. "I have to thank you both. Especially you, girl. I hate to sound clichéd, but maybe giving me a reason to live was better than letting me die. For the time being, at least."

Aurora's cheeks burned, and she had to look away, much to the amusement of the old men.

Daniel approached. He bowed his head to all three of them, humble and respectful.

"I was wondering what you were planning on doing next," he asked Aurora and her grandfather, who looked at one another. It was a good question.

"We've got a City to find," Aurora said. She turned to her grandfather. "Don't we? Everything's moved so fast. To begin with, it was just about getting you out of St Elmo's, then it was escaping the Ne'er DuWells. We've never made it further than that really."

"But it's always been about more than that," her grandfather told her. "It has to be, otherwise we're just surviving, and that's all. That doesn't help us, and makes it only a matter of time before the Ne'er DuWells catch us up. There has to be something bigger, an ideal to aim for. The City *is* that ideal, and how often is an ideal something real?"

Aurora nodded in agreement: it was a big idea, but she thought she understood it. She noticed Daniel watching her and realised he was looking at her aura.

"I think, finally, we understand one another," the Tundra leader said. "All of our work, all of our experiments, everything we've done is to find the City, and for this very reason. To see you both understand it in such a way, makes me realise that perhaps it's not only Avalites who comprehend its purpose, and maybe that's where we've been going wrong."

"What do you mean?" her grandfather asked.

"Mr Hayhoe, you've been looking for the City your entire life. Miss Card, your talents are extraordinary, if somewhat raw." He nodded at Norm. "Your friend and I have spoken, and it's become quite clear that any peace we have will be dependent on staying away from experimentation with the Umbra, for the time being at least. But in order to help maintain the Tundra agenda, we need help, and would like to recruit both of you in order to find the City. We think you could be invaluable in finding it."

"Really?" Excitement edged into Aurora's voice. She looked up at her grandfather: he seemed as eager as she was.

"As a sign of good faith, let me explain something to you: you both know we're not just looking for a 'where.' It's so much more than that. As the gateway to All Worlds Unseen, it has to be. There's an old rhyme we tell our children that we believe holds everything you need to know in order to find it. I hope you appreciate how special it is that we share this with you."

And with that, he recited:

"The Nameless City is not what it seems

Shaped by thoughts and crafted from dreams

Men have looked but it's in no place

All Worlds Unseen is its own space

It's by man's logic they're undone

Reason won't find Avalonne."

Aurora did not share that she had heard all but the last word before, and instead tried to commit it to memory. Daniel repeated it again for their benefit, and stressed that he believed the last few lines were believed to be the most important in terms of finding the Nameless City.

Except it wasn't nameless any more.

This was an Avalite secret. When she had read *Jock Danger and the Phantom Oilrig*, she had seen how excited Drake DuWell had become when he thought he might learn it. She realised they were being trusted with something very important indeed: the name of the Nameless City.

"Avalonne," she breathed. "It's called Avalonne."

*

Aurora didn't let the pleasantries get in her way for long. Questions needed answering, and she hadn't come this far by leaving a mystery unresolved.

A few minutes later, the council meeting began. Aurora and her grandfather were allowed to sit in; they were almost honorary Avalites by now.

There was only one problem: it was *boring*. Aurora hoped for a war council, discussions of Riftrot, fighting, anything interesting, but it quickly descended into semantics on housing, funding and time keeping.

She crept away as soon as she saw her opening.

In the excitement of the day's events, Aurora was afraid she wouldn't remember her way back to the room. It didn't help that all the elegant corridors of the Tundra building seemed to share the same design. Eventually though, she was able to retrace her steps, and with great hesitation came to the door.

The fake doctor's office had been left untouched. It was completely out of character with the rest of the building, and she wondered how long it had taken Drake to set up. A cold pang of fear tugged at her as the memory of her experience in the room returned. The dread that she was as unstable as Drake had implied, the worry that her fantasies had taken on a life of their own. She pushed the uncertainty out of her mind: she had worried about this once already, there would be no benefit reliving it.

The file lay scattered across the floor. Aurora collected up the pages, eyes scouring each one in turn.

They concerned her family. Chances are the Ne'er DuWells would never have paid much attention to it before Aurora had helped her grandfather escape, but it was clear they had done their homework on the Cards. Many of the pages were not interesting; Red's medical history and school records were not the most stimulating things committed to paper, and after a few minutes of searching (and with nothing surfacing about her or her grandfather) Aurora was beginning to suspect that she would never find anything worth worrying about in the folder. This could only be a good thing: she didn't want Drake's insinuations to be true, but she had to know.

Then she found something of interest.

Very much of interest.

One tiny piece of paper that made everything seem a little more uncomfortable.

It was Jim Hayhoe's death certificate.

Aurora's head spun. *He was dead?* What did this mean?

"If it isn't the woman of the hour," said a voice, pulling her out of her ever spiralling well of confusion.

She gasped, looking up. Beth stood in the doorway.

"What are you doing in here?" her wolf asked.

"Drake said some things," Aurora stammered. "They've been bugging me. I thought I'd see for myself. Why aren't you in the council? Has it finished?" The thought sent a jolt of panic through her. If her grandfather knew she was here…

"I'm not one for councils," Beth smiled, then, reading her aura, added, "Your grandfather's still there, he's not going anywhere soon. What's got you so flustered?"

Aurora held up the death certificate. Beth took it from her and scrutinised it.

"This says Jim Hayhoe died, over twenty years ago!" Aurora explained. "What if he's lying, if he's a fake somehow, and he's not really part of my family after all?"

"Aurora," Beth said "the Ne'er DuWells work by spreading lies, rather than getting their hands dirty. You've experienced this first hand. If you start to doubt your granddad now, everything will be lost. It would take little effort on their part to arrange something like this. Who are you more likely to trust?"

She saw her point. "Have you ever met any of them?"

Beth hesitated. "Their father, Thomas," she said, finally. Aurora remembered her grandfather mentioning him: the missing DuWell. The one who had fled.

"The Ne'er DuWells are so evil, they…" Aurora began, but trailed off. The words felt like lumps of coal in her mouth. It seemed like so long ago that she and Norm had played this game in the Loft. Now that she had first-hand experience it didn't seem so funny.

"Pardon?"

"It's a game Norm and I played. I don't think I want to play it anymore."

"Good for you," Beth smiled. "Growing up all the time. You should be very proud of yourself for everything you've done over the last few days."

Aurora made a noise like the one Norm had made when they suggested he become mediator. She was picking up his bad habits already.

"It was nothing," she said modestly, then, reconsidering, "No, actually it was pretty tough."

"I thought so," Beth laughed, "You've been very brave Aurora, both with your... family and with the challenges you faced since you rescued your grandfather."

"How do you know Granddad? I saw him going to your cabin."

"He... got me out of a horrible situation, a... family affair. I wasn't always an Avalite," Beth explained. "In fact, it feels like yesterday when Jim brought me to the Torrid camp. It's why I have all these tattoos; I had to learn how to change shape, fast, and they were the only way." She added the last couple of sentences with a hint of self-consciousness. It was clear she didn't care for the markings that covered her body.

"Well, I think you're as good a shape changer as Bjorn or Daniel. Plus," she added, "the tattoos look *really* cool."

Beth laughed, delighted, and touched Aurora on the shoulder. Her touch lingered but she pulled back. It was clear she wanted to embrace her, but for some reason couldn't bring herself to do it.

What the hell, Aurora thought, and hugged her wolf. She knew the Avalites were proud, and this could be disrespectful, but she didn't care. It felt right.

Beth stiffened for a moment, before relaxing and embracing her in turn. She gripped Aurora tightly, but after a few moments seemed to restrain herself, as if holding back a floodgate.

"Keep your eyes open," she warned, whispering into the girl's ear. "I'm never far away, but it's still not safe. Take it from someone who knows. With them out there, it may never be."

Aurora nodded, she understood. Beth pulled away from the embrace and forced a smile.

"Go back downstairs," she told her. "They'll be wrapping up soon and your granddad will be wondering where you are. I'll clean up here. Get all that doubt out of your mind: it'll do you no good."

Beth waited until she knew for certain Aurora had gone and gathered up the remaining pages from the file, sifting through them. Reaching into her pocket, she extracted a lighter.

Holding the death certificate between her fingertips, she held the flame underneath it, watching it blacken and shrivel into nothingness. Then she took the lighter to the rest of the file, and dropped it into the office's round metal bin, where it proceeded to burn and smoulder.

The information the file held would be lost forever, but it was the omissions, as much as the contents, that were of concern to the Avalite.

Copies of the birth certificates of all the Card family were in the file, save one.

Aurora's was missing.

There were no pictures of her as a newborn, or in the hospital with her mother. All the usual pictures, documents and notes of a new addition to a family were absent. But most puzzling of all, there were photos of a very uneventful holiday in Blackpool that the Cards took for a week in November, over twelve years earlier: the week when

265

Aurora was born. There was no tiny baby present in the photos, and Joan most certainly did not look pregnant.

According to the file, if one had to guess, it would seem that for at least the first six months of her life, Aurora had had nothing to do with the Cards.

*

By the time Aurora made it back to the council, their meeting was at an end. From the auras she read, she could see that it was a mixed success, with frustrations and results on both sides.

Norm looked a tad annoyed, but then he almost always did.

The night wound on, but with the scent of adventure renewed, Aurora's grandfather was determined to make an early start. For once he played the figure of responsibility and ordered Aurora to bed.

"I can't begin to describe how proud I am of you," he beamed, "Just think, a feud that's been brewing for a decade, about to become open war, and you managed to prevent it with only a few words! Outstanding! Not to mention how much the Ne'er DuWells will hate this."

"Norm helped," Aurora said quietly.

"And there's another thing!" he continued, ignoring her response. "You found a use for Norm! I've known that man for decades, and you're the first person I've seen who's ever made him feel useful."

Aurora smiled but it was clear her heart wasn't in it. The girl was unusually quiet, her grandfather thought, as she allowed him to march her into an office that had been turned into a makeshift bedroom upstairs. Maybe she was tired.

"Last stop," the old man said kindly, as he fumbled for a light switch in the room.

"You're right about that," said a horribly familiar voice.

They both jumped. The light came on, revealing Drake, who had a gun levelled at them.

"No more escapes," Drake hissed. "No more tricks. You are both coming with us. *She* wants to meet you."

"Not a chance," her grandfather growled.

"If you don't, I'll shoot the little witch in the stomach," he threatened, chambering a bullet.

"Do you really think you'll be able to smuggle us out without the Avalites knowing?" Aurora asked.

"I do," Drake smiled, and it sent a chill through her. He reached into his jacket pocket and drew out his phone. "Jack, now."

The wall of window behind him exploded noisily, and through the wind and the rain a spotlight shone down. Aurora heard the noise through the wind, and realised the spotlight was coming from a helicopter. Moments later, a rope ladder hung down.

"Grab it and climb up," Drake shouted, his voice struggling over the wind and the rotor blades.

Aurora went to the hole where the window had once been, mindful of the broken glass. The rain and the wind made the edge treacherous, and she was afraid she would slip.

It was a *long* way to fall.

The helicopter banked towards the building, and the ladder swung close. Aurora grabbed it, and with a look at her grandfather, and then Drake, began the climb upwards, feeling sick in her belly.

When she reached the top of the ladder Jack helped her in, looking at her with regret and remorse. Her grandfather climbed in after her, followed by Drake.

"Go," Drake called, and the pilot followed his order.

"They'll come after us," Aurora said.

"Let them try," Drake scoffed, and then, to the pilot, "Give them a hit. Strafe it with everything."

The helicopter turned around, and released a brace of missiles at the building. Four colossal explosions tore through the side of Tundra's headquarters in a mess of glass and fire.

"No!" Aurora screamed, diving at Drake. Jack stopped her and held her back before she could get close.

"What're you, mad?" Jack said into her ear. "He'll kill you!"

Aurora fought in his arms, but went still when she saw the look Drake gave her. "That ought to slow them down, don't you think?" he sneered, "If you try another move like that we'll go back and give them some more.

"Don't you get it, little girl? We're the Ne'er DuWells. We can blow up a building in the heart of the city, and by morning it'll be forgotten. We can do anything. So you should keep your mouth shut, do as we tell you, and with luck you might make it through the night."

Chapter 36

Journey into Darkness

The helicopter travelled to London's edge before setting down in what appeared to be a private airfield. From there, Aurora and her grandfather were rushed into a waiting black saloon. The car rocketed out of London, disregarding speed limits and traffic rules, until the towering buildings and orange lit streets gradually faded away, replaced by a thorough blackness that was illuminated only rarely by the occasional streetlamp that betrayed a rural setting.

The car drove onwards without stopping or hesitation, throughout the night and into what Aurora guessed must have been the depths of the English countryside. Hills crept up and valleys swooped down around them, but in the darkness only vague black shapes were visible and offered no comfort. Aurora had no idea where they were or where they were going. The landscapes blurred into one another and the darkness could have made the journey boring, but fear kept her senses keen at first.

She refused to dwell on what would happen when they reached their destination.

They would learn their fate soon enough.

After what felt like hours the saloon came to a halt, and Drake ordered them out. Aurora was unable to help it and finally had fallen asleep. She had not slept properly since the night before Beth had taken her hunting. Since then she had slain an Umbra, been drugged, scared out of her wits, and had her faith in everything she believed tested. She felt wretched.

The four waited for only a moment until from the blackness emerged an antique horse drawn carriage, which took them up a spiral of winding dark hills. The coach ride was incredibly bumpy and uncomfortable; there would be no rest for Aurora any more.

Drake rode up front with the coach driver, a stout man whose features were masked by a battered top hat and scarf. Jack sat in the coach with the captives and kept an eye on them. "It's tradition," he said, explaining the coach. "The family has ways of doing things that do not change over time."

"Like murder," the old man growled.

"I like your spirit, Aurora," Jack said, ignoring her grandfather, "but I hope you will co-operate with the family. You don't want to make *her* unhappy, believe me."

It started to rain, slowly at first, then coming down in sheets. It worsened the deeper into the country they delved and the higher they ascended. The carriage pulled over, and Drake ordered Jack to swap with him. Jack sighed and got out, pulling up his hood. "Don't do anything to them," he reminded his brother, who rolled his eyes and made himself comfortable inside.

He remained silent but his eyes bored into them. From his coat he drew the knife he had threatened his brother with, and picked under his fingernails with it in a way that Aurora found incredibly unsettling, the knife's tip wedging its way under the immaculate nails and removing minute specks of dirt.

Aurora suddenly wished that Jack would return to the coach and take his brother's place.

*

It was the dead of night when they noticed something unusual in the distance. Aurora saw it first; two milky white objects, glowing in the darkness.

She nudged her grandfather. "Look."

"Oh no," he muttered. "No, no, no, no, no, no. We're here. We're actually here."

As they got closer, the white shapes came into focus, and Aurora realised they were a pair of snow leopards, carved from marble and sitting on top of imposing thirty-foot pillars, poised ready to pounce.

How the leopards were glowing escaped her, but they were. They emitted a murky phosphorous glow, and must have been coated with a paint that caused them to burn in the darkness, or maybe there was something about the rock itself from which they were carved.

In between the pillars were ancient gates adorned with a symbol: it was a globe, gripped tightly by an eagle's claw. The claw's tips dug into the globe, unwilling to surrender it to anyone. At the base of the crest was a monogram: NDW, and under that, a Latin phrase: Lucrum ex damnum.

"Profit from loss," her grandfather whispered.

The gates parted in the centre and they passed through, onto an incredibly long, winding gravel driveway that seemed to stretch forever, and was lined with Victorian lampposts to guide their way.

Further off, Aurora could see lights in the distance looming ever closer. The carriage's windows were small and with the night's harsh weather their vision was limited, but the scale of what they approached refused to be obscured.

It was a mansion.

"What is –" Aurora began to ask, but her grandfather cut her off, looking elsewhere.

"There's the Garden of Death, where the deceased DuWells get the recognition in death that anonymity in life prevents them," he mumbled, more to himself than her. His fingertips stroked the cold glass of the window, as the memories tumbled out of him, "A black rose, grown for each family member."

"Granddad…" Aurora warned quietly. Her eyes were on Drake; the hatred on his face was growing, if that was at all possible. His knife was scoring a line in the seat of the carriage between his thighs. Stuffing from the cushion rushed to the surface like blood from a shallow cut.

Her grandfather was not listening. "The pond, over there. Gone to ruin now. Under the surface of the water is a huge dome that covers an underwater dance floor. The elite few who knew the DuWells would come to dance under the water; circled by carp and surrounded by power. But that all changed when *she* came along."

The old man was shaken out of his recollection by a soft thud on the padded backboard of the carriage. Drake's knife was embedded in the furnishings between their heads, swaying back and forth gently. His aim was perfect.

"*How* is it you've always known so much about us?" Drake insisted. The old man was silent. The mansion grew closer, and Aurora was able to see it in full now. It was vast and gothic, and as they neared it she saw how close they were to the sea. It wore the coastline like a cloak of blackness.

At least four stories high, the manor was crested with battlements, spires and chimneys. Most windows were lit, and in the darkness this created a pumpkin-like effect.

"I made it my business to know," her grandfather said finally, achingly calm. "You have no idea, Drake. The family was always rotten to the core, but it's corrupted beyond recognition now." He turned away from the aristocrat, a defiant move, and pointed at a shape away from the manor.

It was a stack; a massive pillar of rock rising from the sea, its connection to the cliff worn away by years of erosion.

On top of the stack was a small circular building, an observatory, with ghostly white light glowing through its glass-domed roof. A suspension bridge connected the stack to the mainland.

"Then there's that," her grandfather continued. "In there, two very foolish men created something that might have doomed us all. Not that either of them are around to know it."

Drake shot out of his seat, leaning forward to strike the old man. As he drew his hand back, the coach lurched to a stop. The aristocrat managed to keep his balance, but it stopped him from landing the blow. Aurora shrank back, but her grandfather stared up at Drake, refusing to be intimidated. The look on his face was one of anger and disappointment.

The door of the coach opened and Jack stood in its doorway, rain pouring off his hood.

"We're here," he said, eyeing his brother suspiciously.

Aurora urged her grandfather to get out, and Drake followed once he extracted his knife from the headboard. The four of them climbed the broad stone steps up to the mansion while the rain lashed at them relentlessly.

Having never seen anything so immense, Aurora felt compelled to ask, "Where are we?"

"Nowhere House," Her grandfather replied grimly. "The heart of evil."

Chapter 37

The Ne'er DuWells

Mere steps away from the manor the enormous oak doors swung open, and two servants ushered them inside into an enormous sprawling hallway with detached efficiency.

With its high ceilings and classical art it bore a faint resemblance to parts of Norm's loft, while lacking its idiosyncratic charm and individuality.

It was the height of aristocratic decadence. Various stuffed animals adorned the grand marble staircase; amongst others stood a wolf and a bear, bringing to mind uncomfortable associations with the Avalites for Aurora.

More than anything else, the main impression that stuck Aurora was one of utter *gloom*. The wood panelled walls were of the darkest mahogany, and the drab chandeliers were hung too high to properly pierce the darkness. It was as if something vital had died within the manor, and the light was afraid to interrupt the house's mourning.

"Watch them," Drake warned Jack as he left the hallway.

The three stood silently in the lobby, dripping rainwater onto the antique carpet. Jack pulled back his hood and removed his coat. One of the servants held out a hand and Jack handed it over uncomfortably.

"Not used to being waited on?" her grandfather asked. It was strange; he didn't seem to be mocking him, the question was based on curiosity.

"Never have been," Jack admitted, with a hint of shame.

"Good for you." Her grandfather actually seemed impressed.

Towards the end of the hallway hung a huge painting of two men standing in front of an eighteenth century battlefield. From the family resemblance, the taller one had to be a Ne'er DuWell ancestor. The other was very short and smug looking. Aurora stared at it for some time until she realised who it could be.

"Is that… Napoleon?"

Before an answer could be given, another servant appeared, signalling for them to follow him. They passed down a long corridor adorned with drab oil paintings of the grounds of Nowhere House from times past, into an impressively panelled boardroom where Drake and two others were positioned round a massive polished oak table.

Their eyes locked on Aurora's grandfather with the sort of look reserved for a poorly caged tiger: fascination and fear in equal measure.

This was *him*, their enemy, in their home.

In comparison, Aurora might as well not be there.

Drake had changed his clothes and was prepping himself a scotch. His eyes stayed glued on Aurora's grandfather at all times, only leaving him briefly while he fixed his drink, the ice cubes creating an ominous echo as they landed in his glass.

With their smoking jackets, cigarette holders and tailor made suits the three figures resembled 1920's aristocracy. As well as the look of discontent, all three shared a family resemblance.

There could be no mistaking it: they had to be the Ne'er DuWells.

"You know Drake," Jack said, making introductions, desperate to fill the insufferably tense silence. "This is Marcus."

Marcus was a weasel-like figure who resembled a poor copy of Drake; hair receding and figure swamped in a burgundy smoking jacket several sizes too large for his weedy frame.

"Charmed," Marcus drawled, a lungful of smoke accompanying a nervous giggle. His false confidence was horribly transparent, and it made Aurora take an instant dislike to him. She had met his kind at school many times over: he was the bully's right hand man.

Jack moved on to the last member of the group. Unlike the others, she didn't seem too bothered by the presence of Jim Hayhoe in Nowhere House; she had her feet on the table and barely stifled a yawn. Vivian had taken one look at the old adventurer and decided he was not worth bothering with, or at least she wanted to appear this way.

"*This* is why you made me come all the way from Monaco?" she scoffed, rattling the ice in her empty glass, signalling to Jack she wanted her drink topped up. "You know my darling Count can't live without me."

Jack successfully concealed rolling his eyes from his sister and took her glass. Her cruel green eyes passed over Aurora and her grandfather with faked indifference, and she flicked her bleached hair revealing roots as dark as her soul.

Looking at the three aristocrats to Jack and back again, Aurora realised that as much as she disliked him, compared to these three, at least Jack resembled an actual human being.

"There's nowhere left for you to run," Marcus taunted, seeming to rise in confidence. "No more of your little friends to save you, and nowhere for you to hide away."

"So what are you going to do, kill us?" the old man scoffed. He was trying to position himself between Aurora and the DuWells, as if just by being close to them their evil would infect her somehow. The standoff felt odd, rehearsed maybe, as if her grandfather was going through the motions. His chest was puffed out and his chin was raised –

But when she saw the effect the next sentence had on him, she realised everything had changed.

"And why would we do that, when we could have had you killed any time we liked?" said a voice Aurora had not heard before. "And yes, I suppose that does include now."

Everyone stiffened upon hearing this. Vivian took her feet from the table; Marcus choked on his smoke and hastily stubbed his cigarette out.

But the real change came from Aurora's grandfather.

He had previously been stood in front of Aurora, but when they turned she found herself in front of him. His large hands clasped her shoulders, and she felt his grip hold her tight, knuckles whitening. For a moment, she wondered whether he was protecting her or using her as a shield.

The gusto was gone, chest no longer puffed out. What remained was an old man stood in front of the one person he resented more than any other in the whole world, his frame rigid with fear and hatred. Aurora had never seen him like this before.

Because this wasn't just anyone who had entered the room.

This was the figure that had been alluded to in all of Jock Danger's adventures; the black sun that the Ne'er DuWells orbited.

This was *her*.

Catherine DuWell.

Chapter 38

Her

Catherine was a frail looking figure whose wheelchair had been pushed into the room by one of the many mute servants in the Ne'er DuWells' employ. The wheelchair was old but built to last, made from expensive and taboo items that were surprisingly durable; an ivory frame, elephant skin seat and a white tiger fur trim.

If any other soul were to have inhabited Catherine's body, Aurora would have assumed they were mere seconds from death. She had never seen anyone look so old, even in St Elmo's; her skin was wrinkled, hands gnarled and claw-like, and her lips so thin that her mouth was like a paper cut across her face.

Norm may have had centuries on her, but the years washed off him. Every day of her life seemed to have taken its toll on Catherine.

The way she was clothed did nothing to help: her black dress with its lace overlay and veil made the old lady look as if she was draped in cobwebs; this spider's web was its chair, the perfect place to be, and everyone else was at a disadvantage.

But more than anything else, the trait that differentiated her from any other old person Aurora had ever seen, and the reason she knew she was filled with life, was her *eyes*.

They contained the perfect combination of intelligent calculation and a childlike sense of wonder. It was as if everything she laid her eyes on fascinated her, while in the same heartbeat, she had analysed, assessed and judged it expertly. When those eyes locked onto Jim

Hayhoe, Aurora was able to see that she was also the only one of the Ne'er DuWells who showed no fear or hatred towards him, but they widened slightly nonetheless.

He held a special significance to her, and it made Aurora very uncomfortable.

"Well, well," Catherine smiled, her husky voice making the aristocratic drawl of Drake and the others seem like cockney rhyming slang in comparison. "It's certainly been a while. The years haven't been kind, have they?"

"Likewise," Aurora's grandfather replied, his voice a dry croak.

The old lady let the insult slide off her effortlessly, much to the shock of her children. Clearly, no one spoke against Catherine, ever.

"Still, given how long you spent in that ghastly home you're looking better than expected," she continued, then looked at Aurora. The old woman's gaze made her feel cold inside. "I suppose we have you to thank for that, don't we my dear?"

Aurora said nothing. She was terrified.

"Why don't you sit down?" Catherine suggested, as her servant positioned her wheelchair at the head of the boardroom's table, "There's no reason we can't be civil."

Aurora expected her grandfather to make another remark, but instead he took a seat without a word, and gestured for her to do the same.

"I see you're still interfering with our plans," Catherine said in a kindly tone. "Congratulations for reconciling the Avalites. We'd been working on them since just after... Thomas disappeared." She added her late husbands' name thoughtfully, and looked at the old man triumphantly as if she had just moved a valuable chess piece, "And with only words too, from what I hear. When you were a younger man that would have included a punch up and a gun fight."

"It wasn't too hard," the old man replied, trying to appear nonchalant but looking uncomfortable about something. He did not correct her that it had been mostly Aurora and Norm's doing, adding, "You shouldn't have killed Ragnar."

"It was necessary," Catherine shrugged, waving a bony hand. "He was the piece holding them together. After he died, it was almost embarrassing watching the tribes drift apart. Time and pressure, that's all it took. That's all anything takes. I understand you have a new piece in play," her slit of a mouth formed a cruel smile and a wet tongue moistened the corners of her lips. She was clearly referring to Norm. "It was a good move choosing someone we can't kill for a change. How is the old drug addict these days? He must be pleased to have a purpose after all these years, or does he still pray for death like the pathetic wretch he always was?"

"Don't talk about Norm like that," someone snapped, and Aurora realised with horror it was her.

Once again the Ne'er DuWells recoiled, and once again Catherine seemed undisturbed. "So she *can* speak after all," the old lady marvelled, those wide eyes fixed on her once more. "Spirited like your grandfather, same inexplicable loyalties to those beneath you. I'm sorry dear, I didn't realise you two were friends."

"He's a good man," Aurora said, and wanted to say more but couldn't.

"I'm sure he is," Catherine patronised. "I'm sure you feel the same way about your grandfather too, especially after growing up with those…" She paused. "*People*. The standards get lowered somewhat."

"Granddad's a better person than anyone I've ever met," Aurora said, not knowing where she was finding her nerve, and added, "but even *my* family are better than yours. Mine might be a bit thick and selfish; but yours are a collection of murderers and spoiled liars who don't deserve a penny of your crooked fortune."

The glow of any pride Aurora may have received from her grandfather was stopped dead when Catherine looked at her honestly for the first time. She had pushed back too much, Aurora realised.

In that glance, as if she needed any confirmation, was proof that even the slightest shred of kindness Catherine had displayed was the most dishonest of facades.

This was the *she* everyone spoke of with such horror; a dread creature that wilfully wielded darkness in a way the Umbra couldn't begin to understand.

Aurora's heart nearly stopped.

"I like you, but you should really watch that spirit of yours," Catherine warned her, as the mask of civility slipped on again effortlessly. Aurora could still see *her*, lurking in and around Catherine's eyes, and she would never forget who she really was. She added, "It's nice to see this side of you before you learn some truths that knock the wind from your sails."

"So you've got us. Now what?" Hayhoe cut in, eager to tear Catherine's attentions from his granddaughter. "What do you want from us?"

Catherine's children seemed to pay even more attention, as if this was what they wanted to hear.

It was a good question. What indeed?

"I want to make this very clear," Catherine said slowly, making sure Aurora and, more importantly, her grandfather, were following, "I've won. Every single tiny victory you believed you've enjoyed over all your years has been nothing more than a stall to me getting what I want."

Her grandfather snorted. "That's complete –"

"Really? Name one thing you've achieved in fighting this family over all these years. How have any of your struggles or fights made any difference to this family's wealth or power?"

The old adventurer wasn't going to win this argument. With Catherine there was no room for debate. He knew that, so he changed his tack.

"So why take us now?"

"Because your little assistant forced our hand by freeing you," Catherine explained. "Not that that mattered. This would've happened eventually, whether you escaped or I decided to let you out. You've had your fun over the years, but you pushed me too far with your last escapade and St. Elmo's was the only option. But seeing as you were out, it was time to set things to rights."

Aurora couldn't help but wonder: what was his last escapade, the move that had resulted in his incarceration? Given that Catherine had just said nothing he did made any difference, what could he possibly have done to anger her so much?

"Mother," Marcus asked gingerly, "What do you mean 'set things to rights'?"

"You mean kill him," Drake growled.

"I do not mean that," Catherine corrected, and there was a hint of annoyance in her voice. "I'll *not* tell you that again, Drake dear."

Put in his place, Drake sulked into his scotch. He gave Aurora's grandfather a black look. The other DuWell siblings looked at their mother warily. Even if he was second only to Catherine, Drake was skating on thin ice.

"They're both far too important, and you'll see that soon," she said, adding, "but in his own way, Drake does have a point. Unless I find the Nameless City soon, my time left on this earth is limited. I can only stall death for so much longer, and with me gone, I know there's nothing that will stand in Drake's way; he'll kill you, Mister Hayhoe."

Aurora did not need further proof to know this was true, but she glanced at Drake anyway, and immediately regretted it.

"But I believe you're my best chance of finding the Nameless City," she said to Aurora and her grandfather, "and that's exactly what you're going to do."

"Them?" Marcus murmured. "The Nameless City is the DuWell's destiny. It has been ever since Ned DuWell saw it three hundred years ago. It's no business of theirs!"

"That's where you're wrong," sighed Catherine. "They'll find it, and they'll use the resources we have to do so."

"Him?" Vivian asked. "Didn't he kill Michael?"

"I did no such thing!" the old man boomed, with a rage Aurora did not expect. Marcus shrank back and Vivian raised an eyebrow. Apparently the old wolf still had teeth after all.

Her grandfather calmed, seeming to realise that his anger would not help him here. He did, however ask the question on everyone's minds. "So what makes you think we'll help you?"

"I don't think you've any choice," Catherine informed him patiently. "For the first time since we've known you, you've a weakness, and you've brought it with you."

"And what's that?" he asked without thinking.

Aurora flinched. She knew where this was going.

The old woman smirked and pointed a bony finger straight at his granddaughter.

"Her."

Chapter 39

The Hall of Portraits

The Ne'er DuWells, Aurora and her grandfather followed Catherine along the never-ending hallways of Nowhere House in an almost funereal procession. With the exception of the occasional painting, sculpture or mounted artefact, every dreary, dark corridor seemed alike; Aurora was lost immediately.

"Where are we going?" her grandfather asked Catherine.

"To where you'll be helping us," Catherine answered. She did not look back, allowing her servant to continue to push her along.

"This isn't the way to the observatory," he noticed. Aurora wondered how he could tell. The place was a labyrinth.

"It's a detour," Catherine explained casually, "I want to make sure we're all on the same page." She twisted round, craning to look back at them all. "Maybe do something that will ease some of the tension between you." Her gaze lingered on Drake, who glared back as defiantly as he knew how.

They turned a corner and the corridor widened. A set of double doors were open in front of them, revealing a remarkably long room with a high ceiling. It was as impressive as any other room in the house; an intricately decorated darkly patterned rug covered the floor, and heavy black curtains concealed the windows, easily preventing any light entering when day came.

The main feature of the room was dozens of portraits of the DuWell family, stretching back generations.

Aurora looked at her grandfather. He had gone very pale. His jaw was set.

"So what do you need to put right?" Vivian asked, her short attention span making her eager to get to the point.

"Glad to see you're paying attention, darling." Catherine said patronisingly. "I thought I would let our young guest show us."

All six pairs of eyes fixed upon Aurora.

"Me?"

"Have a look around dear," Catherine told her. "Tell me what you see. Put those talents of yours to good use."

"Catherine," her grandfather pleaded. "This isn't going to –"

Silence. The old woman had shot him a withering look that had frozen him in his tracks. Aurora didn't know what grasp she had on him, but the effect confounded her. He didn't seem to understand it either.

She looked at her grandfather, seeking instruction. He nodded his assent: *go on*.

Turning away from the others she faced the huge room. It dwarfed her; she had never felt so tiny.

Aurora shuffled across the room slowly; utterly unsure of what was expected of her. She didn't want to hurry and miss whatever it was she was supposed to see, but neither did she want to waste time. The feeling of the Ne'er DuWells' eyes on her made her skin itch. She tried to block these thoughts from her mind; being self-conscious would not help her to see.

The pictures were arranged in chronological order; that much was obvious from the painting style and the manner of dress. Oddly enough there was a gap where the first picture should have been; a darker square hung on the wall in the shape of a large portrait. She looked back at the DuWells.

"Ned DuWell," Jack offered, sympathising with her awkwardness, "He revolutionised the DuWell family. Before him, the family were aristocrats struggling to obtain power. He was the one who made us secretive, ever since he –"

"That's enough," Drake warned him. He had kept his temper, but there was a growl under his voice. Jack took the hint.

Ned DuWell. Interesting.

The only person she had heard of who had seen Avalonne was also the person who made the Ne'er DuWells what they were today. It couldn't be a coincidence. Judging from the missing portrait, presumably he had taken the anonymity to heart.

She moved on. There wasn't anything to be learnt from this.

How many outsiders had seen this place? How many had seen it and lived?

Within a few minutes, she had seen the full range of portraits. It was a gloomy affair. The family resemblance throughout the DuWells was very strong, it was almost as if a wall of Drakes, Marcus's and Vivian's stared back at her in a dozen different forms of formal attire.

She needed to do something else if she was to find whatever it was she was meant to be looking for. Catherine had referred to her talents, which surely could only mean her ability to see people's auras. It wasn't surprising the old woman knew, the Ne'er DuWells had eyes everywhere, and she was their rotten black core.

Summoning her talent was harder now than it had ever been; it was almost as if she had to learn how to do it from scratch, and was not dissimilar to when she had tried reading her grandfather's aura. The whole house and everyone in it seemed to be was protected from her ability by a thick veil of lies and deceit that surrounded and permeated everything.

"Come on," she urged herself quietly, "You're not looking. *Look*. What do you see?"

On the walls she saw wealth. She saw corruption, and she saw greed. The quarrelling and deception of ten generations or more had led themselves to this: a family so devoid of love, so corrupt and self-centred that to them, other lives did not matter.

Then it hit her.

Other lives.

The book I had read when I had woken up at Norm's was called Other Lives*; and the haunting content of the last story came flooding back. In all the excitement that had followed that day, from Norm being shot, to running from Tundra, to the Umbra attack, and Beth saving me, I had forgotten it.*

A series of locks started to open in my head, and I realised that from the tendrils of light that came from my fingertips that my talent for auras had awoken, finally. It was a little different this time: I'd never seen my own aura before.

Other Lives: the missing scientist; the knowledge of the manor; the in depth information about the family tree. Things were coming together, and I knew I was going to hate where they were heading.

I sprinted across the room, towards the end of the portraits, suddenly desperate to know the truth. Granddad and the Ne'er DuWells followed, realising I had discovered something.

With my mind I cast the ribbons of light that made up my aura towards the walls, and even if only I could see it the gloom temporarily withdrew.

I knew what I was looking for.

I used my aura to illuminate the portraits, moving through the years and generations.

Silus DuWell: 1865-1920; Albert DuWell: 1890-1955. Drake DuWell, Thomas's father and Drake's grandfather. Then, finally, I reached him.

Thomas DuWell.

And with that, my heart dropped. The truth finally hit me.

"Oh my god," I gasped.

The others had gathered behind me, and with two exceptions, watched me with interest. Catherine had that smug thin smile I had come to loathe resting across her mouth, but I didn't care about that. It was the look on Granddad's face that worried me more. For the first time since I had met him, he seemed to be afraid of me.

"What is it?" Jack asked.

"Don't you see it?"

"See what?" this came from Marcus. All the Ne'er DuWells surrounded me; their rage, disinterest and arrogance momentarily forgotten. "What is it?"

I wanted to cry but couldn't. "It's right there, can't you see?"

Somehow, none of them could. But it was there. They all saw their father, missing for decades and most likely dead, but there was more.

The face in the painting was younger, less grizzled and cut from the same aristocratic cloth as the rest of his family, but the resemblance was unmistakable.

The man in the portrait, Thomas DuWell, the leader of the DuWell family, was none other than Jim Hayhoe.

Chapter 40

The Corposant

The Ne'er DuWells were not a family that were easily harmed. They existed as the stuff of rumour and legend, and a rumour could feel no pain. From their cryptic beginnings – they were believed by some to be descendants of an assassin hired by Richard III to dispatch two young princes in 1483 – they grew in power by the year.

For generations they had been masters of their own fates; they knew nothing of want or need, and took whatever they desired from whomever they fancied.

Nowhere House was their stronghold, there was no place in the world that was safer for them.

But in the seconds following Aurora's revelation, in the heart of their sanctuary, they were utterly shattered.

"How is that even possible?" Drake asked, finally. It seemed to be the first time he wasn't angry about something; he just seemed confused. It was inevitable that anger would follow shortly.

"And… why?" this time it was Vivian. With the exception of Aurora, none of them looked at her grandfather. Maybe they couldn't bear to.

Instead, all eyes were on Catherine.

"Come now," she said, a little too casually. "It makes sense, doesn't it? We do this to people all the time, it's not impossible to consider that someone would do it to us."

"You knew? All these years?" Maybe most surprisingly, this question was not asked by one of Catherine's children, but by the man who had been her husband. The old man looked even more deflated than his children.

"Like I said earlier, I let you have your fun, thinking that your little adventures meant something. Little was I to know you weren't to outgrow them and come home like you were supposed to. You always were stubborn, Thomas." He flinched as if he had been slapped. The way Catherine pronounced 'Thomas' sounded infinitely more comfortable in her mouth than Hayhoe, which attracted only disdain.

"But you're back now," she continued, "and just in time to help conclude our quest to find the Nameless City, together. I hoped ten years in St Elmo's would teach you one thing: you can't escape your family."

"Oh god," Jack muttered, the enormity of his own involvement in Catherine's plan bearing down on him. "You had me imprison my own father for ten years?"

"It was necessary, sweetheart," Catherine replied. If any of the others had said this to him, they would have reminded Jack that Thomas wasn't his real father, but Catherine did no such thing. Instead, she added kindly, "I knew I could trust you."

"But why?" Drake said, repeating Vivian's question that still lay unanswered, floating above them like a funeral shroud. He turned to Aurora's grandfather – his father – and the rage that defined his relationship with the old man was slowly starting to seep back in. "Why would you do this to us? Why would you become *him*?"

All eyes now focused on the old man, trying to find Thomas within. He was numb; his secret exposed, he had no idea how to begin. Aurora could guess at the answer, but knew it wouldn't be one the Ne'er DuWells would understand.

"I read this story he wrote," she offered, figuring someone more objective could answer it. She didn't dare try and think beyond that, to who her grandfather was and what he meant to her, and decided to keep talking. "About a scientist who ran away. It –"

"Ah yes," Catherine interrupted. "Well remembered, my dear. You're quite useful to have around, aren't you?"

The old woman lifted a crooked finger asking for patience (as if anyone would dare deny her this) and reached into a pouch sown into the arm of her wheelchair. From it, withdrew her own battered copy of *Other Lives*.

"Once we put you away," Catherine told her once-husband as she flicked through the pages. "We made sure we ruined the publisher of your little Jock Danger stories – Salmon, wasn't it? – and burnt every copy we could find. It seemed cruel not to leave you with copies of your own, but they might be some of the last ones in existence. It just wouldn't do to have you spreading such ghastly rumours about us, but then you knew that. That's why you wrote them." The old man's face had gone dark, but she continued unperturbed. "I kept copies of each of them too. Someone should know what you accomplished. They're quite charming really. You should be proud."

She had reached *The Lament of The Forgotten Scientist* and read it out to the group.

"*Maybe it's the fate of someone born into an evil family to do evil things, even if they don't intend to,*" she began, "*When I'm at my weakest, this is how I justify it to myself...*" It did not take long, it was a very short story, but Catherine's upper class rasp and cynical sneer in the gargantuan hallway gave the words a sense of futility and selfishness.

After what felt like an age, she came to the end: "*She should never have brought them into it. Things are going to change.*"

The old woman closed the book as if it was a bedtime story, not the confession of a man preparing to betray his family.

"That's why," the old man said finally, and his voice was no more than a broken whisper. "I finally saw just how wrong this family was. I tried my best to change it, to put things right, but it was too late." He looked over his family pleadingly, and added, "I did what I thought was right."

He turned to Aurora, and said to her, "I'm so sorry I didn't tell you sooner."

Aurora felt her eyes beginning to well up, and pushed down the emotion that threatened to drown her.

Not now.

She turned to the others.

"But how is that possible?" she asked. "How could you not recognise him? And what is the machine from the story?"

"The answers to both of your questions," Catherine said, "are one and the same."

*

Aurora, her grandfather (if he was still that), and the Ne'er DuWells left Nowhere House.

They headed down a winding pathway that ran through the heart of the endless grounds, towards the observatory her grandfather had picked out when they arrived.

In the impenetrable darkness, Aurora had no way of seeing the extravagant lands the family owned, while the rain continued to lash down, restricting her vision even more.

The mood was worse now than it was when they headed to the Hall of Portraits. Jack, Aurora and her grandfather were especially despondent. Everyone lurked under umbrellas that were so dark and leathery they could have been made from the wings of giant bats.

Aurora felt wetness work its way down her face, and she was so tired she was unsure whether it was the rain, or tears. She couldn't begin to think about the gargantuan lie her grandfather had spun, and ignored the lump in her throat that threatened to claim her composure.

Maybe it was instinct, maybe it was to distract herself, but Aurora tried using her talent again; when she had tried to see the auras in Torrid's camp she saw better than without it. It was darker now, and she thought it might help her to see the way.

Even outside the house, the Ne'er DuWells auras were as impenetrable as my grandfather's was. The only sign of life I could muster was from the servant who pushed Catherine's wheelchair across the gravel pathway, but he was so subdued and fearful he might as well have not been alive.

With the rest of them, it was like they weren't even there.

"Stop that, dear," Catherine said half-heartedly, craning around to look at me. "It's very rude."

I felt sick, but I shouldn't have been surprised.

She knew.

Could she see too?

The path wormed its way up a short hill, and upon reaching the top the view of the sea was revealed, dark and endless, stretching as far as the eye could see. The storm was whipping it into terrifying shapes, and waves exploded on the rocks below relentlessly.

Without the land to shelter them, the group were battered by the winds that came off the water, and Aurora noticed with dizzying concern that they were near a cliff edge.

They followed the path along the cliff until it lowered slightly and reached the suspension bridge that led to the stack where the observatory lay.

The bridge was built to endure such weather, but the prospect of crossing it was not an appealing one. Drake indicated for Aurora and her grandfather to lead the way, and they did so, clinging on to the ropes on either side as if their lives depended on them.

Through the tiny gaps in the bridge they saw the black waters churning underneath them; occasionally two opposing currents fought for dominance, and when they did, small jets of white foam and spray exploded and gurgled noisily.

The group were over the bridge in a matter of minutes, and Aurora watched as Catherine's servant performed the unenviable task of pushing her wheelchair across. "I have every faith in you, Jenkins," Catherine said, "but should you make even the slightest mistake, your children will grow up in an orphanage."

The observatory was perfectly round, maybe forty foot in diameter, twice that in height and topped with a glass dome. The group ascended a small staircase at the observatory's base and entered through its doors, while Catherine's wheelchair followed alongside them on a ramp.

The observatory had only on a single floor, although there must have been a basement below them. The main floor was divided by various walkways and gangways throughout, which allowed access higher up.

The building housed a solitary machine, a device of terrifying proportions. Like any self-respecting mad scientist's creation, it was a huge abomination of glass and metal; tesla coils and glass spheres stood buzzing and glowing atop black steel obelisks, the crackling of electric arcs and the hissing of pneumatic pumps creating a background hum that was quieter than it should have been. An oversized control panel of dozens of gauges, dials and buttons sat turning constantly.

"This," Catherine announced, "is the Corposant." She added to Aurora's grandfather, her husband: "I trust it hasn't changed too much."

Aurora stared up in awe. This was something straight out of a Jock Danger novel.

"You made this?" she whispered, astonished.

"This is what kept me in St Elmo's for all those years," her grandfather explained. Jack lingered close by, looking sheepish and unwilling to look him in the eye, "The radio was linked to it, an outlet in order to keep me sedated. That's just one of the things it can do."

"*Just* one?"

"When Thom –" he caught himself and swallowed. He couldn't deny it any longer and tried again. "When *I* built it, it was a tool to find the Nameless City. Nothing more. Now, who knows what they use it for?"

"You were a scientist? I never knew."

"I was. A lifetime ago."

"On the way here, you said two men created this," she remembered, leaving unsaid that he also mentioned, *they may have doomed us all.* "Who was the other one?"

"The other was a man called Charles Brockman," he sighed, and half smiled to himself. "I haven't said his name in years. He was my best friend. He was..." He paused, and looked over at his adopted son. "He was Jack's father."

"I never knew how he died," Jack said, joining them. "I was only a baby when it happened."

"Why are we here?" Drake cut in. Jack backed off, and Aurora felt a pang of fury towards the elder DuWell sibling. She could sense her grandfather had more to say, and that Jack desperately wanted to hear it.

"Thomas made the Corposant to find the Nameless City," Catherine reminded them. "It makes sense you use it again. This is the best place to start."

"You seriously expect me to begin work immediately?" the old man scoffed, "Just like that?" Catherine raised an eyebrow. Defiance. She was not used to it.

He scrutinised the machine, frowning, "I don't even know what this machine does any more. It's changed. Tell me what you use it for."

"Marcus?" Catherine called. He came forwards, chest puffed out, trying to look bigger than he was. "Why don't you explain?" To her captives, Catherine added, "Marcus has been looking after the Corposant in your absence. He's quite a dab hand with technology. He gets that from you, you know."

"Well, as you know, the Corposant was built to find the Nameless City, the mystical location that's inspired generations of DuWell lore." Marcus spoke as if he was reciting a well-prepared speech. He even cleared his throat beforehand. "A tool to find it has existed in the family in one form or another for generations, but the Corposant was the first time anyone realistically had a chance of finding it.

"Father was reluctant to use the machine for anything else, but Mother and I saw the potential immediately." Aurora noted that Marcus referred to Thomas and her grandfather as two separate people. He was reluctant to accept the theory that they were one and the same. "Then, when he disappeared, the Corposant registered a surge of power like we'd never seen before. It proved to us it could be used for more than just looking for something that no one has ever found. In all the years that followed, there was only once another surge like it." He paused, and his beady eyes fixed on the old man. "If it's true, and you are our father, then I assume the surge in power when you disappeared has something to do with your new identity."

"That's right," the old man agreed. He might as well explain now; the game was up. "The Nameless City is imagination, and the Corposant can tap into that, even if it can't find it. It changes memories, erasing some, creating others. It might as well rewrite history. Jim Hayhoe wasn't anyone; an unsuccessful, widowed writer who adopted a stern girl he never took the time to see. He was my age, so I adopted his identity using the machine. Once I used it, you lot," he gestured at his once-wife and children, "wouldn't recognise me as Thomas, even though physically nothing had changed, and just as importantly, Joan, Jim's daughter, would assume I was her father."

He paused for a moment, and let it all sink in.

"But it can't change people or how they feel. By the time I had adopted his identity, in the real world Jim had been dead for ten years, and Joan had never had the best relationship with him in the first place. So when I became him, there was still a ten year period where her father was absent from her life," he turned to Aurora, and added with a touch of bitterness, "Rather explains why her and I don't get on, wouldn't you say?"

"We knew you weren't Jim Hayhoe," Drake said, "We looked into your past and saw you were faking that. But how could we know who you really were when you had been deceiving us all along? Playing us at our own game, like a coward."

"What about the second surge?" Marcus added, returning to the subject of the Corposant. "There was another one just like it, a little over ten years ago. I've been trying to work out what it was used for, and I know you must have had a hand in it, but its purpose escapes me."

At that, the old man truly looked uncomfortable. His eyes strayed to Aurora and it was clear; this was a secret he would not bear to part with; that he would take to the grave if necessary.

Before anyone could press him further, help came from the most unlikely of sources.

"Why don't we get back to this delightful contraption?" Catherine suggested. "We can discuss the finer details later. Marcus dear, you were saying what it does?"

"Well, there are devices like the radio that kept you in St Elmo's," Marcus sniffed, resuming his speech, slightly put out. "There are dozens of them, subtly placed across the world, working against our enemies. They give us the advantage in whatever we need, be it

303

negotiations, making deals, or keeping our feistier opponents under our influence. After all, a political leader is a much better ally if we do the thinking for him. But then we knew we had to try something different with the Avalites. We knew of their talents and link to the Nameless City of course, but they're a strong people, not easily manipulated or threatened. So we used the Corposant to mask our auras from them so they couldn't see the truth."

"You did that to me too," the old man realised. "Didn't you? That's why Aurora can't see my aura either."

"You were our test subject when we caught you, just after we put you in St Elmo's. It was too obvious though; when Avalites look at you, they find your lack of aura unnerving. We had to make it subtle for us; the trick was they don't think to *look* for it. Instead, they see what we want them to see."

Aurora was both awe-struck and horrified; this machine was almost god-like in its powers. She thought slightly better of the Avalites; she knew that they had been manipulated into nearly going to war with one another, but now she saw how it had been done, she knew they never stood a chance.

"There's one thing I don't understand," her grandfather said. "When Charles and I first activated it, there were side effects. Something awful came from the machine: something that took my thigh and killed him. Ethics aside, that's why I was so reluctant to use the machine. How did you fix that?"

"You said it was a Bengal tiger," Aurora almost whispered, hurt. The lies had piled up upon lies and for a moment she wondered just how much of anything he said was true.

The sneer that resided on Catherine's face did not show the slightest intention of moving. "Fix?" she asked, innocently.

"But, you must have…" he trailed off. "There's no way you could do all this and just let them… There'd be so many by now…"

"What are you talking about?" Aurora had to know. The fear in the old man's voice was apparent, and anything that could impose further dread on him while in the company of the Ne'er DuWells had to be something very unpleasant indeed.

In her gut, Aurora already knew what it was. The powers of the Corposant were too similar for it to be a coincidence.

"What he's talking about is quite straightforward, dear girl," Catherine said, "It's true, we haven't reached the Nameless City, but even the slightest step towards it makes us more powerful. After all, everything casts a shadow, and the City's shadow is very great, and so very dark…"

Chapter 41
The Corposant's Secret

Machines were not evil.

They were not alive, or sentient. They were tools, built for a purpose. But a purpose could be evil.

As its uses and talents were revealed to Aurora, she saw that the Corposant may have been built only to find something hopeful, but a much darker intention had corrupted it.

Thomas had been right when he had written *The Lament of the Forgotten Scientist*: the Corposant had been perverted and blighted. It had made the world a much greyer place. It had been doing so for longer than she had been alive, and Aurora wondered how much brighter the world would be if it had never been built.

She felt sorry for Thomas, Jim, her grandfather, whoever he was, and for the first time felt she understood why he had withheld the truth from her: the Ne'er DuWells were evil, and any association with them could not be a good one.

Their selfishness knew no bounds, as she was just about to witness.

Marcus went to a control panel and tapped a series of keys in quick succession. The keypad was archaic but masterfully designed, like the rest of the machine, with old dials and typewriter buttons; it even needed an old lead key to work.

The air turned electric; Aurora noticed the ends of her hair rise.

"We'll provide you with a demonstration," the younger DuWell shouted over the noise, pleased to have some sense of purpose and control. "Vivian's Count has a particular social rival who's poking his nose in our business. We need to prevent him doing any more damage, and in order to do that, we need to use the Corposant."

From the ceiling hung a cluster of opaque silver spheres – unnoticed until now – each one hanging from a massive chain twenty feet above the ground. The spheres began to crackle with blue energy and drifted in different directions away from one another as if mapping the inflation of an invisible balloon. As they parted, the energy between the spheres stretched, tearing open a rift in the air, from which a blinding light blazed before being channelled into an ornate glass beaker, causing the lights around them to surge.

As the light entered the beaker it cooled into a liquid, bathing the room in an ethereal glow. It was striking, yet wrong somehow. Like a stuffed dead animal, its beauty was marred by being torn from its natural environment, mounted for others entertainment.

"This energy will be used however we choose," Marcus announced over the crackling, "Maybe the Count would like a St Elmo's radio of his very own to use. Maybe he'd like his rival to suddenly adopt a different political stance. The possibilities are endless!"

Once the machine had harnessed its fill, light stopped coming from the rift, leaving a flat black void hanging in the air. Despite the machines continual movement, silence filled the room.

The Ne'er DuWells became restless.

From the void something stirred. A dark, familiar shape stretched in the blackness and emerged from the hole.

Aurora looked to her grandfather, who shared the same look of horror. His hand found hers, and she didn't force it away.

The Umbra dropped from the void like a hideous insect from a cocoon, wet and forsaken, landing hard but silently on the ground. The black disc sealed behind it, leaving no trace in the air. With the energy that held them apart gone, the silver spheres swung back down on their chain, but no noise came when they collided:

The Umbra was awake.

With jerky movements, it got to its clawed feet, uncertain and shaky as an unholy newborn foal. It sniffed the air, recognising something that disturbed it.

The Umbra's head snapped round and its eyes locked onto Aurora; the hive mind that united their kind identified her immediately. Its black lips peeled back revealing teeth of broken glass, and it hissed with hatred.

"It knows her!" Vivian's screech broke the silence. Her family shared her alarm. They had never seen anything like it before. "How does it know you?"

Aurora did not respond. Instead, she continued to hold her grandfather's hand, and mouthed her mantra to herself. "Don't stop thinking. Don't stop thinking."

The old man noticed and squeezed her hand reassuringly.

The Umbra started towards her and Aurora began imagining a spear, a knife, anything to strike it with, all the while mouthing her mantra, but there was no need.

Several feet from them the Umbra recoiled; shrieking as it struck a wall of energy. Blue light flashed as it crackled, giving the room an eerie glow that lingered for several seconds. They were safe: there was no way for the Umbra to escape its invisible cage.

"You've made some unpleasant enemies," Catherine told Aurora, referring to the Umbra.

That was an understatement.

"This is where they've been coming from?" Aurora screamed.

"Actually, we think there's a few other locations too," Catherine corrected her. "Places where the walls between the two worlds are thinner than others and the rift can bleed through. That's what Tundra believes, anyway. Obviously they don't know about this place. But yes, I suppose we have been contributing our fair share."

"What do you do with them?"

"That's what we're about to show you."

Catherine signalled for everyone to move back and they did so, dispersing from the centre of the observatory and backing away towards the walls.

"We can't destroy them," Marcus advised. "Believe me we've tried. But we have another method for disposal."

He pressed a few more buttons and switches, and the floor of the observatory opened like a giant wooden iris, the floorboards rearranging themselves to create a massive pit in the room's centre. The process should have been a noisy one, but like the silver spheres, it was almost utterly silent.

With nothing underneath it, the Umbra fell into the pit, which at first Aurora assumed to be very deep owing to its blackness.

It was not.

It was filled with dozens of Umbra.

The thunderous silence the creatures created was broken only by the occasional hiss or shriek, and the black mass writhed and squirmed uneasily. As their new arrival joined them, a ripple of understanding passed through the creatures as new knowledge spread, and thirty or more pairs of needle like red eyes fixed immediately on Aurora.

She had never, ever, been more scared in her entire life.

The black mass moved in the pit towards the side Aurora and her grandfather were nearest, and the creatures began clambering upon one another to get at her.

The pit was several metres down, but that did not diminish their enthusiasm.

"Oh my god," Jack breathed, having never seen anything like this before.

"Marcus darling, the beasts are getting restless," drawled Catherine. "It seems our young guest has got them rather in a fluster. Maybe we should empty the tank?"

"Certainly mother," Marcus smiled sycophantically. He pressed a few more buttons, and the electrical field that had held back the Umbra stirred again, causing the mass of creatures to screech in panic as one.

A portion of the observatory's round roof peeled back and revealed the stormy sky above. The electrical field lifted the panicked and thrashing Umbra from the ground like an electric net. Within it, the Umbra, resembled a mass of eels in a fishbowl. They made Aurora's skin crawl.

"Where to, Mother?" Marcus asked.

"New York, I think, for a change," the old lady decided. "Wall Street's getting feisty again and it's making life difficult on the stock exchange."

The field trembled slightly, as if charging up, until finally a silent explosion sent shockwaves throughout the room, shooting the screeching mass into the sky, trailing light like a forsaken comet.

With the creatures gone, those in the room seemed to relax, with some notable exceptions.

Aurora and her grandfather were beyond speechless.

"It's normally London," Catherine explained, casually. "I understand they've settled quite nicely in the underground there. We try and place them as close to the financial side as we can, that way they feed on the bankers on their way to work. The less attentive they are, the more we can press our advantage."

"Well, it's clear why you had Ragnar killed," Aurora's grandfather grimaced. "If the Avalites had been united they would've been on to you long ago." He looked up at the Corposant in despair and put a hand over his mouth. "What have I done?"

"Thomas, darling, your lovely machine is the tool that has enabled us to maintain our fortune through the years. You're the one who guaranteed our continued success, and you've come back to us now to realise it. You should be proud of yourself."

It was clear to everyone in the room that the old man was anything but.

"You're... *insane*," Aurora said, finally thinking of something to say.

"Potato-potarto," Catherine shrugged, waving her hand, and then turned to her family. "So defiant. Doesn't she remind you of someone?" she asked with a wicked grin. "Which reminds me, it's time you explained that second surge, Thomas, the one you created just before we caught you."

The old man went pale. "Not a chance."

"If you don't, I will." Catherine threatened, without a trace of malice in her voice.

"You –" the word caught in his throat. "You can't possibly know. There's no way. For you to know I was Thomas was one thing, as mad as it makes you, but for this –"

"One word," the old woman said, and then, with calculated precision added:

"Stephanie."

A ripple of discontent and confusion passed through the rest of the DuWells, but Aurora had no idea what this name meant.

For the time being it did not matter, she was more concerned about her grandfather: the fight left the old man, and for a moment it looked like he was going to collapse.

"You... you've never let me..." he was talking as much to himself as Catherine, and his words resonated with a complete hopelessness, "Even before I was in St Elmo's, you always had me trapped..."

Then he steeled himself and straightened. He glanced over at his granddaughter, then back at his once-wife.

"Let me tell her," he told the old woman. "Let me tell her alone."

Aurora suddenly realised he was talking about her.

"There's not a chance that's happening here," Catherine sneered, gesturing around her, "Sending us away so you can destroy your precious machine. How stupid do you think I –"

"*Catherine*," he said, and it was with such authority, like a man telling his wife something that *mattered*, that for maybe the first time in her life, the old lady stopped in her tracks. The rest of the family could not believe what they were seeing.

He continued to speak, although firm, his voice was now very quiet, "I don't care where. You can tell the others. But this is important. I never asked you for anything, ever. Let me tell her, alone."

Catherine smiled.

"As you wish, my love."

*

The storm was worse than ever when they left the observatory; the sky was obsidian and the wind battered the breath from their chests. A short while later they had relocated to the more hospitable, but equally gloomy setting of Nowhere House.

Aurora and her grandfather were given privacy in the manor's extensive library; a long and sprawling high-ceilinged room that was just as melancholy as the rest of the house. Enormous bookcases of rare and antique volumes lined every wall, stretching from floor to ceiling.

Unbeknownst to the old man, some of the only copies left of the Jock Danger adventures were also concealed in an obscure corner of the library; mementos of the Ne'er DuWells victory over their nemesis. Several framed pictures – mostly of maps – were placed on the small portions of walls that weren't covered in books. Inexplicably, a silver skeleton was arranged in a display case in the centre of the room.

Even as prisoners, they seemed to enjoy a measure of comfort: servants brought them tea and lit the fire before Drake locked them in.

Before he closed the door, he said to his father, "Don't think this changes anything between us. You have half an hour."

They heard the door close and the lock turn loudly.

Then they were alone.

"Rory," her grandfather turned to her, eyes pleading. "It's still me –"

"I know," she said quietly, "You don't have to worry. Even if you were Jim Hayhoe, the real one I mean, the dead one, he wasn't my real granddad, and he wasn't much of a father to my mum from what I've heard. But after all we've experienced over the last few days, I know you care for me. Any idiot can see that. You're still… you're still *you*. I don't blame you for not telling me the truth."

"You may yet," he sighed, and he sat them both down on an ancient and moth-eaten settee. "Because I want to be honest with you. You deserve that. And I've one more thing I have to tell you."

Chapter 42
Stephanie

"Eleven years ago I was ready to take down the Ne'er DuWells once and for all. I had been Jim Hayhoe for over fifteen years by that point, and although I was getting on a bit, I was still at the top of my game. I had seen the world; something that would never have happened if I stayed with the family. But things were escalating. I knew that Drake and Catherine wouldn't tolerate my interfering for much longer, so I had to strike decisively in order to have any real impact.

"But I needed help, and it had to come from inside the family. I couldn't very well reveal myself to be Thomas and assume they would fall into line, Drake would've shot me dead then and there. I had to get them round to my side.

"Jack would've been my first choice. Like I said to you before, he's a good heart and he's loyal, and he loved me as if I was his father. But he was too young at the time, and he wasn't a DuWell by blood. That never mattered to me, but to the others, blood is everything. They would've seen him as a traitor and that would be that.

"The others you've met, and I think you can see why they would be no use. Drake's so much Catherine's puppet now, and the others are lazy and selfish, but there was one who I could turn to.

"Michael was a good lad. Drake and he were twins, but they were nothing alike. He took the very best of Catherine and I: utterly fearless, a man of integrity, and totally loyal to the family. I followed him for days, until finally I was able to get him on his own. When I finally convinced him I was his father, he agreed to help me. You see, he had a young family of his own, and becoming a father had made him realise that the DuWell legacy should not be one of evil. He had one request though: he insisted he get his wife and baby to safety before we tried anything. He knew full well of Catherine's vindictive nature and being her son would not make any difference if she learned he had betrayed her.

"Michael arranged to charter the DuWell dirigible – that's a blimp to you – and made it look as if he was taking it overseas on business. His wife and little girl were on board too. I had smuggled aboard to keep an eye on them, but unfortunately I wasn't the only one…"

The old man trailed off for the first time since he had started telling this story and collected his thoughts.

"This is where my memory gets foggy, so you'll have to bear with me," he coughed, and added, "Even if I could remember it right, this is unpleasant to recall."

"I had lost consciousness somewhere over the Andes, someone had knocked me out cold, probably drugged me, and when I came to, Drake had commandeered the flight with a team of mercenaries he had recruited. I stumbled round the airship, trying to find Michael and his family, when the dirigible erupted into flames.

"Now, an uncontrolled fire in a flying machine is absolutely catastrophic. I was groggy, not myself, and was barely able to fight off Drake and his cronies before we realised the dirigible was crashing, and there was nothing we could do to stop it.

"If we didn't get off the airship immediately we would all die, but it was too late for Michael. He had taken a stray bullet, presumably in my fight with Drake and his men, and before he bled out, insisted I save his family; his wife and little Stephanie."

Once again, the old man stopped, but this time it was to fight back tears. Aurora had never seen someone as dignified as her grandfather cry before: it was absolutely heart breaking.

"My son died in my arms, right there, and I only had minutes to get the rest of us to safety. I knew that Catherine would not allow us the chance to hide, so I decided the three of us should split up to escape detection. It was near impossible for Stephanie's mother to be parted from her daughter, but she understood it would only be temporary, until I could bring down the Ne'er DuWells once and for all.

"But when I returned to Nowhere House – the first time I had done so for over a decade – it all went terribly wrong. Catherine knew I was coming. I was furious, believing this would avenge the death of my son, and no sooner was I in the mansion than she stunned me with the Corposant.

"This was the first time the Corposant had been used like that, and I was able to resist the effects at first, but it was quickly becoming obvious that they had me. I made my way to the observatory, and fought them off for long enough to use it myself. I knew I had to protect Michael's family if nothing else. I owed him that. His wife, Catherine wouldn't care for, she wasn't blood, and you know how they feel about blood. But Stephanie was a different matter altogether. She was the next generation of the family, and Catherine would want to mould her into another Drake. I could not, would not accept that.

"So I triggered the second surge, the one Marcus wanted to know about. The first one transformed Thomas DuWell into Jim Hayhoe, the second... turned Stephanie DuWell into Aurora Card."

Aurora took a sharp intake of air. She wanted to stand up and sit down at the same time.

She didn't know what she wanted to do.

"No..." she mumbled. "You're lying... You've lied about so much already..."

"I'm so sorry," sighed her grandfather. Her real grandfather, it turned out. He looked vaguely like a huge load had been lifted from his shoulder, but it brought him no relief. "I couldn't let Catherine tell you. I never knew that she knew; I assumed she never did or she would've retrieved you years ago. Maybe she was waiting for you to come for me for some reason. It had all gone wrong; you were never meant to stay with the Cards for long, just until I brought the family down, but instead they raised you as their own, never realising you weren't theirs: the Corposant had done its work well. As for me, I spent ten years in St Elmo's, a prisoner of a device I had made. Jack never knew that the man he was guarding for so long with such determination was his father. And that's where you came in."

Her grandfather was reciting the rest of what happened, but in some ways it was more for his benefit than hers. No one except for him and Catherine knew his sad tale, and he had to share it with someone. The truth would be held back no longer.

But Aurora wasn't really listening now.

A month ago she had been, well, she hadn't been *happy*. She had never fitted in with her family, and they had never gelled with her. They were selfish and could be mean, but in a way that could be understood. Even her mother – who wasn't her mother – had been distant and disinterested, and Aurora wondered if that was because even if she didn't consciously recognise it, she had never been hers.

But now? Now, if this story, which was too far-fetched to be believed, was true, then the Cards were not her family. Not really.

But the alternative was too much to bear.

"Norm... he said you chose my name... that my parents couldn't decide..."

"It's a story," the old man said softly. "Maybe the only kind memory to come of all this. Not all lies have to hurt. Norm's helped me for years. He was only doing as I asked him to."

"But... I don't *want* to be a DuWell," she protested feebly.

"Aurora?"

She looked up, tearing herself from her thoughts. Her grandfather looked so concerned he could die of worry at any second.

"I'm fine," she said, but her voice came out like a croak. Her eyes were sore for some reason. She blinked, but that didn't seem to fix them. There must be something in them. She gave them a rub, and when she looked down at her hands, realised they were wet.

"Rory, it's okay."

She had only cried once in recent memory, when the Umbra chased her through the darkness of an underground tube tunnel, and she was dealing with certain death.

Since then the Umbra had nearly killed her, draining the thoughts from her body, until she was saved by a saint in the shape of a hunter.

She had slain an Umbra of her own, and been abducted.

Drugged. Made to doubt her sanity.

Abducted again, terrified. Threatened. Learned that the person she cared the most about in the world (for he had become that) had lied to her about who he really was, and was a member of the worst group of people she had ever met.

Even then, after all that, she had remained composed.

But now, this final blow delivered its sting, and Aurora finally collapsed against her grandfather's chest, and burst into tears.

Chapter 43
Jack's Decision

Which lasted for all of twenty seconds.

Aurora forced herself to stop. It wasn't easy, but she was an adventurer after all; Jock Danger's granddaughter, and crying was simply not acceptable.

Stop it.

If being Jock Danger's granddaughter wasn't enough, she was a DuWell too, and they were too evil to shed a tear.

Stop.

Crying.

Now.

She pushed herself away from her grandfather's embrace, noticing the wet patch she had left on his jacket, and stood up.

"Rory?"

"Is… is it okay if I deal with this later?" she sniffed, forcing an awkward smile onto her face. The last thing she felt like doing was smiling. "It's too much for me to take in right now."

Her grandfather stood up and wiped the tears from her cheeks.

"You're a piece of work, lady, you know that?" he said fondly.

"What are we going to do?" she asked, composing herself. If she kept moving, she could keep herself together.

"We're going to destroy the Corposant, of course," the old man declared, "The damage that monstrosity's caused, there's no way I'm going to let it carry on for a second longer."

"Won't she be expecting that?"

"Oh, most definitely," he beamed.

"So…" she trailed off, leaving the question unsaid.

"Yes, she's expecting that, and yes, she knows me well enough to predict what I'm going to do. But she knows Thomas DuWell; she doesn't know Jim Hayhoe," he smiled, and this was when the troublemaker's grin Aurora had learned to love came back for the first time in what seemed like an age. "And, most importantly, she certainly doesn't know you."

"So that means I'm coming with you?" She was dreading the noble hero routine; the bit where he sent her somewhere for her own safety.

"In a place like this? The safest place you could possibly be is right beside me."

Now *that* was more like it.

The old man approached the door. He put his ear to it and listened. After a few moments he awkwardly lowered himself on to his knees (which cracked) and reached into his pocket, extracting a pick. He set to work on the lock.

"You know, there'll probably be guards or something on the other side of that door," Aurora observed.

"I'm well aware of that."

"Then why –"

"Ssh! Let an old man concentrate."

The old man had not worked a lock for years. It took a few more attempts than he expected as his old fingers stumbled over the pick, and several times he mumbled something that Aurora guessed was a particularly vicious combination of swear words.

She watched him impatiently, when a very important thought struck her.

"You said my father was dead, but what about my –"

The lock clicked noisily, cutting her off. The question dissipated noiselessly into the air. "Ah!" her grandfather announced, and, getting to his feet, was about to turn the handle when the door swung open.

Jack entered the room, checking behind him warily and closing the door. He pocketed a key, and Aurora realised her grandfather's lock picking skills were rustier than he thought.

"What are you doing here?" the old man asked.

"She just told us," Jack said, glancing over at Aurora. "You're one of us, it seems."

"Guess so," Aurora muttered.

"She's ordered me to come get you both."

"Not Drake? I thought he'd prefer to take charge of these sorts of things."

"Drake won't even look you in the eye right now," Jack said. He paused, before adding, "Is it true? Are you really my father?"

"Charles…" He drifted off. "Yes, I am."

"Wow," Jack said, pacing somewhat. Aurora could see now the influence her grandfather had had on his children; the way Jack carried himself, spoke, and even paced the room was very similar to him. Finally, he said, "I'm so sorry. If I'd known I never would have kept you in St Elmo's. I can't believe she would do such a thing –"

"Can't you?" The question hung in the air, and it was obvious Jack knew full well this was a lie.

"Those things... I've never been in the observatory."

"It didn't seem right to let you," the old man explained, "Not after what happened to Charles."

"But what we do with them. I never knew..." he seemed to come to a realisation, and said, "The rest of the family doesn't know the world like I do, they've not been out in it. What we're doing to the world; it's *wrong*."

"I know. That's why we're going to destroy the Corposant."

Aurora couldn't believe her grandfather was telling Jack this. Anyone could see he was the best of the bunch, but still.

He was a Ne'er DuWell. They could not be trusted.

She almost laughed. She was one too, as it turned out. Could the same be said of her?

"Then I'll help you too," Jack volunteered, straightening for duty.

"Not a chance," the old man told him.

"Why? Those things killed my father, surely that in itself should be enough."

"It's not about that," the old man said kindly. "I don't want to test your loyalties, that's unfair. And more importantly, I refuse to put my family in harm's way again."

"What about her?" Jack asked, indicating Aurora. He had a point.

"That's different. She can handle herself around the Umbra," Aurora felt a rush of pride when she heard that, although it rather diminished when her grandfather added, "Plus I'm never letting her out of my sight again."

He laid a hand on Jack's shoulder. "I should never have hit you, back at St Elmo's. I'm sorry. No father should do that to his son."

"I had it coming," Jack shrugged. "And you're wrong. Drake deserves a smack."

A small laugh forced its way from Aurora, to Jack's amusement. He returned his attention to his father, and pleaded, "Let me *help*."

Keeping his hand on his son's shoulder, the old man gave a sad, proud smile, and said, "Not this time, son."

And with that, Jack collapsed.

"What happened?" Aurora cried, rushing to his side. Jack was out cold.

"Nerve pinch," her grandfather explained, "A little trick I picked up in Tibet. He'll be fine, but he'll be out for a while. Help me move him."

Jack wasn't a particularly heavy man, but he was large enough to make an old man and a twelve-year-old girl struggle as they dragged him to one of the numerous armchairs that filled the library.

"What now?" she asked.

"One minute." Her grandfather was busy rummaging through a small cabinet in the library's corner, until finally he found what he was looking for. He removed a cane. It was long and black, with a gold

325

tip on one end and a golden ball with a familiar design in place of a handle at the other.

"This was my grandfather's," he said. "I remember him using it back when I was little. I always liked it, but it seemed like something an old man would use." He smiled, "I think I've grown into it." Holding the handle towards his granddaughter, he explained, "See? The globe held by the eagle's claw is the DuWell crest. Given the family's secretive nature it's rare for anyone to see it. Rumour has it the points where the claw tips touch the globe are of great significance, but no one knows why."

"Um, I don't need to be rude," she said, making her way to the door, "but shouldn't we –"

"All in good time." He moved closer to the bookshelves, away from the door "Anyway, if we leave that way, Drake will find us in no time." He turned towards the books and ran his fingertips along their spines, muttering to himself. The collection was immaculate; leather bound first editions, many with gold leaf trimmings, they would put most libraries to shame. "Come here."

She did as he told her, becoming gradually more and more impatient. "I want you to look for *Crime and Punishment*, by Dostoyevsky. Don't touch it, but tell me when you find it."

Perplexed, she did so while the old man continued to scour the shelves. At the same time, she heard him cry "Ah!" He had obviously found what he was looking for, and within moments, so had she.

"He had a great sense of humour, did Grandpa Albert. Or at least I thought he did, until I realised he actually tended to mean what he said, and what he said wasn't very nice at all. Turns out the man did not believe in irony. I suppose he would have been your Great-great-granddad," He put his fingertips on the edge of the book he was looking for – *Bleak House*, by Charles Dickens – and said, "Tilt the book towards you on three.

"But more than anything else, there's one other thing about my grandfather that's worth knowing," he lowered his voice and counted: "One, two, three."

They pulled the two hardbacks as one, and with a creak and groan, the entire bookcase swung open, revealing a long tunnel that disappeared into the darkness.

"Grandpa Albert was insanely paranoid."

Opening the bookcase triggered a series of small sounds; cogs turning, pulleys lifting, and a row of torches ignited one by one, creating a gloomy but adequate light to show them the way.

"Okay, that's really cool," admitted Aurora.

"Isn't it?" he beamed, "There's dozens of little touches like this across the house. Hundreds, maybe. Catherine doesn't know the family as well as she thinks. She may have learnt the family lore when she married me, but this is *my* house."

He lifted the cane and pointed into the gloom of the tunnel.

"Come on, let's go blow up something expensive."

Chapter 44
Second Chances

The tunnel was long and winding, but fortunately it only went in one direction, and all they had to do was follow it to the end.

Occasional ghostly whispers could be heard, but Aurora assured herself it was just the wind. Ghosts on top of everything else would be a bit too much to bear, although if they existed anywhere, Nowhere House was probably the most likely candidate.

Every now and then tiny gaps in the walls let in slivers of light, and Aurora realised they were passing behind family rooms. This was when they had to move silently, or risk detection.

The tunnel dipped and made its way underground. A small staircase at its end led to the surface.

Through years of neglect the passage to the outside had become choked and congested with weeds, and it took a few minutes to clear a path through into the night air.

The storm had arrived in full force as they crossed the grounds to the cliff edge. Aurora struggled for breath as the winds battered her, and she struggled to keep her balance on the wet grass in the darkness. Her grandfather kept a hand on her arm to stop her falling, and it was only when they made it to the cliff edge that she realised it had been the other way round: he had been relying on her for support.

Their route to the stack where the observatory lay passed near the Garden of Death her grandfather had mentioned when they arrived, and she wondered whether Michael, the father she never knew she had, had a black rose growing for him somewhere amongst its dark recesses. She wondered what she was supposed to think of him, or how he had felt about her. What sort of a person had he expected her to become? Would he be disappointed? Proud? He was a Ne'er DuWell, should she even care what he thought? But then the circle came round in full and she remembered once more that she was one too, as was her granddad, as was Jack.

Even in total darkness there were shades of grey.

They crossed the bridge as they had before, but after hours of rain the wooden slats were wet and slippery. Every step she took forwards was potentially fatal, and the only thing which stopped her worrying about her grandfather was the more pressing concern of her own survival, as the bridge swayed in the howling wind.

Finally, they made it across, and her grandfather patted her on the back reassuringly, "Don't worry, every good adventure story requires a hazardous bridge crossing. It's mandatory."

They entered the observatory, making sure to lock the doors behind them, and stared up at the monstrous device. How they were supposed to damage something as massive and solid as this was beyond her.

"Ideas?" Aurora asked, "I don't suppose you happened to include a failsafe or self-destruct button no one else knows about?"

"That's an idea!" the old man exclaimed, "Where were you when I was building this thing first time around? Sadly not. Well, unless you count hitting it with something really rather heavy as a failsafe. We'll have to turn it against itself."

He approached one of the control panels Marcus had operated earlier and threw several levers and switches. The panel, which had been calmly ticking over, flared up; dials and gauges starting to react to the surge of energy passing through the device.

The silver spheres that had torn the hole in the air earlier came to life, but before they started to part, the old man pressed a few more buttons and dials, causing them to sway from side to side like a giant pendulum.

The arc grew larger as it swung, and the air became alive with energy, as coils of lightning grew angry, arcing and crackling thirty feet above. "It shouldn't be able to handle a consistent increase in energy, so we overload it, then make sure it destroys itself," her grandfather said, "There's one problem though."

"What?"

"Marcus emptied the pit of all the Umbra it had accumulated earlier, but I don't know how rapidly it fills up again. There could very well be a few of the creatures in there right now. If we destroy the Corposant, no more will come through from the Rift, but any that are already in the pit will be able to get out. We'll have to be careful."

Aurora swallowed. She had only killed one Umbra before, and not only had that one been wounded, but Beth and Bjorn had been there too. Against multiple creatures at full strength, alone...

Looking at his cane, she realised something. "How come I don't have a weapon?"

"You've got your wits," he quipped. "They're razor sharp."

A booming sound came from the other side of the doors, loud enough to be heard over the Corposant's frantic crackling.

"What was that?"

"They've found us," her grandfather said grimly. "Quicker than I would have thought too. We haven't much time."

The crashing sound continued, and the doors shook on their hinges. A third crash and they began to splinter.

"How much time have we got?" Aurora asked, suddenly feeling very scared. "Can we destroy it before they get through?"

"No, the machine's taking too long to charge up," he told her. "I'll have to hold them off. You need to climb that gantry and get to the top."

"I'm not leaving you," she said, although she knew it was pointless to argue.

"You're not. There's another control panel up there. If you can reach that, you should be able to speed it up."

"How do I –" she began, when the doors finally gave in.

"Go!" the old man shouted, and she had no choice but to tear up the metal staircase and leave her grandfather to his fate.

Drake burst through, more enraged than she had ever seen him – or anyone – before. In his wake followed a few servants, who advanced on the old man.

"No!" the aristocrat yelled, "Hold back. I'll handle him."

Her grandfather tried his best to appear unthreatened. Drake was an intimidating opponent at the best of times, but the hatred he held for his nemesis only made him more so. He was *seething*.

"I've been waiting a long time for this," he hissed.

"And now you know the truth?"

"Truth is subjective." Denial. Big surprise.

"It's not too late for you Drake," his father pleaded, "You've been manipulated your entire life, but that doesn't have to continue. Listen to me, I'm your father –"

"You are *not* my father!" Drake yelled, flying at him. The old man was fortunate; Drake's rage impaired his aim, and he had enough time to throw himself clear. Drake picked himself up, straightened his tie, smoothed back his hair, forcing calm.

"Lucky," he smirked, a nervous laugh, "Lucky old fool."

Reaching into his jacket, he drew his stiletto knife. The blade danced in his grip like an extension of his hand.

"I should take my time," he told himself, circling his prey. "Do it slowly."

Hayhoe raised his grandfather's cane. Holding it like a rapier, he forced Drake to keep his distance. Drake recognised the family heirloom, and his eyes narrowed.

"That won't save you," he threatened, and lunged at him.

By this point Aurora had reached the balcony, and was watching the fight. She flinched when Drake lunged. She couldn't bear to watch, nor could she tear herself away.

She didn't have a choice either way, as something grabbed hold of her hair and violently pulled her up.

Fighting like a wildcat, she twisted and scratched until the grip released her. Turning, she saw Vivian standing over her. She had crept in behind Drake and his cronies, and had identified the real danger immediately.

"Mother filled us in about our little niece," she purred, "I must say, I'm disappointed. Look at you; you wouldn't know style if it was staring you in the face. Anyway, I figured the boys may have reservations about hurting Michael's daughter, but I've no such qualms, especially if said brat intends to interfere with our rather sweet set up here."

She went for Aurora; hands clawed and face a mask of hate, no longer the lazy creature. Aurora dived aside at the last moment, and Vivian struck the bars. Aurora landed hard on the gantry's steel grating, but wouldn't allow herself to feel the pain. Vivian was on top of her again moments later.

"This is not... yours to break!" her aunt spat, trying to gets her hands round Aurora's throat. In the heat of the moment, Aurora could swear that despite their precautions, she could see Vivian's aura leap to life, a murderous, ugly thing.

Aurora had fought dirty before; she had been raised with two brothers twice her size, and had to play dirty now. Vivian deserved it and more.

She poked her aunt in the eye, a move that surprised and hurt the older woman.

The grip on her throat released and Vivian fell back, screaming obscenities and holding her face.

"Don't... be so... bloody selfish!" Aurora gasped, rising, struggling for air.

Forcing herself to her feet, before Vivian could get up, she delivered a kick Red would have been proud of, right in the stomach. The aristocrat went down, heavily winded.

Aurora turned her attention back to the Corposant; she had reached the other control panel, and looked at it in despair, unsure of what to do. She flicked every switch she could, then decided something more drastic was needed.

She spotted a fire axe on the wall. It was high up and heavy, and she dropped it as she removed it from the case, jumping back to avoid losing her toes.

Dragging it to the control panel, she struggled to raise the axe, and was about to bring it down when she heard Vivian scream, "Stephanie!"

Vivian had levelled a small pistol at her. Stunned, Aurora stopped and waited for the shot.

The gun went off.

Chapter 45
Collateral Damage

Although Aurora presently had more pressing concerns, it would have comforted her to know her grandfather was a much better fighter than she could have hoped. His footwork excelled as he nimbly sidestepped his opponent and in the same step, the cane flicked up and struck Drake hard in the cheek.

"You're going to have to accept it, son," the old man said. "I'm your father."

Drake swiped his blade, screaming, but the old man avoided it with ease and it cut through only air. Drake's face was bleeding now, the cut on one cheek matching the scar that was already present on the other.

"I've had a lot of time to reflect on why I left you all," he continued. "Believe me, it wasn't an easy decision. In some ways, I regret it every day."

This only angered Drake further, and his father knew it. "I'm going to rip you apart!" he roared, diving forwards with the knife once more.

There was plenty of time to parry the blow. It was part of Hayhoe's strategy: angry, Drake was lethal, but the more furious he became, the sloppier he was too. The old man's only chance was to exploit this weakness, and he did just that, sidestepping his son and tripping him in the process. As Drake fell, the cane shot out and struck his wrist, smacking the blade from his grip.

"That's so you didn't hurt yourself," his father said, "You should never run with a blade. You'll have your eye out."

Drake tried to grasp the fallen knife, but another two flashes and the cane struck him on both sides of his head, stunning him.

"As I was saying, my biggest mistake was leaving you. Not because I loved you, and I do love you, son, even though you're clearly in need of therapy, but because you needed a firm hand growing up."

Drake stood, and the cane hit him across the face. Too angry to feel it, he went for his father once more, forcing Hayhoe to step away. Drake used the opportunity to scoop up his knife from the ground.

"You've grown up to be a right nasty piece of work," the old man continued, "and you've done some rotten things in your life."

"You have no idea."

"I might. Just before you took me down, I had a theory about something you could have done, but I wouldn't dare let myself consider something so unforgivable. Something you don't want anyone to know about, not even *her*. If I'm right, then you've got a lot to answer for."

"Who do you think you are?" Drake screamed, and it seemed likely that the old man had hit a nerve.

The cane shot out three times, a rap across the knuckles to hurt him; one in the gut to bend him over; and one across the back to bring him to his knees.

"I'm Jim Hayhoe. I'm Jock Danger. I'm the worst threat this family has ever faced. I've seen the whole world, I've fought monsters you could never believe existed and escaped death a thousand times.

"I'm Thomas DuWell. I'm your father. And I'm shutting this family down."

Drake tried to rise, but the fight was leaving him.

"I'm warning you now," the old man said sternly. "Don't get up."

Drake didn't. He couldn't: he was beaten.

He had no way of knowing, but his father was on his last legs. If he went for him once more Hayhoe would have no way of fighting him off.

But Drake had one last trick to play.

He waited for his father to look away – the adventurer's eyes left him for a moment, glancing to see where Aurora was – and raised the knife, ready to pitch it at the old man.

As he was about to release it, a shot rang out and Drake screamed, dropping the blade and clutching his bloodied and ruined hand.

Hayhoe was pointing the cane at him. The end had exploded, smoke rising from where the shot concealed in its tip had gone off.

"Your great-grandfather was a cunning bugger, wasn't he?" his father said.

The fight was over. The guards took this as a sign to take the initiative and stepped forwards, raising their weapons. Hayhoe straightened and looked at them in turn while Drake rolled on the floor, moaning in agony.

"Well gentlemen," the old man addressed them, fighting to steady his breathing. "You all heard that. You're smart men; the DuWell family doesn't employ fools, only people with flexible morals. What do you want to do now?"

*

Aurora's life had been in danger several times since she sprung her grandfather from St Elmo's, but staring down the barrel of a gun was the most brutal and obvious way she had seen so far.

As Vivian's finger squeezed down on the trigger, a large blur knocked her to the floor.

The bullet went wide, chipping the wall behind Aurora, whose heart skipped a beat. Her legs had turned to jelly, but there was reassurance:

Beth had saved her once again. The wolf had Vivian's trembling form pinned to the gantry and Aurora could tell that the Avalite was *furious*. She roared in Vivian's face, making the Ne'er DuWell cower in terror.

"Don't – don't, please…" she mewled, causing Beth to only growl more.

Aurora ran over to them and laid a hand on the wolf's shoulder. Vivian noticed, her eyes turning to her niece, desperate and wide.

"Best not eat her," Aurora advised, "Too bitter."

She ran to the edge of the gantry and looked through the splintered doors of the observatory. Away from the cliff top, towards the manor, a small fleet of vehicles tore across the lands, kicking up dirt and grass in their wake.

It was the Avalites.

Aurora did not watch them approach for long: she had a job to do.

The cluster of silver spheres was swinging dangerously now, but she picked up the axe anyway. It was almost too heavy for her to use effectively, so she spun round with it a few times trying to build some momentum, well aware of how insanely dangerous this was. She had no desire to throw it at Beth.

On the third spin, she released her grasp; hammer tossing the axe at the console.

It tore through the machine, shredding the intricately designed control panel.

And that appeared to be it.

Aurora's heart sank; that was the only trick she had. Worse, in doing so she had destroyed the console, and had exhausted all her other options.

Then suddenly without warning a few sparks came from the console. More followed. A resonant metallic sound filled the observatory, a deep creaking that made everyone pause. Beth released her grip on Vivian and trotted over to Aurora, and the aristocrat wasted no time in fleeing the giant wolf.

Halfway through their pendulous swing, the winch controlling the chains attached to the cluster of silver spheres released suddenly. They dropped, forcing those on the ground floor of the observatory to scatter or be crushed. They crashed into the Corposant's huge base, the electricity they channelled crackling manically.

The tumbling mess of metal was heavy and fell with force, denting, and then tearing through the smooth black metal casing, triggering an uneven chain reaction of explosions that tore through the observatory, igniting fires and setting off alarms.

Chaos exploded in the observatory.

"We should probably go," Aurora suggested to Beth as they watched the explosions spread. She flinched as a particularly violent one struck close to them. Even in her wolf form, the Avalite was able to give her a glance that read: *You think?*

Vivian had already fled the observatory. As the fires and explosions took hold, Drake and his men wasted no time in following. Aurora's grandfather lingered and was unprepared to leave until she had descended the gantry and was by his side.

He was so busy watching her descend that he had not noticed that the noise from the explosions around him had diminished slightly, yet the blasts were no less violent. Neither did he notice the dirty black mass clambering through a hole in the floor behind him. The iris-like opening that led to the pit in the basement had released slightly, and its occupant wanted out. The only thing in its way was the old man.

Aurora saw it though. She could see the Umbra lifting itself out by its claws as she descended the gantry, mere feet from her grandfather. She shouted, but he could not hear her, the explosions and the Umbra's ability to mute sound working in conjunction to muddy the noise around them.

The Umbra's head and shoulders were out of the pit.

"Beth!" she screamed. Beth saw it too, and went to leap from the gantry, but an explosion from above sent a fiery mess of metallic debris her way, forcing her to jump back or be crushed. Her path obscured, the wolf would have to find another way to the ground.

It was down to Aurora.

The Umbra was out of the pit.

Vivian's gun lay on the deck. Aurora knew from first-hand experience it would not kill the Umbra, but she had an idea. She clasped the pistol by the barrel and uttering her mantra

Don'tstopthinkingdon'tstopthinkingdon'tstopthinking

like crazy and she pitched the weapon at the creature. She couldn't afford for this not to work.

It was Granddad.

The Umbra hissed and drew back a claw.

Even cast from her hand, Aurora managed to retain control of the gun. It spun in the air, blurring as it did so. It changed; retaining the same right angled shape, but morphed and twisted into a razor sharp bladed boomerang.

The weapon passed over her grandfather's shoulder. It sliced through the top layer of his jacket but went no deeper, embedding itself in the Umbra's open mouth.

The creature fell back, killed instantly, and the sound returned with a bang as the explosions continued.

Aurora and Beth wasted no time in reaching the ground floor as her grandfather watched the Umbra fade away, amazed. The old man wanted to say something, but the explosions made him think twice. "Get out!" he yelled instead.

Beth, in her wolf form, led the way, shooting out of the building and across the bridge in a matter of moments, but in the confusion and in her haste she hadn't realised that Aurora and her grandfather had failed to keep up. In seconds she spun around and started back towards the observatory, while the Avalites gathered on the other side of the cliff and watched it come down in the fire and rain. Norm, Bjorn and Rory were amongst their number. Of Drake, his men or Vivian there was no sign.

Beth had started her way back to them as Aurora and her grandfather left the observatory, stepping on to the bridge and beginning the journey across, when a particularly violent explosion tore through the building, sending a mass of something huge and fiery into the air. The flaming heap came down on the bridge, tearing it from the stack and flinging it into the black waters below. Beth would have fallen too, but her animal reflexes saved her from harm. She managed to leap from the collapsing bridge and scramble to safety, but instead of re-joining the Avalites on the cliff, she sprinted back and forth along its edge, desperately trying to find her way back to Aurora.

She was unsuccessful. The bridge was gone, and Aurora and her grandfather were trapped on the stack as the observatory continued to come down around them.

Beth let out a howl of fury and despair.

They were stranded.

Chapter 46

Certain Death

The collected Avalites watched their friends across the water in despair as the death knell of the Corposant wreaked havoc on the stack.

In addition to the explosions and fires, a blade of white energy cleaved through the air, shooting straight up and blasting through the observatory's roof and into the night sky, where it illuminated the storm clouds above.

The rain hounded them as relentlessly as it had all night, and as the explosions continued Aurora's grandfather took charge, leading her away from the missing bridge and towards the side of the observatory, where the white light revealed a narrow path that twisted down the stack to the beach below. They clung to each other as they tried to navigate the slippery trail without falling into the stormy waters beneath them. What they would do when they reached the bottom, where the path ended in the black waters, she could only guess.

From above, more explosions betrayed the observatory's destruction. Arcs of energy split from the white blade and rained down, illuminating the depths of the dark waters for fleeting moments like dying fireworks.

As they neared the base of the stack a final explosion that dwarfed all others sent the observatory, Corposant and a chunk of the stack itself hurtling towards the water, with Aurora and her grandfather in its way.

When Aurora looked up she saw something dark obscuring the fires above them. She knew what it was. There was no time to think.

"Jump!" she yelled, pulling her grandfather with her. The old man saw the huge boulder too, and together they threw themselves into the savage waters below as the path disappeared.

*

Aurora had only swum in the sea a few times. Near Watford, the local swimming pool had a wave machine, and she hoped landing in the water would be a bit like that, only colder.

She had no idea.

The water was freezing, sapping her thoughts and strength immediately.

She fought to the surface where a wave slapped her face, knocking the breath from her lungs and blinding her with salt water.

The blackness of the ocean and the dark skies above made sight almost pointless; there was nothing to see. The world underneath her shifted horribly, making her feel sick.

"Granddad?" she cried, "Granddad!"

She called a third time, and a large wave caught her unawares. She took in a mouthful of water, choking. Another larger wave struck her, and knocked her underwater. The roaring in her ears was absolute.

She tried to surface but another wave hit, pinning her under.

Aurora sank.

She fell into the blackness, unable to fight any longer. Her clothes were too heavy, the water too cold.

Then something happened.

Her sight switched on, involuntarily.

As I descended, my stinging eyes made out a light shining from the blackness.

In the depths of my mind I knew what this was. It was delirium, the light at the end of the tunnel, my death.

Except as my eyes got used to what I was seeing – the air pounding for release in my chest – I realised that whatever it was, it really was there. Perfect blue, calming and radiant, it shone up in the shape of a disc, the opposite of the Umbra's void. Whatever it was, it was real.

And it gave us a chance.

I knew I had to fight. I had to find my granddad and show him, when

A hand clutched at her collar, pulling her above water.

Her grandfather held her as tight as he could. He clutched a chunk of driftwood under one arm to keep him above water and held her with the other.

"You're not going anywhere," he told her, kissing her forehead as she gasped for air. His cheeks were wet with tears as well as seawater; he thought he had lost her.

"I saw something," she spluttered, catching her breath, "Down there."

"You nearly died!" he shouted, his voice hardly audible over the roaring storm.

"I think it's our way out!"

"What was it?"

"I don't know!" she admitted. "But we have to try!"

"Rory, going down will kill us!"

"It's the rhyme," she tried to explain, so cold she could hardly think. "Reason won't find Avalonne!"

"This isn't the time to find the City," her grandfather cried. "We've got to get to safety!"

A wave crashed over them and they spluttered for air. Her grandfather struggled to keep his grip on the driftwood.

They weren't going to last much longer.

"It's the same thing!" she shouted back.

"If you're wrong about this, we'll die."

"I know." She was reminded of the first time she met Drake. In amongst the tangle of lies he had told her, he said that passing into another realm would mean madness. For a second she wondered if that was the choice she was facing now: death or insanity.

She dismissed the thought. Regardless of who her family was, of what that might mean, she knew who *she* was, and she was not afraid.

The water under them shifted and withdrew, and they turned; a black wall of water, the stuff of nightmares, was drawing itself up, towering twenty feet above them and preparing to topple.

Only death would follow in its wake.

"Do you trust me, Granddad?"

He smiled. "Lead the way."

They would not waste any more time watching the black wave grow. They descended.

*

Only once in living memory had Nowhere House been attacked before, and the Ne'er DuWells learnt from their mistakes. They survived by preparing for every eventuality.

It was locked down, and would be impenetrable to the Avalites, should they turn their intentions to assault instead of rescue.

Drake had managed to make his way back before the manor had been secured. Many of his men had not been so lucky. He had no idea where Vivian was, and at that moment he did not particularly care.

Soaking wet, he stalked through the corridors like a wounded tiger, cradling his ruined hand in an increasingly bloody handkerchief.

He had to find his mother. He had to tell her what had happened.

"What's going on?" Marcus asked, intercepting him en route. He would want to know about his precious machine.

Drake did not stop to answer, and Marcus nipped at his heels.

"Where are the others?"

"They never made it across the bridge, they're probably dead," Drake grunted.

Marcus paused to glance out of the window. Even with the foul weather pounding against the glass the flames were visible in the distance.

"I can't believe it," Marcus muttered. "Unbelievable."

He ran to catch Drake up again. "What are we –"

He stopped. A sound drifted through the corridors of the mansion, freezing them both in their tracks.

It was something no one had heard in decades.

Catherine was laughing.

"It's all coming true," the old lady chuckled. "They did it."

It was as if they weren't even there.

"Mother?" Marcus didn't want to disturb her, but had no choice. He had never seen her like this before.

"They've found it," she said. True, mad, elation tainted her voice.

"What do you mean?" Drake asked. "They never made it off the stack. They're dead."

"They're not. They're *there*."

"Where?"

"The Nameless City."

Chapter 47

Through the Blue Disc

The Nameless City is not what it seems, remembered Aurora. She heard the words in Daniel's voice.

Shaped by thoughts and crafted from dreams.

They pushed downwards, the pressure building on their skulls.

Men have looked but it's in no place.

All Worlds Unseen is its own space.

Swimming beside her, her grandfather could see the blue disc too. Undisturbed by the powerful waves that threatened to end the adventurers, the disc lay flat, like a spot of light suspended several metres from the floor.

As she swam, Aurora briefly wondered what its reverse looked like.

It's by man's logic they're undone.

This was where the rhyme was most important. Therein lay the answer.

Reason won't find Avalonne.

She prayed she was right. If she were responsible for both their deaths, her grandfather would kill her.

Passing through the disc was an experience both awe-inspiring and terrible. It was more than just passing through water. A tide of emotion struck Aurora, and with crystal clarity her short life flashed before her. She relived the horror and excitement of the last few days:

The Corposant.

The Hall of Portraits.

Catherine.

Her fear in Nowhere House.

Norm, fearlessly fighting the Avalite chiefs.

Slaying the Umbra in the woods.

Beth.

Crawling through the underground tunnel, Umbra on her heels.

Norm's loft.

Fleeing St Elmo's, and the radio.

Granddad.

She remembered the Cards, and thought of them fondly despite everything. The memory of her mother, in particular, brought longing. Would she ever see her again?

Her memories stretched back further, to early childhood; to things she never thought she would remember – her blue doggie, as she had called Beth, always there, always watching – and then she remembered further still, until the distortion of time and the limits of her experience brought her to an abstract place, of fire and noise where her fate would be shaped forever.

And one place more, a place of warmth and colour, where a large pair of eyes shone on her with love.

They were very familiar: eyes that knew her soul intimately.

Was this death? She couldn't help but wonder. It was too late now, the only way was forward.

The feeling passed as they came out the other side of the disc, and the burning in Aurora's lungs was an urgent reminder that they needed to reach the surface now.

Desperate for air, they swam through into calmer waters where, disorientated, they pushed on downwards. Somehow here the water pressure relaxed and it felt like they were ascending.

Down was leading them up.

Suddenly they surfaced, and when she opened her eyes, everything was different.

We inhaled as one, our lungs screaming.

There was no trace of the storm. The seas were calm, warm and blue; the sun beat down upon us.

I looked down into the water at the circular portal we had passed through. On this side the disc was black, the darkness created by the stormy seas in another world.

In the deepest, darkest part of my mind, I wondered if I had gone mad, if I was sitting in a hospital ward somewhere, unable to tell what was real anymore and what was fantasy.

"Wow," I heard. Granddad's voice brought me out of my wondering.

He floated next to me, ecstatic, and I smiled at him. He grinned back, and gently splashed water at me, confirming that my surroundings were real. I wondered if he knew my thoughts, but all I could see was relief and excitement on his face.

Swimming to shore, the water put up little resistance; in fact, it felt as if it was aiding us, that in some way it wasn't really water, but the idea of water, that maybe we could control it if we knew how. The air was the same; I'd never tasted anything as pure or as cool before.

Soft waves carried us to shore, and lowered us onto white sands. We lay there exhausted; appreciating solid ground while the sea gently broke around us. When the light struck the waves it shone like crystal.

We could not rest for long. We were a little frayed, but it paled to the excitement rising in my chest. I knew Granddad felt the same.

"Did we –" I managed but didn't need to finish.

Moments later we were standing on uncertain feet in a new world.

We looked over the sea behind us, and saw way out that the water from all around flowed into a huge basin, miles across.

As the water fell into the abyss it kicked up a dense cloud of mist, making it almost impossible to see the sight before us.

Above the pit, obscured by the mist, hung a mountain, suspended in the air.

The mountain was floating.

It was completely impossible, and beyond amazing, held in place by three massive chains that stopped it drifting away.

I realised what the mountain was. How could it be anything else?

Built on a giant floating country of mankind's earliest hopes, it grew and flourished. The crystal of impossible thought that was its base trained over millennia to become habitable, crudely at first, but developing as it went. Walls and halls, tunnels and rooms, parapets and battlements all carving it into a place that was worth every ounce of the obsession that had been devoted to it.

As my gaze trailed further up I could see that the imagination that shaped it was more sophisticated, and domes, twisting towers and spires of the most unfathomable aspirations curved and climbed, piercing the very top of the velvet sky.

Crested with clouds and illuminated in its ethereal aura it was something to see.

Just how I had imagined it, like in my dreams; the source of Granddad's quest all his long life and the obsession that had fuelled the Ne'er DuWells for generations.

The Nameless City.

Avalonne.

Acknowledgements

I have a lot of people to thank for donating their time in both reading this and offering their opinions.

I'm indebted to Rob Bell, who forensically read this last draft and offered meticulous suggestions and revisions with saint-like patience. If the acknowledgements don't feel as precise in their composition, it's because they're the one section he didn't read. This book wouldn't be half of what it is without him or Christian Zante. The two of them have read every word I've written and offered loads of feedback and suggestions. Most of them were even good.

The following all read this book in various incarnations, and I'm very grateful they took the time to either massage my ego with their kind words or set me straight. Amongst others were Seb Allen, Clyde Baehr, Matt Bolton, Sarah Bredl-Jones, Katie Catt (who provided gorgeous hand drawn illustrations), Andy Clark, Nigel Crow, Caroline Hunt (who tracked down this book and its sequel online, and then was gracious enough to tell me how much she enjoyed them,) Marcia Lecky, Andrew Mills, Andy O'Donnell, Jim Powell, Adam Rayner (another excellent editor and writer), Dom Spong, Katie Warnes, Bethan Williams, and James Winfield-Straker (who endured hours of rants in the pub as this was being developed). I may have forgotten others, and if so, I'm very sorry that you've not been included in this list.

Richard Wheelhouse also read this, and, most amazingly, provided the cover, sparing me from becoming an entry on the kindle cover disasters list. So far he has provided three covers to this series, and – I'm hoping – he'll provide the fourth in time.

Thanks go to my parents, who both read this and offered their opinions. I know this isn't your genre, so I appreciate it all the more. My love of reading and stories comes from you both, so technically this book is your fault.

Finally, my wife, Jenny listened to me go on and on about this book and the world it's a part of for years. She's offered countless ideas, too many to list here. The one that springs to mind is Beth, and how stupid I was to miss it.

They say writing a book isn't a solo endeavour, but I didn't realise how true this was until I wrote one of my own. To everyone who's helped me with this: I hope you're all proud of your efforts, I am, and I think Aurora would be too.

Printed in Great Britain
by Amazon.co.uk, Ltd.,
Marston Gate.